Bob!

Another tidbit of lit
as you goin' south. A
morsel of words to cork
your ear. Happy Birthday
Reading!!

X Y

MR.
C. & D.
MS.

DEATH OF A
TENOR MAN

Also by Bill Moody

Solo Hand

DEATH OF A TENOR MAN

An Evan Horne Mystery

BILL MOODY

WALKER AND COMPANY
NEW YORK

For Helen Louise

First published in the United States of America in 1995 by Walker
Publishing Company, Inc.

Published simultaneously in Canada by Thomas Allen & Son Canada,
Limited, Markham, Ontario

Library of Congress Cataloging-in-Publication Data
Moody, Bill, 1941–
Death of a tenor man : an Evan Horne mystery / Bill Moody.
p.   cm.
ISBN 0-8027-3269-0
I. Title.
PS3563.0552D43   1995
813' .54—dc20   95-13048
CIP

Printed in the United States of America
2 4 6 8 10 9 7 5 3 1

DEATH OF A TENOR MAN

INTRO

I'M *LOOKING AT* old photos, a collection of jazz history, a gift someone has given me in a well-meaning gesture, designed probably to help fill the silent hours of my recuperation. The coffee-table book is filled with black-and-white moments from an era never to be seen again. This photograph is of twin tenors, Dexter Gordon and Wardell Gray, taken at a club in Los Angeles in the early fifties, probably the Club Alabam or the Bird Basket. Central Avenue all the way.

In this grainy framed moment, the photographer has caught Dexter in full flight, his huge body blocking all but the bass player's hands, towering over the microphone and Wardell, who stands a few feet behind him. Gordon's eyes are closed, his shoulders raised slightly, both hands gripping the horn like he's choking it, his face caught in a grimace as if the note he's searching for won't come out of the horn.

Behind him, ultra-cool Wardell, a baggy suit hanging on his slight frame, a hat on the back of his head, looks on stoically. But when I look closer, a pencil-thin mustache is curled slightly upward as if a smile is about to begin. Was it something Dexter had just played, or is Wardell amused by Dex's struggle to get that note out? Maybe he's thinking about what he's going to play. And what were they playing when this photo was taken? A blues?

*A standard? Maybe it was "The Chase," their most famous col-
laboration, and Wardell is waiting for his turn.*

*Wardell's hands are crossed over the tenor saxophone that
hangs from his neck strap. A cigarette is wedged between the
fingers of his left hand. A wisp of smoke curls up around his eyes.*

*The drummer, I think it's Roy Haynes, is leaning forward,
his right hand a blur on the cymbal. His eyes are wide open and
there's a white flash of teeth against his dark face. It's not a smile
exactly, more like an expression of euphoria. The pianist, who
looks to be no more than a teenager, is looking toward Dexter
expectantly, for approval perhaps. Both hands are locked on the
keys. Who is it? Al Haig? The caption doesn't identify all the
band, just the date—1953.*

*I close my right hand into a fist and unconsciously think
about the rubber ball, then instantly remember I don't use it
anymore. It's like remembering someone you were close to who is
gone, and you haven't come to terms with their absence yet.*

*If I had been born thirty years earlier, maybe I could have
been the pianist in the photo. I grew up in L.A., I was into jazz
from an early age. Would I have hung out on Central Avenue like
Art Pepper? What would that gig have been like? What would it
have been like to know and play with Dexter Gordon and Wardell
Gray in an era when personal sound was everything, an era before
synthesizers and electric pianos?*

*With Dexter, or Roy Haynes, it could have been possible. But
our paths never crossed. Dexter was around until a few years ago
after sixteen years in Europe, an Academy Award nomination for
his role in* Round Midnight, *and scores of records. Roy Haynes
is still playing better than ever.*

*But with Wardell Gray there was no chance. He was gone
two years before I was born, left to die mysteriously in the Nevada
desert.*

And me? I hardly ever play the piano anymore.

1

"IT HAPPENED RIGHT here," Ace Buffington says. "At least, this is about where his body was found."

I've only been in Las Vegas thirty minutes, and already I'm bathed in sweat, wilting fast under the 107-degree heat, standing in the middle of a vacant lot next to a convenience store. The scorching dry air beats down on us like some huge hair dryer.

I shield my eyes from the glare with my bad hand. Ace, standing a few feet away, is no more than a tall shadow. The heat doesn't seem to bother him. He came straight to the airport from the courts, dressed in tennis clothes.

"How can you be sure?" I ask.

"Well, I'm not really," Ace admits. "There's been a lot of building since 1955, but the Moulin Rouge is not far from here. It certainly could have been here."

By now I thought I'd be in an air-conditioned house, sipping on a Henry Weinhard or floating in the cool, soothing relief of Ace's swimming pool. Instead I'm standing in the middle of a vacant lot Ace thinks is the murder site of an all-but-forgotten jazz musician named Wardell Gray, a tenor saxophonist whose big sound and tone belied his skinny body.

There's no historical marker here though, no weathered sign that reads "Wardell Gray died on this spot, May 1955." Dirt, sand, and scrub weeds, a patch of desert strewn with fast-food wrappers, drink cups, bottles, even an abandoned truck tire, is all that's here.

"Ace, that was thirty-seven years ago."

"I know, I know," Ace says. He walks closer, his enthusiasm undiminished. "But this could have been it." He points to a spot on the ground.

There's a tinge of sadness, even romanticism, to his voice that I understand. A devoted fan, record collector, and occasionally historian, Ace is intrigued by the legendary figures of jazz. The only memorial to Wardell is a legacy of out-of-print albums and some reissued CDs. "Imagine, Evan, Wardell Gray found out here."

I shake my head, listen to the traffic noise filtering down from the expressway behind us, and watch the steady stream of cars pull in and out of the convenience-store parking lot fifty feet away.

"I'm trying to, Ace." My shirt is sticking to my body, and I can feel droplets of sweat running into my eyes. "Can we go now?"

"Sure," Ace says. He thrives on the heat, plays tennis no matter what the weather is, and subscribes to the theory of all locals that this is hot, but it's dry heat.

We climb back into his red Jeep Cherokee. Seconds later the soothing cold air from the air conditioner is blowing in my face. I take one last look at the vacant lot and wonder why I agreed to come to Las Vegas in July.

The last time I was up for the Lonnie Cole investigation, interviewing country singer Charlie Crisp at the Frontier—my debut as a detective. That turned out reasonably well, at least financially. Lonnie Cole is still in jail; I saved Charlie Crisp a considerable sum of money. Now, I was going to see if I could play piano again. That and Ace are two reasons I'm in Las Vegas.

I watch Ace drive. Both hands on the wheel, shoulders hunched forward, the bucket seat barely able to accommodate his huge frame. His face is burned brown, and there's a light sheen of perspiration on his forehead. I try to imagine him at a podium before a class of UNLV undergraduates, lecturing on literature. Ace looks nothing like an English professor. Over there, he's Dr. Charles Buffington.

While we wait at a traffic light he looks over, slaps my shoulder, and grins broadly. "Evan, great to see you."

"You too, Ace. How's the backhand?"

"Never better. Just went three sets with a history prof before I picked you up. How's *your* hand?"

We both glance at my right wrist as I flex my fingers. Except for two tiny scars, there are no other visible signs. The surgery was long ago, and I've stopped carrying around the rubber ball I used to squeeze for therapy.

I close my fingers into a fist. There's only a slight twinge of pain now. "We'll find out soon enough," I say.

Ace nods and heads the jeep onto the expressway. The Strip skyline is on our left. In the distance, I spot the first hint of a pyramid.

"The Luxor Hotel," Ace says, noticing my gaze. "They're even going to have a scale-model sphinx in front of it."

Ace exits at Flamingo, just past a sign for the University of Nevada Las Vegas. "How are things in academia?" I ask.

"Oh, you know. English-department election, new chair, petty politics, professors jealous of each other's publications, and the NCAA is still after Jerry Tarkanian. Business as usual."

A few miles farther west Ace turns into the Spring Valley area, a part of Las Vegas most tourists never see. It could be Phoenix or Scottsdale or any Southwest city with its shopping centers, supermarkets, gas stations, fast-food places, and ranch-style homes. Ace turns off busy Spring Mountain Road and guides the Jeep through a residential neighborhood. He pulls into the half-circle drive in front of the house that will be my home for the next few weeks.

We grab my bags, and I follow Ace around the side of the house, down a long walkway. It's a rambling one-story ranch-style, surrounded by trees and shrubs. In back is a self-contained apartment originally added for Janey's mother, complete with wrought-iron security gates on the doors and windows.

"Not my idea," Ace says, noticing my frown as he unlocks the door. "Janey was always worried about burglars. Her mother was worse."

I nod silently. The death of a loved one is always tough, and it's still an open wound with Ace—barely six months since his wife was shockingly and swiftly ravaged by cancer.

"Well, here we are," Ace says. "I'm sure you'll be comfortable here, and you can come and go as you please." The two rooms and kitchen are furnished with castoffs from the main house, but Ace has thought of everything. There's a small TV, stereo, and a refrigerator well stocked with Henry Weinhard, cold cuts, and a pound of gourmet coffee. I'm genuinely touched as Ace hands me the keys.

"Of course, you know about the piano in the house. Use it whenever you want. The phone is a separate line, and, well, just make yourself at home. I serviced Janey's VW so you'll have some transportation."

We walk outside to the patio and pool area. "That's what I want first," I say looking at the still, blue water shimmering in the fierce sun.

"You got it," Ace says. "I've got some papers to grade, but how about I throw a couple of steaks on the grill later?"

"Sounds great." There's a momentary awkward silence as memories of Janey, my accident, and a long friendship pass between us. "Look, I really appreciate all this, and the gig of course, it's—"

"Hey, forget it," Ace says, holding up his hand. "You may

not like playing for shoppers, and I'll be glad for the company. Besides, you're going to help me."

"Help you? With what?"

"Solving Wardell Gray's murder."

REFRESHED AFTER A quick swim, I pop open a Henry Weinhard and think about Wardell Gray. I load the tape player with one of the cassettes Ace has left me, and suddenly it's the fifties again. Wardell and Dexter Gordon, two of the great tenor players in jazz, sparring with each other in a tune appropriately titled "The Chase."

It was a hit on jukeboxes across America. Wardell and Dex got a lot of publicity but only a hundred dollars apiece for the record. Dexter went on to New York and eventually Europe for a stay of sixteen years. When he came back, his career went into high gear. He was "rediscovered" by American audiences and nominated for an Academy Award for his portrayal of an exiled American jazz musician in the film 'Round Midnight. Wardell Gray wasn't so lucky.

After stints with Count Basie and Benny Goodman, Gray came to Las Vegas with little notice as a member of Benny Carter's band for the opening of Moulin Rouge, the first black hotel-casino in Las Vegas. He died the second night. His murder—it was never officially called that—has never been investigated to anyone's satisfaction.

Like everyone else, I know only the unofficial accounts, the myths that pop up in the jazz world when one of its own dies suddenly. A known heroin addict, Wardell was found in the desert, the apparent victim of an overdose. Many people thought there was more to it than that, but in those days the police in Las Vegas didn't think the death of a black junkie jazz musician warranted much of an investigation. They probably wouldn't today, either. There were other theories about Gray's death, but no one wanted to talk about them, and that's all they were—theories.

I decide on a shower, then stretch out on the couch, letting the hum of the air conditioner lull me to sleep. In what seems like only minutes, Ace is tapping on the sliding glass door. "Hey, Evan," he says, "these steaks are almost ready."

"Be right with you." I shake off the nap, throw on some shorts and a T-shirt, and join Ace just as he's pulling two T-bones off the grill.

"Too hot out here," Ace says. "Let's go inside." We settle in at the kitchen table with the steaks, large baked potatoes, and a tossed salad. The steaks are tender and juicy, marinated in some mixture Ace has concocted. We wash it all down with a couple of beers. Later, with plates pushed aside and coffee brewing, Ace fills me in on his plans to research Wardell Gray and the Moulin Rouge, and why he needs my help.

"I'm doing an article for a popular culture journal," Ace says. "There's a conference coming up in September where I'll present the paper. My colleagues frown on it, but I get credit and it's a helluva lot more fun than rehashing nineteenth-century fiction."

Ace has two books to his credit: one is a study of Charles Dickens, the other an argument that Herman Melville stole the plot for *Billy Budd* from Nathaniel Hawthorne. I really tried, but I had trouble getting through either of them. I'm convinced they were mostly the result of the publish-or-perish syndrome that keeps him alive in academia.

"Is this article just about Wardell?"

"Not really," Ace says, warming to the subject. He pours us two mugs of coffee. "A number of jazz musicians have met rather untimely ends. Clifford Brown and Bud Powell's brother Richie were killed in a car crash. Lee Morgan was shot at Slugs in New York City, Albert Ayler was found in the East River. Supposedly a suicide, but he was handcuffed—hands behind his back. Wardell is another story. I'm sure it probably was a drug overdose, everyone agrees on that, but what was he doing in the desert, and how did he get there?"

Good point. A hotel room would be more likely, or an alley behind the Moulin Rouge. "So where do I come in?"

Ace opens another beer. "There are a couple of old-time musicians still around here, but they're not likely to talk to me, at least not very freely. You, Evan Horne, a musician, on the other hand, have some immediate common ground. There's also another lead, a dancer. She's in real estate now, but she was one of the chorus line girls at the Moulin Rouge when it opened. I tracked her down through a newspaper reporter friend, but when I told her what I was doing, she clammed up. Really strange."

"Did she say why?"

"No, just that she was sorry, she didn't remember or know anything about Wardell Gray. I don't see how that's possible."

I sip some coffee and light a cigarette despite Ace's frown. "Okay if I smoke?" Ace just shrugs. "I know, I know, when am I going to quit. Well, sounds like you have some good leads, but maybe there isn't anything to tell. Some people prefer to keep the past just that."

Ace shakes his head. "I don't buy it. She sounded as if I were asking about something that happened last week. It's been more than thirty-five years. Maybe I'm imagining it, but I swear I heard fear in her voice. At the very least she was uncomfortable. Anyway, what do you say?"

I have to admit it's intriguing. The gig, if I stick with it, won't take up much time, and helping Ace would give me something to do. But two voices are arguing in my head. This sounds too much like investigating, and once was enough. In trying to help Lonnie Cole I'd been beaten up, nearly killed, and, in the end, betrayed. But the other voice is saying, Relax, this is the past. How could that get you into trouble? Sometimes the wrong voice wins. "Hey, why not, I'll give it a try."

"Great," Ace says, beaming at me. "I'll get you the names

of the musicians. You can find them at the Four Queens most Monday nights. Alan Grant still has the only game in town as far as jazz goes. There are some clipping files on the Moulin Rouge at Special Collections in the campus library. I'll pave the way there."

"What about the dancer?"

"I've got a number for her. I'll leave it to you as to how to contact her." Ace smiles. "Maybe we'll get lucky, and she'll find you."

Who knows, maybe she will. This is the first gig I've had in a shopping mall. "By the way, Ace."

"Yeah?"

"What are you calling this article?"

He grins and looks like he's been waiting for me to ask.

"Death of a Tenor Man."

2

BRENT TYLER IS curly blond hair, white shirt, tie, and suspenders holding up expensive trousers. He probably has a BMW parked outside to go with the cellular phone tucked in his hip pocket. He has a clipboard in his hand, so already I don't like him.

We're standing before a white grand piano—already a bad sign—on the lower level of the Fashion Show Mall, just off the Strip near the Frontier Hotel. A red velvet rope shields us from the steady stream of morning shoppers that troop past carrying bags with the logos of Neiman Marcus, Saks, and The Sharper Image.

Directly opposite is the mall food court, a collection of up-scale fast-food outlets—everything from gourmet coffee and muffins to baked potatoes with nacho sauce. The Fashion Show management decided piano background would soothe the shoppers, get them to linger, and give the mall some added class. They also contribute to the UNLV music department and get most of the pianists from there. I'm one of two exceptions to the graduate student pool, mainly thanks to Ace's contacts at the university.

"You got your own music, right?" Brent Tyler asks. He's used to the music students who come in with a briefcase full of sheet music—show tunes, classics, and the occasional concerto to practice for a recital. Most of them probably figure this gig as paid practice. For me it's going to be therapy.

"I'll fake it," I say, running my fingers over the keyboard. No stuck keys, but I'll be surprised if it's in tune. I hope Brent doesn't offer to paint it. Once when I pointed out to a club owner several stuck keys that produced no sound whatsoever on his piano, he'd said quite seriously, "Can't you play some songs that don't use those notes?"

"Whatever," Tyler says. He takes in my dark suit, white shirt, and Miles Davis print tie. "You got a tux?"

I nod. Tyler and I met earlier in his office to sign a contract, and this is the end of the mall tour he insisted on—to give me a feel for the place, as he puts it. I told him I'd actually been to a mall before, but Brent was adamant.

"Okay, here's the deal. Music starts at noon. Two-hour shifts. Except today, you come on at two and relieve Roger Baldwin," Tyler says, consulting his clipboard. "Like the piano, get it?"

"Cute."

"Mary Lou relieves you."

Somehow I manage to avoid rolling my eyes as Tyler continues. "If she's late or doesn't show, you stay on, understood?" I nod my compliance.

"Good luck," he says, flashing me his best smile. "You have four weeks, then we'll see. Nice to have you at the Fashion Show." He shakes hands briefly, then his phone rings. He pulls it out of his pocket, waves at me, and heads up the mall, phone to his ear, a smile on his face, a friendly wave for the shoppers. What a guy.

I sit down at the piano and tentatively try a few chords. Action is okay and, amazingly, it is in tune. The sound is dampened by the crowd, and I'm far enough away from the food court area that I doubt whether anyone can hear very well, which suits me fine.

The customers are staff on their lunch break wearing name tags from their respective stores, shoppers taking a break, and weary husbands or boyfriends looking at their watches, wondering where their wives are.

Anybody looking my way just sees someone in a suit sitting at a white piano, and once in a while think they hear a note or two over the din of conversation. It's an illusion, a musical illusion. I glance back over my shoulder and smile at the escalator riders coming down from the upper level above me.

I clench my fists a few times, take a deep breath, and try a few bars of a ballad I can't even remember the name of. I have to concentrate, willing the fingers of my right hand to follow the right pattern. The rubber ball I used to squeeze for strength is behind me, but the flexibility is still not there like it should be.

Before the accident I could play this tune, keep a cigarette, a drink, and a conversation going with no trouble at all. Hand feels okay, but this is only the first tune. Two hours to go, and I don't know how quickly my fingers will tire.

I start a second chorus, begin to stretch out a bit. Nothing fancy, just some easy runs. My mind is way ahead of my fingers. Going into the bridge, I falter momentarily. I haven't forgotten the chords, but my fingers are just a hair slow. I look up and see a gray-haired woman in a warmup suit who catches my eye, her head nodding to the music, a dreamy look in her eyes.

"That's really nice," she says, clutching her shopping bag. I smile back and nod a thanks and almost lose my place.

I'm a long way from jazz clubs and concert stages.

I HAD A VW when I was in college, but it's been years since I've driven one. This one is in excellent condition—I'm sure

Janey Buffington never drove it more than to the store or short trips around town. She and Ace had installed an add-on air conditioner, but it does little more than turn down the blow-dryer heat to low. I keep one of the wing windows open to create some air flow.

Jacket off and tie loosened, I leave the Fashion Show parking lot and head west on Spring Mountain, across the railroad tracks—after a slow freight holds things up for ten minutes—and on to Decatur, where I turn right. With the rest of the afternoon still ahead of me, I can't resist taking a look at the Moulin Rouge, the site of Wardell Gray's last gig.

Bypassing downtown and the freeway, I turn east on Bonanza. I pull up to a warehouse parking lot across the street from the casino and get my first look at the Moulin Rouge. In its neglected state the large red-and-white structure looks like a small transplanted Strip hotel that's been abandoned. From what Ace has told me, the inside is worse.

Opening in 1955, the Moulin Rouge quickly became a celebrity hangout, packed nightly. I try to imagine opening night. A jammed parking lot, limos pulling up to deposit the likes of Frank Sinatra, Dean Martin, and Sammy Davis, Jr. Benny Carter's band onstage, a line of show girls, celebrities, and skinny Wardell, the thin man of the tenor, standing up to solo. A gig for Wardell that was his last; a dream of an interracial hotel-casino that was over in six months. Ace tells me there's a move underway to raise money, renovate, and try again.

All I can think of is, what happened to Wardell Gray?

Time for some research. I leave the warehouse lot and continue east on Bonanza, all the way to Maryland Parkway, then south to the UNLV campus. The summer-school rush is on, but thanks to Ace's temporary faculty permit hanging from the rearview mirror, I manage to find a parking spot near the library.

I've visited Ace at the campus several times in the past, so I generally know my way around. It's a short but hot walk to the library. The students, male and female, are dressed mostly in shorts and T-shirts, and many of them carry water bottles or Big Gulp drinks from the 7-Eleven. Something I'll have to look into.

At the library building I make my way to the elevator, where, following Ace's instructions, I got to the fourth floor, Special Collections. A thin blond man I take for a graduate student looks up from his computer when I walk in. There are no other takers.

"Hi," he says, as if glad for the interruption. "Can I help you?"

"My name is Evan Horne," I say. "Professor Buffington in English may have called you."

"Oh yeah, right," he says, consulting a pad in front of him. "You're looking for stuff on the Moulin Rouge." He shakes hands and gives me a file folder. "Ted Rollings," he says. "I pulled what we have. You can look at it over there," he says, indicating a row of tables. "Anything you want copied, I'll do it for you."

"Thanks," I say, taking the file. While Rollings goes back to his computer, I sit down and flip through the clippings, newspaper stories and photos documenting the brief history of the Moulin Rouge.

Halfway into the pile, after a number of articles about the building of the hotel-casino and its opening, I find the first mention of the saxophonist's death in a series of newspaper articles.

NOTED JAZZ SAXOPHONIST
WARDELL GRAY FOUND SLAIN

The body of one of the nation's leading Negro jazz musicians, Wardell Carl Gray, was found in a weed patch at the side of the road in Vegas Heights yesterday. Sheriff's deputies said the well-dressed man apparently had been slain.

The story goes on to say that robbery was ruled out, since Gray's watch, wallet, and ring were still on his person. Accord-

ing to the testimony of another musician, Gray owed someone
in Los Angeles $900. Investigators theorized that that person
might have followed Gray to Las Vegas to collect.

Would someone murder Gray for $900? Today it happens
all the time for much lesser amounts, and if Gray was involved
with drug dealers, it's certainly a possibility.

Another story cites dancer Theodore Haley, professional
name Teddy Hale, member of the Moulin Rouge show, as a
suspect. Hale's story was that he met Gray after the second show,
and the two of them went to Hale's apartment for a "joy pop" of
heroin. Both passed out. When Hale regained consciousness, he
tried to revive Gray, but the saxophonist fell off the bed and hit his
head on the floor. Hale panicked, fearful he would be prosecuted
for narcotics possession, and drove Gray to the desert, where he left
the saxophonist's body. Hale sticks to his story even with a lie
detector test, which he apparently passes. Another headline:

DANCER CLEARS SELF IN DEATH OF SAX PLAYER.

The police evidently bought Hale's version of what happened;
he describes in detail the events leading up to the discovery of
Gray's body. The police reported that they discovered several nee-
dles and spoons in Hale's home but did not find any actual heroin.

In still another article, a different theory is offered by the
deputy coroner. The headline stops me cold.

HINT JAZZ MUSICIAN STILL ALIVE WHEN
BODY DUMPED BY DOPED DANCER
The possibility that jazz musician Wardell Gray was
still alive when his body was dumped in a weed patch
near a remote ranch Thursday is being considered by
police here.

The coroner explains that a heavy shot of heroin sometimes
produces a comalike state resembling death in a human body,
with hardly detectable breathing and heartbeat.

Hale, however, claims he checked for a heartbeat and even

put a mirror against Gray's nose and mouth to see if he was breathing. Murder or manslaughter charges would not be filed against Hale unless there was some new development in the case. Apparently there was none. Hale was released with the possibility that he could only face charges of illegal use of narcotics and illegally disposing of a body.

There are subsequent articles with background on Gray and quotes from friends and other musicians, but the story ends on that note.

Like most musicians, I've heard the stories of Gray's death that get passed around the music world, embellished in the retelling until they reach mythic proportions, but I'd never seen anything in print, nor had I ever heard this theory that Gray might have been alive when Hale dumped the body. The coroner's report citing head wounds consistent with blows from a blunt instrument also pops off the page. Blunt instrument? Head wounds? Caused by the floor when Gray fell?

There are several more follow-up articles, which I gather up and ask Ted Rollings to photocopy for me. "I'll be back in a few minutes."

I find the stairs exit, step into the hall, and light a cigarette, musing over the clippings. Did Gray and Hale have an argument? Had Hale accidentally killed Gray? You don't get head wounds from a blunt instrument by falling out of bed, do you? This sounds as improbable as trumpeter Chet Baker's alleged suicide, caused, some theorized, by Baker jumping off the second-floor balcony of an Amsterdam hotel.

Did someone else kill Gray and dump his body in the desert? Who, if not Teddy Hale? Junkies can get into trouble with all kinds of people. Or maybe it was because of something at the Moulin Rouge. That was a different time and place.

I go back inside and find Ted finishing up the photocopying. He puts the copies in a manila envelope. "Come back any time," he says.

"Thanks for your help," I say.

I take the agonizingly slow elevator back to the first floor and walk across campus to the student union, where I'm to meet Ace before his late-afternoon class. The heat is relentless, and I envy the students in shorts. The coolness of the student union is welcome, and after fighting the lines of students and faculty, I get a giant Coke, filling the paper cup with ice.

A few minutes later Ace joins me. No tennis gear today. He's in sandals, chinos, and a golf shirt, with a pile of books under his arm. He takes in my tie and smiles. "Better watch it, you'll be taken for faculty," he says, sitting down, "or worse yet, an administrator."

"Not if you all dress like that. How's the molding of young minds coming?"

Ace shakes his head in disgust. "The students are fine, it's the new idiot department chair that's the problem. The man is determined to get even for all the slights he's felt over the years, at the expense of some damned good programs and people." Ace shakes his head in disgust. "And we teach the humanities. What a joke." He takes a long drink and glances at his watch. "So how did it go with you?"

"My wrist is aching, Brent Tyler's certainly interesting, but I got through the set okay."

Ace nods. "Did you get to the library?"

I tap the envelope of clippings on the table. "Yeah, Rollings was very helpful."

"And?"

It's hard to talk over the din of students. "I think you may be onto something. According to several newspaper accounts, it sounds like Wardell might have done more than fall out of bed."

"I've seen some of that stuff," Ace says, his eyes lighting up, "but I'm more interested in what, if anything, you find out from some of the old musicians in town. I've got a couple of jazz history books you can look through. There's not much. There

are a couple of accounts of Wardell's time at the Moulin Rouge."
I watch Ace for a moment until he catches my expression.
"I know, I know, it was nearly forty years ago, but you've got to admit it's damned intriguing."
The safest kind of thing to investigate—the past. That other voice I hear keeps trying to get in. After the Lonnie Cole case, the past suits me fine.
"So how about we grab something to eat tonight, and you have a relaxing weekend. You can check out the Four Queens on Monday. Alan Grant should be able to give you some leads."
"Sounds good to me," I say. "I'm going home, get out of this suit and soak in your pool."
Ace stands up to go. "Just imagine how it was before air conditioning. See you later." I watch him shoulder his way through the crowd of students, wondering how anyone can keep his mind on nineteenth-century literature when it's 110 degrees.

I finish my drink and look through the clippings again. Most of it is background stuff about the construction and later the casino's demise, when the owners of the $3,000,000 resort filed for bankruptcy. Bad management, financial troubles, or even pressure from competing resorts are possible reasons given for the closing.

Bandleader Benny Carter's statement is ambiguous at best, calling Gray one of the most dependable musicians he's ever employed. Benny is still around, still blowing at eighty-four. I wonder what he remembers. Gray, the story said, was replaced by a local musician. Who was that, and is he still around? One more lead to check for the ace detective.

Reluctantly I leave the coolness of the student union and head for my car. It's all I can do to resist running through the sprinklers, but then that wouldn't do if someone took me for faculty.

3

AFTER A RESTLESS night of tossing and turning, worrying over the gig, listening to music, and wondering whether I should invest in another rubber ball, I sleep in on Saturday morning. I decide to pass on Ace's offer of using his piano to practice and save my strength for the Fashion Show Mall and Brent Tyler. If I've read Tyler right, he'll be around to check me out.

Cindy Fuller is also much on my mind. We didn't exactly break up, but after the Lonnie Cole thing was wrapped up, we kind of drifted apart, saw less of each other, even though our apartments are in the same building in Los Angeles. We had gotten pretty intense for a while, but one or both of us was scared off, at least temporarily.

We still saw each other occasionally for dinner, but there was a tension neither of us could ease. Maybe we both knew we had crossed a line. Cindy was looking for commitment. I didn't know what I wanted. Still, with all this time on my hands it would be nice to see her.

I try her number. She's still got Sinatra's "Come Fly with Me" on her answering machine, but she's not picking up. I leave her my number and a short message. She's probably on a flight, but I'm hopeful she might be back on the Las Vegas run.

Ace's Jeep is gone when I check the driveway, so I decide on breakfast at a nearby coffee shop I'd seen earlier while I sample the local paper. It's a short walk, but the heat is already more intense, beating down on me without mercy. Vic's Coffee Shop looks like it might be a hard-hat breakfast stop most mornings, but there are only a couple of tables occupied today. I get a paper from the rack out front, settle into a booth, and order ham and eggs.

The *Las Vegas Review-Journal* is not exactly the *Los Angeles Times*. From a quick scan it looks to be made up mostly of news-wire releases, right-wing editorials, some syndicated columns, and a very slim entertainment section dominated by hotel casino ads, with the biggest spreads given to Wayne Newton and Tom Jones.

The food is good, the waitress friendly. I drag things out with two cups of coffee too many until almost noon, then wander back to the apartment. Still no sign of Ace. I try the number for the woman he mentioned who had been a dancer at the Moulin Rouge, but there's no answer and no machine. How refreshing.

The pool looks too good to resist, so I bake a while, swim, and skim through the jazz reference books Ace has left. They mostly give one version or another of the highlights of Wardell Gray's career, listing dates and who he played with, stuff I already know, but all the bios end simply with "died Las Vegas, May 1955." Two months after Charlie Parker, and both were the same age.

I'm surprised how caught up I am in all this. I remind myself that this entire research-investigation is only for a paper Ace is writing, but I realize—maybe because of all the spare time—I'm hooked. Unanswered questions always bother me, and Wardell Gray's death has gone unanswered for too many years.

The file of newspaper clippings is probably all the written

stuff I'll find. But if I can find a connection, maybe I can get a look at the police records. All of which triggers a thought of Danny Cooper. Maybe he can wield his influence with the Las Vegas police. It's worth a try.

I jump in the pool for one last cooling dip. I'm almost dry by the time I gather up the books and go inside the apartment to call Coop.

"Santa Monica Police. How can I help you?" a pleasant voice asks.

"Homicide, please."

"Just a moment."

A much less pleasant male voice this time comes on the line.

"Is Detective Cooper on today?"

"Yeah. Name?"

"Evan Horne."

"Hang on." There's a click before Coop picks up.

"I hope you don't want anything," Coop says. "I'm having a bad hair day."

"That's hard to do with a crew cut, isn't it? How did they get you to work on Saturday?"

"Fuck you, Horne. We serve and protect, even on weekends. Where are you, and what do you want?"

"Las Vegas, and just a little information."

"Las Vegas?" I hear a noise that can only be Coop's feet hitting the floor. He'd probably been in his usual phone position—feet crossed on the desk, leaning back in his chair. "Doing what?"

"A gig. Nothing big, just some solo piano in an upscale shopping mall." For once Coop doesn't make a crack. We go back too far. He's one of the people who knows what it's like for me not playing anymore.

"And I thought I could avoid you for a while," Coop says. "It just so happens that I'll be coming up next Thursday for a weekend of decadence and debauchery."

"That's hard to do by yourself."

"Thanks, Horne, I needed that. By myself is not how I do it. For your information, my companion on this pleasure excursion is a very attractive young lady."

"Who's the lucky woman?"

"A blond in Traffic. I'm trying to exercise my immense influence and get her promoted from meter maid."

"I don't think I want to hear it."

"Weekend or not, she deserves the promotion. Maybe as a former conductor to big stars you can pull some strings and get us into a couple of shows."

"Sure. Wayne Newton is working at the Hilton. I know he's your favorite."

"Nothing wrong with Wayne Newton," Coop shoots back. "The man is immensely talented, a legend. So what information? You're not playing detective again, I hope."

"Only on paper. Just doing some research for a friend on a musician's death."

"Oh, for Christ's sake, Horne, you—"

"Relax. This happened in 1955. I just want to look at the police reports. This is for an article in a very scholarly journal."

"Yeah, sure. Let me think." There's a long pause while Coop decides whether he wants to get involved in this or not. "I know a guy in Homicide up there. Worked with him on an extradition case a couple of years ago. He might help, but Vegas is not my turf, and in case you didn't know, the police aren't happy about disclosing their files to mere civilians, let alone musicians."

"Hey, tell him he might be a footnote in the article."

"I'm sure he'll be thrilled. If it's an open case, you're out of luck. Do you know for sure it was murder?"

"No, that's just a legend in the jazz world. There were some funny circumstances, though."

"Such as?"

"Wardell Gray is the name. He was a heroin addict and

supposedly died falling out of bed during a drug party, but the newspaper story says there were head wounds from a blunt instrument, as you police types call it."

Coop snorts. "If he was a musician I'm sure there were strange circumstances. When was this again?"

"May 1955."

"That sounds safe enough even for you. All right, I'll give this guy a call, but don't hold your breath. Meanwhile, get me in to see Wayne Newton."

"I'll try. Want me to pick you up?"

"Absolutely not. The blond meter maid and I will be taking the hotel limo as befitting a man of my position."

"Have it your way. Call me when you get in." I give him my number and promise again to try with Wayne Newton. "Thanks, Coop."

"I haven't done anything yet."

WHEN I'VE HAD enough of the pool and apartment, I decide to brave the heat and go exploring. I remember that driving around on Friday, I'd found a jazz station. I head the VW in the general direction of UNLV and flip around the dial until I catch some Coltrane, followed by announcements and station ID by the DJ. The sleepy, laid-back voice calls himself "The Breeze."

"This is KUNV Las Vegas, your jazz connection for southern Nevada, where the airwaves are my playground, The Breeze blowing tunes at you. Give me a call at 895-5555. Now back to the sounds with Miles Davis."

While Miles's muted horn comes over the car radio, I start looking for a pay phone. I pull into a gas station just past the Strip and call the station.

"KUNV, Jazzline. You are talking to The Breeze."

"Yeah, I was just driving around and caught your show. How about some Wardell Gray?"

"Wow, jazz buddy, an informed caller. We got lots of Wardell. Anything special?"

"How about 'Twisted'?" It's the first tune that comes to mind, and I remember Annie Ross's lyrics crafted to Wardell's solo.

"Way cool, man. I know we got that. Listen up in about ten minutes."

"Thanks. Listen, I'm in the area. Any chance I could drop by the station? I'm a musician."

"Can you hold a minute?"

"Sure." I watch the traffic backing up from the Strip, thankful I'm not sweating in a phone booth. After a couple of more minutes The Breeze is back.

"Sorry man. Dude wants to know why I don't play big bands. I told him Glenn Miller died in a plane crash. What's your name? Do I know you?"

"Evan Horne, piano. Used to work with Lonnie Cole."

"Lonnie Cole? I think we got him, too. Sure, come on by. I'm here till three. UNLV, student union building, third floor."

"Thanks. See you in a bit."

"Later."

The Breeze rings off. A psuedo-hipster? No one really talks like that, even if they do jazz radio. By the time I reached Maryland Parkway, I hear myself noodling behind Lonnie Cole on a blues. One of the first things I did when I joined him. It feels good listening to my own two very respectable choruses before Lonnie comes back with the vocal. The downside is, I know this is how I used to play. True to his word, The Breeze follows with Wardell Gray and "Twisted."

The campus is pretty deserted being Saturday, so there's no problem finding a parking place near the student union. I sit in the car listening until Wardell is finished. Inside there are a few scattered tables occupied in the snack bar, and a couple of students are watching a baseball game on a giant TV. School is definitely out.

I take the elevator to the third floor. As soon as the doors open, the music hits me—Stan Getz in full flight. I follow the sound around the corner and find someone who can only be The Breeze, leaning against the studio doorway. Neither the cigarette hanging from his mouth nor the Las Vegas Jazz Society baseball cap resting on the back of his head go with the slacks, loafers, dress shirt, and tie. He's also older looking than his voice sounds.

"Horne?"

"Yeah, thanks for the airplay."

He extends his hand and snuffs out his cigarette in an overflowing ashtray. "No problem, jazz buddy. Come on in. About time to put up something else." I follow him into the tiny studio. CDs and records are scattered everywhere. The Breeze motions me to a chair and sits down at the board in front of the microphone. Two turntables to his left with records cued up; two CD players stacked to his right. As the Getz group winds down, he watches the seconds tick off on the top CD player. He presses a button on the control board as Getz finishes and Bill Evans comes out of his studio speaker monitors. "Cool," says The Breeze.

There's not a piano player in jazz who doesn't list Bill Evans as an influence, and I'm no exception. Neither are Chick Corea, Keith Jarrett, and Herbie Hancock. It was Evans's touch, sound, and voicings that led me to the piano.

The Breeze spins in the swivel chair, adjusts the volume to conversation level, and faces me. "One of great ones," he says, "but, hey, so was Wardell." He picks up an album cover. "Maybe they'll get around to reissuing this on CD." He passes it over to me. I glance at the sidemen. Al Haig, piano; Tommy Potter, bass; Roy Haynes, drums.

"Yeah, great group. You have any more Wardell?"

"We got a few on vinyl in the back." I'm still taking in the dichotomy of The Breeze's dress and his radio persona as he asks me, "How come you're so interested in Wardell Gray?"

I fill him in on the research I'm doing for Ace. He smiles and snaps his fingers. "Now I got it. You're the cat brought down Lonnie Cole. Record scam, blackmail, or something. I remember reading about it. Hey, you gonna solve Wardell's murder?"

Given Lonnie Cole's popularity, coverage in the jazz press was extensive, and my name was thrown around a lot. I shrug. "In the first place, we don't know it was murder."

The Breeze just shakes his head. "No, man, he was whacked by someone in the mob. They were heavy here in the fifties. Not like now, with the corporations running everything. Man, they don't even have live music with these shows now. It's all on tape."

"Why do you say it was the mob?"

The Breeze glances at the CD player. "Hang on a minute, okay? Time to go live." He swivels around, puts on headphones, and pulls the mike toward him. As the music stops, he hits another button on the board.

"Bill Evans on 91 FM, with Scott Lafaro on bass and Paul Motian on drums playing the Miles Davis tune 'Israel.' I'll be right back with more swingin' sounds after these brief messages." The Breeze presses another button to activate the tape carts that play public service announcements, then he's back on mike.

"All right, back to the sounds and a nice ballad from my man Dexter Gordon." He punches off the mike button as Dexter slides into "Darn That Dream." The Breeze replaces a CD in the player, checks everything out, and turns back to me.

"As I was sayin', man, Wardell was whacked. Figure it out for yourself. Young, good-looking dude like Wardell, comes up here with Benny Carter to blow his tenor for the opening of a new casino. Celebrities everywhere and lots of chicks. Wardell scores but with the wrong one. Turns out to be one of the wiseguys' women. Now they can't have no brother hittin' on one of their women. They know he's a junkie, so it's easy to give him a hot shot, and there you go. Wardell in the desert. Cops are in the mob's pocket, and Wardell is just another colored-boy musician. This is a redneck town, man, was then, still is now. A real drag, man, a real drag."

Except for The Breeze's embellishments, it's a story I've heard many times. Interesting, maybe even possible, but all speculation. As if reading my mind, The Breeze smiles. "Hey, it could have gone down like that, right?"

"I guess so," I say. "How about a look at the other Gray things?"

"Sure. Follow me." He takes me around the corner to a small room that houses the jazz library, floor-to-ceiling records and CDs in alphabetical order. "Help yourself, man. I'll be in the studio."

Even a quick glance tells me the station is well stocked. I find several of Wardell's early records, made in the days when liner notes with detailed histories of the musicians and the music were written by people like Nat Hentoff and Leonard Feather and Ira Gitler. But reading the covers tell me no more than I already know. I slide the records back into the rack and head back to the studio.

The Breeze is lounging outside the studio again. We share a smoke, talk music, and generally strike a chord with each other. He glances at his watch. "I got to get organized, man. My relief will be in soon."

"Well, thanks for your time," I say.

"Anytime, man." He digs for his wallet and pulls out a card. "Give me a call whenever."

I glance at the card and do a double take. Now at least the dress makes sense. The card reads:

JONATHAN COUNTS, ATTORNEY
SPECIALIST IN COPYRIGHT LAW

I look up and find The Breeze grinning at me. "Gotcha, eh,

man." The Breeze points a finger at me. "Yeah, this is my weekend gig, keeps me sane for dealing with the legal system. I'm good at that too."

"I'm sure you are, Jon."

"Hey, one more thing," The Breeze says, now dropping the jazz character completely. "Have you thought of looking into the police records on Wardell's death?"

"Yeah, as a matter of fact."

"Don't bother. I already have."

"And?"

"There's no record of any investigation on Wardell Gray."

4

IN A CITY known for its live shows and touted as the Entertainment Capital of the World, Las Vegas has made some abrupt changes to the contrary. The music for the production shows at the major Strip hotels is now tape, replacing the live bands with music prerecorded by musicians who are now out of work.

The majority of the other hotels that feature star policies—big-name singers and comedians—have reduced their house bands to skeleton combos or in some cases eliminated them altogether. The lounges for the most part hire self-contained groups with fewer and fewer musicians. Thanks to synthesizers, drum machines, and the weakening of the musician's union, Top Forty groups dominate the entertainment for audiences that are only killing time between gambling and eating.

The jazz scene is another story. A handful of bars try jazz for a few weeks or a few months, refuse to advertise or pay decent money, then blame it on the musicians if it doesn't pan out. The owners quickly move on to something else.

Despite the number of former big-band sidemen who flocked here after getting off the band buses and the grueling life on the road, there's only one constant on the jazz scene—

Alan Grant's Monday Night Jazz at the Four Queens Hotel and Casino downtown.

Grant, a former WABC New York DJ, who came to town in the early eighties, originally to open an ice cream franchise, was offered an opportunity to present jazz at the Four Queens. He agreed to try it for four weeks, but only if he could do it on Monday night. That was more than ten years ago. Grant knew Monday is a travel day for musicians, and figured he could catch enough of them on the way in or out of Los Angeles for a once-a-week schedule that would provide top names.

Grant, who discovered the likes of George Benson, the Thad Jones–Mel Lewis Band, and Grammy winner Joe Henderson, has missed only one Monday since he began at the Four Queens, and that was because he was in Sydney accepting an award from Australian radio. The Four Queens sets are recorded and broadcast on American Public Radio on 140 stations here and overseas. If anyone knows anything about Wardell Gray, it's Alan Grant.

I get to the Four Queens toward the end of the first set. Tonight it's trumpeter Art Farmer, working with a rhythm section. The casino is crowded with gamblers who probably have no idea who Art Farmer is, much less care that he's one of the world's premier jazz musicians.

Near the lounge the air rings with the sounds of slot-machine bells and coins dropping into trays. Inside the French Quarter the faithful are in attendance. The bar is three deep with musicians, hard-core fans, and surprised tourists clutching coupon books and cups of quarters, who didn't expect to find jazz in Las Vegas. Some have stayed around to see what it's all about.

I know there are some musicians at the bar, but I don't see any familiar faces. Scanning the audience for Grant, I find him in a booth at the back of the lounge, nodding his head in time to Art Farmer's elegant lines. I envy the pianist feeding him chords. The bassist and drummer both look familiar, but I can't place them.

Grant has become something of a legend over the years. When he was at WABC in New York, Alan Grant literally pushed some musicians through the door of labels such as Blue Note and Impulse, introduced them to record company executives, and got them recording contracts. There are more than a few musicians who owe the jump-starting of their careers to Grant.

I've met him a couple of times, but I'm not sure he even remembers me. When I catch his eye, he gives me one of those where-do-I-know-you-from? looks. He's got a bushel of graying hair and thick glasses, but still looks nowhere near what must be his seventy-odd years.

I wave in response, get a drink from the bar, and wait for Farmer to finish his set. When the final note is played, Grant climbs up onstage to reintroduce Farmer and the group, give a rundown of coming attractions, and thank everyone for coming. The applause is genuine for both Farmer and Grant.

Grant clearly loves the spotlight as he grins at the audience. "In this day and age, jazz is probably the only thing that makes sense, so keep supporting live music. Thanks for coming by. We'll have another set in about an hour." The lights go up and the packed lounge starts to empty out while Grant lingers onstage for a couple of minutes, talking with the musicians.

I make my way to Grant's booth and prepare to introduce myself. He beats me to it.

"Evan Horne," Grant says, pointing at me as he walks up. "Piano with Lonnie Cole, one album on your own, but something happened." He shakes my hand, then looks at it. "I got it. Car accident." He drops into the booth and looks up at me as if he's already asked me to sit down. "How am I doing?"

I'm speechless, just long enough for Grant to laugh. "No, the old memory isn't that good anymore. Your friend at UNLV called me. Ace Buffington? What kind of name is that for an English professor? Sit down, and I'll tell you all I know about Wardell Gray's death."

I slide into the booth and wait for a few minutes while Grant jokes with some of the customers passing by. He signals one of the waitresses and orders us a drink. Finally he turns to me. "Nothing," he says. "That's what I know about Wardell's death."

He shrugs. "Hey, everyone knows he was a junkie. It probably happened just like the papers said. An overdose. A shame, he was a great talent. I wasn't here then. I was working at a station in Florida, the only white jock on a black station."

We both look up as a well-groomed, very attractive woman I guess to be in her late fifties approaches the table. She pauses, gives me a brief glance, but speaks to Grant. "Art sounds great."

"Thanks," Grant says. "Come by next week. We've got Miles."

The woman's eyes widen. "But Miles Davis is—"

"Miles Schwartz, great clarinetist." Grant nudges my shoulder. "I get 'em every time with that one." He turns back to the woman. "Still haven't seen her."

The woman shakes her head slowly, a look of resignation on her face, then continues out of the lounge.

"What's all that about?"

Grant pulls out a huge cigar and takes three matches to get it going. "She's in here every Monday night. Her daughter, so she says, is a singer. Christ, everybody is a singer, and they all want to work here. Dropped out of sight, and she thinks she might show up here some time."

"And has she?"

"Hell, how should I know? Hey, I remember where we met now. That benefit for Woody Herman at the Hollywood Bowl."

"Right, your memory is better than you think." It's hard to keep him on track. His mind seems to flit everywhere. I try again. "Anyone still around who might know something about Wardell? A musician maybe?"

Grant puffs on the stogie and engulfs us in a cloud of smoke. "Let me think." He taps his fingers on the table, then stabs at the air with his cigar. "There is a bass player, Elgin 'Pappy' Dean. Everybody just calls him Pappy. Doesn't play much anymore. He's almost as old as me. He was around then. Jesus, man, that was 1955."

"I know, I know. You know where I could find this Dean guy?"

Grant looks around the lounge. "Yeah, that's him, standing right over there at the bar. Guy in the Panama hat."

I follow Grant's gaze. Elgin Dean is a very big, very dark black man with a white beard, talking animatedly with Art Farmer's bass player. His tan suit, white shirt, and tie make him, except for Art Farmer, the best-dressed man in the lounge.

"Well," I say to Grant. "I'll give him a try. Thanks for the drink."

"Anytime. Stick around for the next set."

I leave Grant and head for the bar. It's thinned out considerably now, although a line is already forming for the next show. I wait a minute or two until I see the bass player moving off, then introduce myself to Dean.

"Elgin Dean? I'm Evan Horne." I offer my hand, which Dean takes more by reflex than courtesy. "Alan said you might be able to help me."

Dean glances quickly toward Grant's booth, then back at me with slight suspicion in his eyes. "Oh yeah?"

I launch into my research speech as quickly as possible. "You a writer?" Dean asks.

I know this tune. Musicians, myself included, are naturally suspicious of writers. They often don't know who they're talking to, they usually don't know music, and generally they ask stupid questions. "No, piano player. Just helping out a friend over at UNLV."

Dean holds up his empty glass. "Who you work with?"

"Lonnie Cole for a few years." I signal the bartender to order a beer and look at Dean. "Scotch?"

"Cognac. You play on the live album?"

"That's me." The bartender brings our drinks. I offer Dean a cigarette. He takes one, lights up, and gives me a good going-over with eyes that have seen everything. "So, whatta you want that an old bass player knows? You call me Pappy."

"Okay, Pappy. Wardell Gray. My friend is writing an article about him. Alan said you were around when he died."

"Wow, Wardell." Pappy throws his head back and laughs. "I haven't thought of him for years." He shakes his head. "That skinny little junkie sure could play." He pauses for a moment, looking at his glass, then downs half the cognac. "Yeah, I was around then. Came out here with a territory band from Oklahoma. Stayed around, got some gigs here and there. Even made the Strip hotels when they needed a black face or two in the band, when Lena Horne or Sammy Davis was here. You know how that shit goes." He doesn't wait for my answer. "Well, that's history now, and so is Wardell. Come on, let's take a walk."

I get Dean another cognac, and we walk over to a less-crowded part of the casino and take a couple of stools at a bank of slot machines. He fumbles in his pocket for a quarter, drops it in a machine, and pulls a handle. Not even a cherry. He shrugs. "Keno is my game."

"Did you ever work at the Moulin Rouge, after Benny Carter left?"

Dean smiles at me for the first time. "You done your home-work, huh? Yeah, a few times. The west side was cool then, not all this gang shit we got now. These young bloods are crazy. I worked in a six-piece group, did some shows, that kind of thing."

"And Wardell?"

"I was working that night, not at the Rouge. Little bar that had some jazz. Heard about it the next day. We was all shocked, man. Not about the drugs, but that the cat was dead, in the desert." Dean shakes his head sadly. "Wardell was bad, man, bad. You ever heard those sides he did with Dexter? Wardell could have made it big."

"So what do you think happened? Papers say he was with the dancer Teddy Hale and fell out of bed, broke his neck."

Dean laughs outright at that. "Yeah, he might have been with Teddy, but I never bought that fall-out-of-bed shit. What else the papers say?"

"Head wounds, possibly from a blunt instrument," I say.

Dean nods in agreement. "Yeah, that sounds right, like a pipe or a gun. Teddy coulda been bought off. Easy to make it look like Wardell OD'd."

"By who?"

"Who do you think, man? You never seen that movie *The Godfather*? They ran this town, man." Dean looks around as if someone might overhear us. I keep reminding myself we're talking about a thirty-seven-year-old case that is apparently not even a case.

"I knew a couple of cats in the band," Pappy continues. "They say Wardell had eyes for a woman hung out at the Rouge or was a dancer in the show. If she belonged to one of them godfather dudes, well . . ." Dean's voice trails off, and he spreads his hands and smiles.

Maybe this was more than a theory. "But what about the police? There must have been some kind of investigation."

Dean looks at me, puzzled. "You know what this town was like then? Selma. Redneck, baby, redneck. Sammy, Lena, they couldn't even stay in the hotels they was playin' in. Sammy went in the pool at the Sands and they drained it. Took Harry Belafonte and his calypso ass to break into the blackjack tables."

Dean takes a deep breath and sighs audibly even over the bells of the slot machines all around us. "Far as the police cared, Wardell was just another dead spook in the desert. They didn't investigate shit."

"So that's it, then. There's no way to prove any of this, I guess."

He points a finger at me. "There's one way. You find that woman, you might be onto something. If I was you, I'd be careful though."

"Why?"

"There's still some of them godfather dudes around."

5

THOSE "GODFATHER DUDES" Pappy Dean mentioned are still on my mind as I ease into the final tune of my first set of the day at the Fashion Show Mall. So is Brent Tyler. I can see him walking toward me, phone to his ear, gesturing with his other hand. Must be a big deal mall emergency. I'm sure it's more than a coincidence that his stroll to this end of the mall is at 2:45 P.M. The timing is to see that my breaks are coming on schedule. Tyler runs a tight ship.

A piano player I knew in Los Angeles was once faced with a similar situation when the club owner insisted on a precise schedule—forty minutes on, twenty minutes off. Sometimes in a club the music runs over, the solos are longer, or someone requests something near the end of the set. And sometimes the breaks run over. Customers want to talk, someone wants to buy you a drink. This club owner wasn't hearing it. Stick to the schedule, he'd said.

The next night this pianist brought in an alarm clock, set it on top of the piano, and at the end of forty minutes it rang loudly. He stopped playing even though he was in the middle of a song. The owner went berserk. The pianist had made his point. He was fired for his trouble. Brent Tyler, I decide, would make a good club owner.

My hand is tired and sore, but I've made it through in respectable fashion by keeping mostly to ballads. No complaints or response from the Las Vegas shopping public as yet. I finish with a flourish, feeling my right hand tighten up as I try to stretch over an octave.

Tyler steps over the velvet rope and leans on the piano. "How's it going? What was that you were playing?"

"Old Tadd Dameron tune. Never was a hit or anything."

Tyler nods. "You might try some of the Carpenters' songs. They're big again. Saw them advertising on TV."

I let that one pass while Tyler looks at his watch. "Your fifteen-minute break is about due, eh?"

I stand up and stretch. "Gosh, time flies when you're having fun. Think I'll get a cup of coffee." I close the keyboard cover and head for the coffee concession, where, according to the sign, they roast their own beans. Tyler tags along and decides to join me. We order and he picks up the tab, checks his watch, and heads off to handle yet another mall emergency.

"You're doing a great job, Evan," he calls over his shoulder. Mission accomplished.

I find a free table in the smoking section, feeling just a little self-conscious in a tux while everyone around me is in casual clothes, but no one says anything. I'm sipping the coffee and watching the passing parade of shoppers when a voice behind me says, "You were with Alan Grant last night, weren't you?"

I turn to see the same woman that stopped by Grant's table. Today she's dressed in a smartly tailored suit and carries a bag from Saks. Last night it was difficult to tell her age, but in the harsh mall lighting I can see she's older than I thought, but still has a striking complexion and features like Lena Horne. "Yeah, that's right."

"Mind if I join you for a minute?"

"Sure, sit down. I've got to go back in a couple of minutes."
She takes in my tux and glances toward the piano, then back
at me. "Now I remember," she says. "About two years ago, you
were here with Lonnie Cole at . . . Caesar's Palace?"

"Golden Nugget downtown."

"Of course. My daughter and I went. She loves Lonnie. She's
a singer herself. Maybe you've heard of her. Rachel Cody?" She
smiles, then shakes her head. "I'm sorry, I'm Louise Cody." She
offers her hand. It's cool and firm. When she leans in, I catch a
slight whiff of some very subtle perfume.

"Evan Horne."

"And you're a friend of Alan Grant?"

"Not really. He was just helping me out with an old mystery."

"Sounds intriguing."

"Well, it was a long time ago. I'm doing some research on
the Moulin Rouge for a friend of mine at the university. One of
the musicians died the second night. Wardell Gray. He was a
saxophone player."

Louise Cody smiles briefly again, and her eyelashes flutter.
She has to be nearly sixty but she's still a beautiful woman.
"Your friend's name wouldn't happen to be Professor Buffington?" She catches my look. "Somehow he got my phone number, asked me lots of questions about the Moulin Rouge, but I
told him I don't remember much."

"You there at the time?"

"Well, yes. Just a few weeks. After the trouble, my mother,
well I was just a young girl then, and she thought it was too
dangerous. That was pretty much the end of my dancing career.
I went away to college, and now I'm a boring old real estate
career woman."

"And your daughter?"

Her eyes cloud over. She looks away and stares into space.
"I haven't seen her for some time now. That's why I go to the
Four Queens."

"I'm sorry." This was getting too heavy too quickly. I glance at my watch. "About time for me to go back to work. I'd like to talk to you about the Moulin Rouge sometime."

"Well, I suppose I . . . what time do you finish?" She glances toward the piano. "This *is* a rather different engagement for you, isn't it?"

"Four o'clock. Yeah, you could say that." I didn't feel like going through the story of my accident and how this was my big comeback.

"I have a house to show at four. I'm free after that. Perhaps we could meet someplace."

"Fine, just tell me where."

"There's a coffee bar out near Desert Shores called Capio's. It's right near the freeway. Are you familiar with the city?"

"I'll find it. See you then."

She gets up with me and goes to the escalator. I can feel her eyes on me as I sit down at the piano, flex my fingers, and think about what I'm going to play. When I turn around she's gone.

By the end of the next hour I'm scanning the mall for Mary Lou, my relief. My right hand is cramping badly, and I'm grateful I don't have to play another set. Two hours and I'm finished. I feel like smashing the keyboard with my fist. I've been taking longer between tunes to save my hand. Maybe this wasn't such a good idea after all.

I look over my shoulder and feel relieved to see Mary Lou coming down the escalator with her briefcase full of music. She waves and joins me at the piano. Despite the heat outside, Mary Lou looks remarkably cool in a long black skirt, white blouse, and bow tie. I'm guessing she's mid-twenties. Her hair is pulled back and held in place with a black beret.

"God, the traffic was a bitch," she says, dropping the briefcase on the floor. Mary Lou, I learned the first day, is a piano major at UNLV. She's aiming for a symphony career but will probably settle for a public school music gig.

"What are you going to share with the shoppers today?" I ask.

"Mozart," she says, digging into the briefcase for a stack of music. "I've got a recital coming up." She notices me massaging my right hand. "Still bothering you, huh? Have you thought of trying a cortisone shot?"

"No, thanks. I don't like drugs. I'll put some ice on it later." I surrender the piano bench to Mary Lou and head for the escalator. As I glide up to the second level, I look down at her. She arranges the music on the piano and launches into a concerto as if it were a Carnegie Hall recital.

CAPIO'S ISN'T HARD to find. The Desert Shores signs are all along U.S. 95. I take the Cheyenne exit and cruise the shopping center till I spot some patio tables and the Capio's sign. It's wedged between a Family Fitness gym and a greeting card shop. Louise Cody is already seated and waiting for me.

I leave my tux jacket and tie in the VW and suffer the hot fifty-yard walk, wondering if anyone ever gets used to it. The TV weatherman had talked about cooling trends with the temperature dipping to 102 degrees.

Heat doesn't seem to bother Louise Cody. She has draped her suit jacket over the back of the chair. Her face is half covered by large, stylish sunglasses.

"It's not as bad as you think," she says as she notices my glance into Capio's cool interior. "These misters really work." Above our heads is a network of thin pipes that send off a cool welcoming spray. The mist is so fine, it evaporates before you get wet. Louise's drink is okay, so I go inside, get an iced cappuccino, and join her.

"At least you can smoke out here," she says.

I take a long drink of my coffee, get a cigarette going, and wonder why she's so agreeable. I haven't picked up any of the apprehension or reluctance Ace described when he talked to her. I put it down to what I hope is her connection to me as a musician, or rather my potential connection to her daughter. Maybe she just likes musicians. "So, tell me what it was like when the Moulin Rouge opened."

She takes off her glasses and shakes her head. "I've been thinking a lot of about it since your friend called me, more this afternoon. I'm afraid I wasn't very nice when I talked to him, but I had other things on my mind."

"Your daughter? Alan Grant told me you've kind of lost touch."

"Yes, I haven't seen her for weeks, and I'm getting very worried. Well, she's a big girl. I guess I shouldn't fret so much about it." She forces a smile. "Anyway, you want to hear about the Moulin Rouge."

"And Wardell Gray," I remind her. "If you can recall anything."

"That place jumped around the clock, but especially late at night. Once the shows were over at other casinos, everybody came by the Moulin Rouge. People never knew what big names they were going to see at the Rouge. Black and white entertainers who had known each other for years and worked on the same stages found this was the only place they could socialize together. A lot of the hotels would be deserted after two o'clock because everyone was at the Rouge."

"And the musicians?"

"Same thing. You wouldn't believe how much sitting in there was after the shows, but I don't think anyone thought of it as making history even though it was the first interracial hotel-casino. But six months, and it was all over." Louise shakes her head and stares out at endless rows of cars in the parking lot.

"What happened?"

"The night before it closed, the place was packed as usual.

We were devastated. We had a show to do, and the next thing you know, they told us it was closed."

"I thought you were only there a few weeks."

Louise smiles but won't meet my eyes. "Caught me. I went back, very much against my mother's wishes, the last month. I was eighteen, hooked on the glamour, the celebrities, the excitement. I had to go back. Can you understand that?"

"I think so, but in a different way." Maybe what I didn't want to admit, even to myself, was that same feeling was pushing me to play a solo piano gig at a shopping mall.

"Well," Louise says, "at least you're still doing it. I sell homes to casino executives and retired Californians."

"And I bet you're good at it."

"I've been lucky. This town runs on juice, they call it—influence, connections."

"Did the Moulin Rouge have anything to do with that?"

"No," she says, but her answer is too quick. "Why do you ask?"

"Just curious. What about Wardell Gray?"

Louise shrugs. "I just remember a swinging band and Wardell being a nice, good-looking man who played great saxophone. He was too fast and too old for me, and the word was he was doing drugs."

"What was the feeling the night he died?"

"Of course everybody was shocked, sad, but there was a show-must-go-on kind of thing, and it was kept pretty quiet."

I could imagine. Two nights into the opening of a new hotel, and one of the musicians is found dead in the desert. Not the kind of publicity any business would want. I drink the last of the iced coffee and chew on an ice cube, letting some silence pass between us, but I sense Louise has told me all she's going to, and now she'll get to her real reason for meeting with me.

I glance at my watch. Misters or not, I'm thinking about Ace's pool, but I'm too late.

"Look," Louise says, "maybe I can help. I kept a journal during the Moulin Rouge days. I didn't tell your friend that. I'll go through it, see if there's something else that might be helpful." She sits up straighter in her chair and assumes what I guess is her closing posture. "I read about the Lonnie Cole thing. I know you were pretty involved in that investigation, and I thought—"

"That was a one-time thing," I say, cutting her off. "If you read all the accounts, you know I was named in the blackmail note as a go-between. I didn't have much choice about getting involved."

"Oh, I know. I wasn't thinking about anything like that."

"What then?"

"My daughter. I am worried, and I don't know how to look for her other than hoping she might show up some night at the Four Queens. You're a musician, you must know a lot of musicians in town, the hangouts. You could ask around. I would certainly pay you for your trouble."

I stub out my cigarette before answering her. She's a nice woman, so I measure my words carefully. "Louise, this is the first time I've been able to even remotely play the piano in more than a year. That's the only thing I want to think about at the moment. Wardell Gray—the Moulin Rouge thing—is just to help out a friend. I'm not a detective or an investigator or whatever they call them in Nevada, and believe me, I wouldn't know where to start looking for your daughter, whether you pay me or not." I pause for a moment and try to take the edge off my voice. "I'm sorry."

"You're right," Louise says. "I had no right to ask. It's just, I'm afraid something might have happened to her."

"Call the police. File a missing persons report. You don't even know if she's still in Las Vegas."

"No, I don't want . . . can't do that. I don't want to go into it, but I just can't."

"Well, I don't know what else to tell you." I try to be firm, but I find I just can't walk away either. "Look, tell you what I will do. You're right. I know some musicians, some of the clubs here. I'll ask around a bit, see if anyone knows her, but I don't want your money and I'm not promising anything."

"Thank you, I would appreciate any news." She digs into her purse and pulls out a photograph. "Just in case." She hands me the photograph and I flash on photos of Lonnie Cole and Charlie Crisp. This is how that all started.

Rachel Cody, blond, her hair cut short, is smiling at the camera like she hasn't a care in the world. "When was this taken?"

Louise sees my look of surprise. "I know, even light-skinned black girls aren't usually blond. She wanted a new image. That was taken about a year ago at my house. By the way, if you're free for dinner some time I'd love to have you out." She digs in her purse again and comes out with a business card.

I nod and start for my car. "Evan? There's just one more thing."

"Yes."

"Rachel is a very good singer." Her smile is like a plea.

I sit in the car for a minute, Rachel Cody's photo in one hand, her mother's business card in the other.

A possible murder out of the past, a missing person in the present. Where do I go from here? I start the car and drive off, wondering what Danny Cooper will think of all this.

6

THERE'S A NOTE on my door from Ace when I get back
to the apartment. He wants me to join him at a tennis club in
Green Valley. I look longingly at the pool. A drive across town
in this relentless heat isn't appealing, but I think Ace needs
some company, and there is a sense of urgency in his note.

"Please try to make it by five," Ace has written, along with
directions to the club. I check my watch and find there's still
time for a quick dip if I hurry.

Ten years ago Green Valley was nothing but desert, several
hundred acres of it, owned by the Greenspun family, who also
owned and published the *Las Vegas Sun* newspaper. In the far
southeast corner of the city, Green Valley is now a sprawl of
comfortable homes, shopping centers, restaurants, and apartment complexes. A development pushing Las Vegas ever closer
to Los Angeles.

The tennis club is just off Sunset Road and upscale all the
way. I park in the busy lot and hope shorts and T-shirt are
adequate for whatever Ace has in mind. A pretty blond at the
front desk, dressed in a tennis skirt and top, directs me to the
courts on the lower level.

"Almost finished," Ace yells, and waves as I take a seat on the bench at his court. For his size, Ace moves amazingly well and his height is a real asset at the net. But his opponent, a chunky man with a gray beard, moves faster and is too much. He passes Ace with a blistering shot down the line for match point, then throws his racket in the air.

Ace drops his racket and applauds the shot. "Next time, Jim, next time," Ace says. The other man waves, and Ace flops on the bench beside me and towels off. "I'm beat," Ace says.

"Now I know your secret. Playing on an air-conditioned court."

"Once in a while," Ace says. "I'm just his guest today. This club is too expensive for college professors."

I know Ace well enough to sense that he's stalling, avoiding telling me something. "So, what's up?"

Ace gathers up his things and shoves them in his tennis bag. "Let me grab a shower and I'll meet you up in the juice bar, okay?"

"Sure." I go back upstairs. The bar is across from the front desk. Two guys in workout clothes are doing their best to interest the bartender, but she looks to be in better shape than both of them. I order some kind of juice shake that's the special of the day and watch an aerobics class through a wall of glass opposite the bar.

The women are dressed in outfits ranging from leotards to warmup suits to shorts and T-shirts. The sound of heavy rock music leaks through the wall. Watching these women grind it out before a disciplinarian instructor makes me think of Cindy.

"She called today," Ace says, dropping his bag on the floor. "A bottled water, please," he calls to the girl behind the bar.

"Who?" I watch Ace pour the water into an ice-filled glass.

"Cindy." Ace nods toward the aerobics class. "You told me how much she was into working out."

"That I did. What did she want?"

"Just, you know, how you were doing." Ace takes a long pull of his water. "The girl is nuts about you, my friend. You know that, don't you? Love is the pump that inflates the soul."

"You going poetic on me, Ace?"

"That's from a Czech writer, Milan Kundera. He's right you know."

I'm not one to spill everything to my friends, but I know Ace means well. "Yeah, I know. You didn't drag me all the way over here for advice to the lovelorn, did you?"

Ace laughs. "No, not from me, but Cindy and I had quite a little talk. She just wonders why you haven't called her. She's worried about you. You know, how the gig is going, that kind of thing."

"It's not going, Ace." I reach for a cigarette but remember this is a health club. The smoking police will probably surround the club if I light up. "I can barely get through the two hours. Two hours, Ace. I've played club gigs backing two or three horns for six hours and I was still ready to play more. Now I can't get through a solo gig for a third of the time." I flex my fingers and stare at my hand as if it's betrayed me.

"Hey, it's early," Ace says. "You just started. It'll just take time to get back in the swing of things."

"I'd like to believe that, but I think I know better."

Ace is silent for a few moments. He knows better than to push it, and I know he wants me to make it.

"So how are you doing?"

"You mean with Janey gone? Okay, I guess." He shrugs. "The days are long. You know, we never spent a night apart since I was in graduate school. Sometimes it just doesn't seem possible that she's gone." He blinks back a couple of tears and takes another drink. He stares off into space for a few moments, lost in memory. "Anyway, a lot of teaching, writing to do. I don't know why, but this article has become really important to me, Evan."

Cindy's call was not the urgency in Ace's note. He just wanted some company. Glad for the change of subject, I tell him about my talk with Pappy Dean and Louise Cody. Ace immediately discounts Pappy's apprehension and is excited by Louise Cody's revelations.

"C'mon, Evan. Wardell's death is ancient history. Who would be interested in it now except a professor who needs to get published? The mafia is history too. These days the town is run by corporations."

"So they tell me." That was certainly true as far as music goes. The bean counters in suits closed lounges, cut back on entertainment, and installed more slot machines in its place.

"Well, there might be some leftovers, but who would be left from the fifties?"

"Maybe I'll find out."

Ace ignores that. "It sure would be nice to get a look at Louise Cody's diary. You know there could even be a book in all this. Maybe you'll get lucky and find her daughter and—"

"Settle down, Ace. I'll do your research for you, but I'm not in the missing persons business."

Ace puts up his hands in surrender. "Okay, okay," he says. "Just do me one favor. Call Cindy."

"I did. Left a message."

"Yeah, well, talk to her next time."

ACE IS RIGHT about one thing. Corporations do run Las Vegas now, and that mentality extends into complimentary tickets for shows. Before my shift at the Fashion Show I make a few calls to some musicians to see if I can line up something for Coop and his meter maid, but it's not until I get through to Wayne Newton's conductor that I have any luck.

"Yeah, it's tough these days," Tommy Redman says. "Tony Orlando couldn't even get his mother comped, and the hotel charged him for every bottle of champagne he gave away at the show."

"How is the Midnight Idol?"

"Wayne? He's putting my kids through college, thank you very much. They'll owe their education to 'Danke Schön.' "

I've heard Tommy play many times. He isn't Bill Evans or Oscar Peterson, but he knows how to play for singers and conduct an orchestra. "Well, do what you can, Tommy."

"You got it, man. I'll tell Wayne Lonnie Cole's conductor wants to see the show. That should do it. I'll try for Friday night."

"Thanks, Tommy. Let me know."

THANKS TO TOMMY, when Coop calls from the Rio Hotel on Friday, I can tell him we have ringside seats to Wayne Newton's show. "You owe me big-time, Coop."

"Why? I thought this was a freebie."

"It is, but if I have to sit through the show, you're heavily in my debt."

"You jazz guys are all alike. How about if I introduce you to my friend from Metro after the show?"

"That would do it."

"Okay, I'll check with him. No promises though."

"I know you'll do your best to further relations with the Santa Monica police."

"Fuck you, Horne."

COOP IS CHECKING his watch and pacing around in front of the showroom entrance when I get to the Sands. A line snakes from the desk back through the casino. The tables are crowded with players, and the banks of slots and video poker machines are crammed with hopefuls, eyes glazed, palms blackened from the slot handles. When Coop sees me he charges forward, a scowl on his face.

"We're going to be late, aren't we? We'll never get a seat."

"Relax. Where's your companion?"

"Huh?" Coop spins around, scanning the crowd. A tallish blond in a black cocktail dress waves at him from a video poker machine. She gathers up some quarters from the tray and comes over.

"Winning already? Hi, I'm Evan Horne."

"Natalie Beamer." She holds out her hand. I try to imagine her in a police uniform. Even a quick glance tells me I wouldn't mind a parking ticket from her. Coop has outdone himself. He looks proud but is assessing the line to the showroom.

"Hadn't we better go?"

"Yeah, c'mon," I say. I lead them to the invited guest line. Miraculously, all the arrangements have been made. We're quickly ushered into the showroom and shown to a booth near the stage. Coop slips a folded bill to the maître d', and the three of us slide into the booth. It's nearly center stage. Coop is beaming.

The room is quickly filling up. There's a buzz of conversation, and the waiters and waitresses are bustling about, trying to get drink orders in before the show. Coop orders a split of champagne for himself and Natalie. I settle for a couple of beers.

"All right," Coop says. He pats Natalie on the shoulder. "I told you my man would come through."

I raise my glass to them. "Here's to a happy weekend."

"This is awfully nice of you, Evan," Natalie says.

"No problem. It wasn't that difficult."

"No, I mean to sit through this show." She gives me a big smile and nudges Coop.

He rolls his eyes. "Yeah, I forgot to tell you. Natalie here claims to like jazz. Just don't get any ideas, sport."

I like her already. "Any favorites?" I think I can see this coming, but I'm wrong. Natalie knows her stuff.

"I love Chick Corea," she says, "and I just bought all the early Stan Getz that was reissued on CD."

"I'm impressed."

"Lot of money for a sax player," Coop says. "Kenny G, now there's a sax player."

Natalie and I both scowl. "There isn't any early Kenny G, Coop," I say. "He hasn't been around long enough." Natalie and I are going to be good friends.

The house lights dim, a timpani roll signals a booming voice from off stage that dramatically announces, "The Sands Hotel proudly presents Mr. Las Vegas, the Midnight Idol, Wayne Newton."

A wave of applause sweeps the room as the curtain goes up, the band kicks in, and Wayne strides onstage in a white suit, waving and smiling, shaking hands with the ringsiders. He grabs the mike at center stage and launches into a fast version of "Country Roads."

Coop is mesmerized. Natalie sips her champagne and stares curiously at the stage. I recognize several of the musicians and Tommy, of course, his back to the stage, watching Newton out of the corner of his eye, putting the band through its paces.

For one reason or another a lot of jazz musicians have passed through hotel house bands. James Moody, Dizzy's long-time partner, and Red Rodney, who toured with Charlie Parker, are two who labored behind the Las Vegas stars while nobody in the audience would give them a second look or know who they were if you told them.

After nearly two hours of nonstop Newtonizing, which includes the obligatory "Danke Schoen" and numbers by Wayne on banjo, guitar, drums, and just about anything else, the audience prepares for the finale. Tie loosened, Wayne starts talking to the audience, introduces Tommy and the band.

I lean in close to Coop. "Now he's going to say, 'We normally finish about now but you're such a great audience, we want to play some more for you. Right, guys?' "

Newton says exactly that, and right on cue, the horn section rises in unison and dons McDonald's hats. "You deserve a break today!" they shout.

"How about these guys?" Newton asks the audience. The crowd breaks up, and naturally, they love it. "Hit it," Wayne shouts. The band goes into "Mack the Knife," Wayne's tribute to Bobby Darin. That's followed by "America the Beautiful" as a huge screen rolls down behind the band and an American flag flutters in the breeze. Wayne hits his last notes and salutes the audience, who are on their feet before the last chord for the twice-nightly standing ovation.

Coop jumps up to join in and claps so hard my ears sting. Natalie, I notice, is as reluctant as me to rise. The house lights come up, and Coop drops back into his seat, looking nearly as tired as Wayne must be.

"Well, I've got to admit," Natalie says, "he gives them their money's worth."

"That was fucking great," Coop says. He slaps me on the back. "Thanks, sport."

"The best thing Wayne Newton does is make large contributions to the UNLV jazz program."

"No shit," Coop says.

We wait a few minutes for the room to clear out a bit, then make our way toward the exit, jostled by the happy group of tourists who will return to Iowa or Indiana raving about what they've just seen. I don't have the heart to tell Coop that exactly the same thing will happen almost word for word at the midnight show and for the next two weeks as well.

We finally emerge in the casino. Coop looks at his watch. "We're supposed to meet this guy at the casino bar. Natalie, why don't you—?" but she's already ahead of him.

"I've got a date with a poker machine," she says. "I'll catch up with you guys later." She disappears into the crowd and Coop and I head for the bar.

"Nice, Coop, very nice," I say. "I don't think you deserve her."

"We'll see," Coop says.

At the bar Coop looks around and heads for a short stocky man with a brush cut and a dark suit. "That's him," Coop says. There are no other seats at the bar, so the man picks up his drink and follows us to a table.

"Hi, John, how you doing? Evan, John Trask, Metro Homicide." We shake hands briefly while Trask sizes me up.

A stunning brunette with exceptionally long legs takes our drink order. Trask shakes his head as she walks away. "That's why I don't come into the casinos," he says. Except for his eyes, which seem to take everything in, there's not much cop about Trask. He glances once at Coop and turns to me. I have the feeling they've already worked out something between them.

"So," Trask begins, "Coop tells me you're investigating an old murder."

"I don't think 'investigate' is the right word. Research is more like it, for a friend at the university. I also don't know that it was a murder."

"It wasn't," Trask says. He's all business now. "I checked our files. Of course they weren't computerized in 1955, but it's not listed as an unsolved. We wouldn't be having this conversation if it was. In fact, it's not listed at all. I did check with the coroner's office, but all they have is an incident report. Wardell Gray is shown as a drug overdose."

Coop listens passively. I'm sure he knows all this already but wants me to hear it from Trask.

"Wouldn't there have been some kind of an investigation?"

"Probably not," Trask says.

Even though I knew Trask was going to tell me this, it's still disappointing. Then I remember what Pappy Dean told me. "Just out of curiosity, is there still any kind of organized crime presence in Las Vegas?"

What I would describe as a meaningful look passes between Coop and Trask.

"Sure," Trask says. "That's why the FBI has a task force here."

"Is it possible there are relatives left over from that era?" I don't know where I'm going with this but it elicits a smile from Trask and Coop both.

"Tony Spilatro was the last of the big guys from Chicago, and he and his brother were found in an Indiana corn field. You're not planning to hunt up old mob guys and ask them if they know anything about Wardell Gray?"

"No, I don't think so."

"Good," Trask says. He puts his empty glass on the table. "Sorry I couldn't be more help." He reaches in his coat pocket and takes out a business card. "If you have any more questions, give me a call."

"Thanks." I glance at the card and think of something else. "Are there any guys still on with Metro who might remember the case?"

"Like I said, there wasn't any case." Trask pauses and glances again at Coop, who seems preoccupied with the casino crowd. "There is a guy, he's retired now, but he was a sergeant then. He might talk to you." Trask takes his card back and writes a number and name on the back. "Buddy Herman. He'll entertain you. He's got a lot of stories about the old days."

"Thanks," I say, pocketing the card.

Trask gets to his feet. "Well, gentlemen, it's been nice. Good to meet you, Horne. Thanks for the drink. Coop, you too. Drop by and say hello." Trask leaves the bar and is quickly swallowed up by the crowd of gamblers.

"Well, are we even?" Coop lights one of his little cigars.

"All square. Thanks, Coop."

"Take his advice," Coop says.

"What advice was that?"

"Leave the past alone."

7

DRUMMERS WALK IN four-four time; bass players just walk. When I get to the Hob Nob, that's exactly what Pappy Dean is about to do—walk on two hundred years of German wood he wouldn't trust to skycaps but which survives in a canvas bag and gets around on one wheel with Pappy's arm cradling it like an old friend.

B. B. King calls his guitar Lucille; Pappy calls his bass Trouble. "That's what it is," he says as he unzips the bag and pulls it off the bass. He neatly folds the bag and lays it near his amp. "Keeping it in tune, keeping it safe, keeping it working. It's all trouble."

He cradles the bass and reaches for a key on the piano, a battered spinet covered with cigarette burns and stains from hundreds of forgotten drinks.

"Don't know why I bother," Pappy says, banging on the key. "This motherfucker hasn't been in tune for years." He carefully lays the bass on its side and glares at the drummer, a tall thin black man who's just beginning to set up.

"We hit in fifteen minutes," he says to the drummer. Turning to me, he shakes his head. "My gigs start on time. C'mon, I'll buy you a drink."

I hadn't planned on the Hob Nob, but Pappy had called right after I got back from the Sands. His call was more than an invitation. I knew I wasn't going to sleep, so I took him up on it. The Hob Nob is light years from the Strip, literally across the tracks in an industrial area on Highland next to a sex tease club called—this week—Runway 69. I doubt if a single tourist has even been to the Hob Nob.

The bandstand is nothing more than a cleared-away corner in the cavernous bar that was once a country-and-western club. Huge paintings of Kenny Rogers, Elvis, and Willie Nelson hang on one wall, and a half dozen pool tables fill up one end of the room.

Heavy metal bands are featured on weekends, or nothing, but tonight is jazz night, which I assume management feels is better than nothing. The bands play for a percentage of the bar, which usually amounts to only a few dollars. Musicians who gig at the Hob Nob view it as a paid rehearsal. It's the nature of jazz musicians to play, paid or not. Club owners know this, and often take advantage. I don't know who's smarter, the club owners who get a band cheap or the musicians who get a place to play.

Pappy and I sit at the long bar—we're the only two customers at the moment—and sip on the two beers the bartender has brought without asking. "Dude I want you to meet," Pappy says. He tilts the Panama hat on the back of his head. "Tenor player named Sonny Wells. He ain't saying much these days, but there was a time." Pappy shakes his head remembering the past. "He's been scuffling for years. If he ain't crashed with somebody—sometimes me—he sleeps on the street downtown, plays for change in a storefront."

The name doesn't ring a bell with me, but there are a lot of lost jazz orphans out there. "He knew Wardell?"

Pappy nods. "He was around then. I think he knew Wardell in L.A. Might be able to help you. 'Course is brain is fried now."

I wonder about Pappy's interest in this. He certainly has no reason to help me. I don't want to ask, but I do anyway.

"I don't know, man," he says. "People do a lot of funny things. This whole Wardell thing never set well with me or a lot of people. No tellin' what he would have done if he'd lived. Look at Dexter Gordon. If there was more to it than a drug thing, I'd like to know." Pappy looks at his watch, then toward the door. "Don't look like Sonny's gonna make it."

"If he doesn't?"

Pappy smiles and adjusts his hat to a rakish angle. "Then it's trio time." He swivels on the bar stool and watches the drummer finish setting up. The piano player has arrived, and the two of them are laughing and joking but glancing occasionally toward Pappy.

I decide to push my luck with Pappy. I take out the photo of Rachel Cody and show it to him. "You know this girl?"

Pappy takes the photo and frowns at it for a moment. "She a singer?"

"Yeah, her mother was a dancer at the Moulin Rouge when it first opened."

Pappy looks from me to the photo and back a couple of times. His face creases into a huge grin. "Shit, you some kind of detective too, ain't you?" He hands me back the photo and looks at me with a new expression.

"No, no, nothing like that. Her mother just wants me to ask around."

"Uh huh," Pappy says. He's not really buying it. "I think I do know her. I seen her around couple of places, sittin' in."

"You remember where?"

"Nah, couple of places on the west side, maybe out at Pogo's. I think she's doing some heavy coke, and that's trouble."

"I thought your bass was trouble." Pappy grins and slaps my outstretched palm.

"You want to play?" Pappy asks me. He gets off the bar stool and brushes off some lint from his jacket.

I knew this was coming. I knew I'd be tempted, and I know how I'm going to answer. I feel like I've walked into a party without an invitation, and the host is embarrassed but accommodating. Pappy is this party's host, but he's not embarrassed. "I don't think so," I say.

Pappy nods again. "When you *know*, just holler." He heads for the bandstand, picks up Trouble, and starts walking a blues line the drummer and piano player quickly pick up. The drummer rushes slightly, but Pappy reins him in. After the head, the piano player spins off a few adequate choruses, but his heart is not in it, despite Pappy's prodding. He knows the tunes but does nothing more than run the chords. Maybe it's too early.

They do better on a couple of standards. Pappy is solid as a rock and plays decent lines against the pianist's chords. I listen, mentally playing the substitute chord game with myself, realizing I wouldn't sound any better if I had played.

Forty minutes later there is still no sign of Sonny Wells, nor any more customers, except for two guys in jeans and T-shirts who shoot a couple of games of pool. The crack of the balls competes with the band, and between shots they stare at Pappy's trio like they are aliens. Not everybody likes jazz.

Just after midnight the door opens, and two guys in their mid-thirties dressed like they've just come from Armani walk in. They scan the room, then take barstools on either side of me. When the bartender comes over, they wave him away. The biggest one stares impassively at the band. Expensive or not, his suit is too tight. His arms bulge at the sleeves, and I imagine he spends a lot of time with heavy weights.

"Your name Evan Horne?" the other one says. He's about my height and weight, wears his hair in a ponytail, and chews vigorously on a wad of gum.

"Yeah. Do I know you?" I glance toward the bandstand.

Pappy is pulling on his bass, eyes closed, head nodding in time to the music.

"Not likely, but for the record it's Tony." He doesn't offer his hand. He shifts on the bar stool and unbuttons his coat. "This is a dump, Horne," Tony says, looking around the bar. "Bad neighborhood. All kinds of things could happen to someone in a place like this. I think there was a knifing here just last week. Isn't that right, Karl?"

Karl doesn't look at either of us. "That's right, Tony."

"You see what I mean," Tony says. "Karl is up on these things."

Karl looks like he could make some of those bad things happen. Pappy and the trio have stopped playing. They hover around the piano, talking, lighting cigarettes, and glancing our way. I'm beginning to regret not taking Pappy up on his offer to play.

Tony pops another stick of gum in his mouth and smiles at me. His eyes are cold. "Horne, you look like a smart man. I've got some advice for you." He pauses, then looks directly at me. "Do your research in the library, you know what I mean?"

"I think so."

"Good. Then we understand each other. I can tell my boss that our conversation was very positive. He'll be pleased to hear that."

"And who is your boss?"

Tony smiles again. "That's not important, Horne. What's important is that I can give him a positive report." He gets up. "Nice talking to you, Horne." He heads for the door with Karl trailing close behind.

Pappy walks over, wiping his forehead with a towel, and stands for a moment watching the door.

"Godfather dudes," he says.

———

I WAIT UNTIL Pappy and the trio start another set, but Sonny Wells never shows. Pappy promises to try and get in touch with the saxophonist, and we say good-bye.

"Watch yourself, man," Pappy says.

I do. When I go out to my car, I'm extra careful checking the parking lot, but there's no sign of Tony and Karl.

Back at the apartment I turn on some music, Miles's *Kind of Blue,* and sit up a long time debating whether to tell Ace or Coop or even John Trask at Metro about Tony and Karl's visit to the Hob Nob. Ace would panic; Coop and Trask would say I told you so.

I think about calling Cindy as well. A friendly voice would be welcome about now, but I put it off, settling instead for Miles, Cannonball, and Coltrane weaving their way through the haunting "All Blues." It's like three guys talking on a street corner.

Bill Evans's piano makes me regret not sitting in with Pappy's group. What could be more safe? A deserted bar and, except for Pappy, musicians I'd probably never see again. I'd come close, but I couldn't make myself take the plunge, not yet. Maybe I was kidding myself.

After the accident, when I was going through therapy and squeezing my rubber ball, there was a time I didn't even want to hear any live music, much less play it. There's no way you can prepare for something like that, when a few seconds change your life forever.

I'd never once contemplated not having a career in jazz, playing the piano. Suddenly and perhaps permanently not being able to do what I'd always done left me drained emotionally and physically. I tried to make analogies with athletes—promising quarterbacks who blow out a knee, sit out a season, then return and take their teams to the Superbowl.

I visualized myself in a recording studio making an album or a jazz club in New York on tour with my own trio. It helped, but when the facility failed to return, when things seemed beyond my control, I nearly gave up. Weary of sympathetic looks, well-meaning advice, and words of encouragement, I avoided jazz clubs for the most part and lost contact with a lot of musician friends. It didn't take long for me to be out of the jazz loop.

Then one morning when I was at about the lowest point, I woke up, flexed my hand, and felt a difference. It was slight, almost imperceptible, but I felt it, enough that I approached my piano for the first time in weeks. I sat down with apprehension for a companion and struggled through a ballad.

One solo chorus told me. I knew I was on the way back. It might be a long, tortuous journey, but I was convinced I would make it. Enough to take the Las Vegas gig. But now I'd gotten more than I bargained for.

What I should do is pack my bags, make my apologies to Ace, plead injury to Brent Tyler at the Fashion Show Mall, and go back to L.A. Las Vegas was a bad idea. But I know I won't. I hate unanswered questions, which is why my dad and I never got along and my mother was peacemaker in the family.

What started as a favor to Ace and curiosity to me is now more intriguing than ever. Who would send two central-casting mob types to warn me off investigating the death of a jazz musician more than thirty-five years ago? More importantly, why? Does it have something to do with Louise Cody and her daughter? What did whoever sent Tony and Karl think I was going to find?

I run this around for another hour or so and get nowhere. I finally drop off to sleep with Coop's last words running through my mind.

Leave the past alone.

8

IT'S THE PHONE that finally wakes me. I grope for the receiver and find out it's only Ace. "How about some breakfast? I got coffee going already."

"Sure, sounds good, I think. Give me a few minutes."

"You got it," Ace says. He sounds entirely too cheery. I fight off the grogginess from sleeping too little and starting too late. My head begins to clear as I stand under the shower for several minutes. I throw on some shorts and a T-shirt and feel almost human when I join Ace in the kitchen of the main house.

I bring the jazz reference books with me, and while Ace busies himself with some scrambled-egg-and-peppers concoction, I work on a cup of coffee and stave off the desire for that first cigarette. I look up Sonny Wells and Pappy Dean. Both get a couple of short paragraphs, Pappy's being the longer one.

Pappy is from Detroit. He's spent considerable time on the road with some of the early territory bands, had a short stint with Count Basie and a number of singers before settling in Las Vegas. Sonny Wells—now I know why the name is familiar—was part of the West Coast contingent that worked on Central Avenue in Los Angeles. The writer describes him as "a hard-edged tenor player who was influenced by Don Byas." He has two recordings to his credit, but the last mention of him was in Las Vegas in the early eighties. All roads, it seems, lead to Las Vegas.

Ace delivers his breakfast special, which includes a stack of sourdough toast. "So how was last night?" He joins me at the table and starts to wolf down the eggs. "Your friend enjoy Wayne Newton? He's a cop, isn't he?"

I fill Ace in on Coop's big night but leave out the Hob Nob and Tony and Karl. I don't want to panic Ace, and I don't know what I'm going to do yet.

Ace eyes the reference books. "Something new?"

"Just looking up a couple of musicians. One of them might be a lead."

"Really?" Ace says. He pours me some more coffee and waits to hear more.

"Nothing much to tell, really. Just a guy who might have been around here when Wardell was. I'm going to check it out today."

"Hey, how about if I come along? Maybe we could tape him, you know, get an interview."

"I don't think so, Ace. This guy has been on some hard times. I don't think he's going to feel like being grilled by a college professor. Let me see what he has to say first."

"Yeah, sure, you're probably right," Ace says, but I can see he's clearly disappointed.

"Can I give you a hand with the dishes?"

"No, you go ahead. Listen, take the Jeep if you want. I'm just going to hang around here today. Lots of papers to grade, and I've got to write a test for Monday."

The air-conditioned Cherokee sounds appealing. I go back to my place and dress in my tux. Standing in front of the mirror, flexing my hand a few times, I stare at my own reflection. A not-too-bad-looking thirty-five-year-old piano player who doesn't know when to quit. In the clarity of morning Tony and Karl don't seem quite so threatening. Tony was very cocky; he probably reported to his boss that their veiled threats were more than enough to let me know I should back off. Who the boss is still intrigues me.

The one aspect of their visit I don't like is that they probably know where I live. The only way they could have known I was at the Hob Nob was to have tailed me from the Sands, which means they had to have seen me with Coop and John Trask. Coop they wouldn't know, but they might have made Trask. Nobody—Trask, Coop, or Natalie-knew I was going to the Hob Nob. I didn't know myself until Pappy Dean called me.

It's a short ride to the Fashion Show. The Jeep rides smoothly, and the wonderful air-conditioning staves off the heat, which according to the radio is 107 degrees. I park in back of the mall and take the escalator down to the piano just a minute or two ahead of Brent Tyler.

It's much busier today. The shoppers are out in legions, and the food court is full. Long lines stretch in front of each outlet. A few of the curious watch me take my place at the white grand and kick off the afternoon with a Duke Ellington medley. Tyler is at my shoulder almost immediately.

"Doing great, Horne, just great."

"Thanks, Brent." I give him my best mall smile, but again, I know better. Tyler is typical of people who say something to the band when they come off about how good they sounded when the musicians know it wasn't happening. Maybe ignorance is bliss.

I segue into "Sophisticated Lady." Actually, my hand feels better today. There's no cramping yet, but the two hours stretch ahead. Tyler, relieved that I'm on the job, waves and heads off to do whatever he does.

On an unscheduled break I find a pay phone and call Louise Cody. I get her on the third ring.

"Hi, it's Evan Horne."

"Oh, hello. I was going to call you today. Are you free this evening?"

"We must be on the same wave length. I was going to invite myself to dinner if your offer is still good."

"Of course, that would be nice."

"No news on your daughter yet, if that's what you're wondering."

"I know, it's too soon," Louise says. There's a long pause, which I don't fill. "I've been looking through that diary I told you about. I think I may have some information, something I forgot myself."

"Sounds interesting. What time do you want me?"

"How about seven?"

"That's fine. I've got a couple of things to do after my shift here." She gives me an address in Desert Shores and directions to her house.

I grab a cup of coffee from one of the outlets, and when I get back to the piano, Coop and Natalie are standing just outside the velvet rope. Coop looks a little sheepish.

"Not my idea, sport," Coop says. "Natalie wanted to hear you play."

I nod, somehow irritated to see them there. This isn't a gig I want advertised, even for friends. "Any luck on the machines?"

"I won fifty dollars," Natalie says. "I've already blown it, though." She holds up a Neiman Marcus shopping bag.

"Well, it's time for me to go to work. Anything you'd like to hear? You, I mean," I say to Natalie. "Coop would probably want a Willie Nelson song."

Natalie has one trait I like already. Before she speaks, her eyes close, then flick open and almost catch you unawares. She smiles, thinks for a moment, and asks for a Charlie Parker line. "I'll give it a shot." I flex my hand and begin the intricate line while Coop and Natalie take a table in the food court area. For some reason I'm very aware of Natalie watching me, and when I look up, Coop has gone to get them both drinks. I get through the tune in fair style and finish just when Coop sits down again.

I play four more songs. When I look up again, Natalie is gone, probably for more shopping. She's still not back when I finish the set and join Coop at his table.

"Sounds pretty good to me," Coop says, "if you'll take a compliment from an uninformed listener."

"Thanks, Coop." He watches me light a cigarette and rub my wrist. I realize this is only the second time Coop has heard me play.

"Still stiff, eh?"

I nod and look around the food court. The aroma of hamburgers, pizza, coffee, and frying onions permeates the air. Unconsciously, I'm looking for Tony and Karl.

"I had some strange visitors last night." When I describe the dynamic duo's visit to the Hob Nob, Coop's eyebrows go up and down several times, but his response is uncharacteristically calm.

"Sounds like someone wants you to leave Wardell Gray dead and buried," he says.

"What do you think I should do?"

"How important is this research you're doing?" Coop asks. "Is it really just for your friend?"

"What do you mean?"

Coop sighs and stubs out his cigar in a black plastic ashtray. "What I mean is you're calmly telling me you got some heat from a couple of goons—never mind who they are—but I don't hear you talking about backing off or going back to L.A. like you should. We both know telling you to back off is like waving a red cape at a bull. You always have to know why, and you usually don't give up until you find out, right?"

"Yeah, but—"

"Just hear me out," Coop puts his hand firmly on my arm.

"You remember in high school the campaign to get rid of Mr. Ortega, the Spanish teacher, when all the rumors were flying around that he was gay? You got up a petition and got all those students to sign it saying what a great teacher he was and then mailed it to the Board of Education. Christ, I signed it myself. And what did everybody tell you?"

I smile in spite of myself. I hadn't thought about that for years. Ortega was reinstated, and I was labeled a "fag lover" for some time after the incident.

"Right," Coop says, seeing me remember. "You were the only one who stood up to be counted. Jesus, you're about as gay as Mel Gibson. Which reminds me, I don't like the way Natalie is looking at you."

"Aw c'mon, Coop."

"Just kidding. Anyway, this Wardell Gray thing is something more for you, but keep this in mind. The past may seem safe, but sometimes there are things buried there people don't want dug up. The deeper you go, the more you'll find out, especially if it's connected to the present." He pauses again. "Somebody may not like that." He takes out another miniature and pats his pockets. "You got a light?"

I hand Coop my lighter. "Okay, I think it's more than just an article. Ace is getting a bit obsessed with it. I think it's more than just wanting or needing to get published. He's up for a promotion, and this could do it."

"And you?"

"Okay, it's more for me, too."

"Fine," Coop says. "Now we're being straight. You want me to check out these guys? I can call Trask. He might know them."

I'm surprised at Coop's show of cooperation and tell him so. "Are you saying I shouldn't worry about these guys?"

"You should worry about them plenty. What I'm saying is no matter how the piano is going, this has got you out of your fog. You're doing something you know and care a lot about, and that may be the best therapy. Face it, man, playing piano in a mall might be the best you can look forward to."

I know Coop means well, but anger momentarily flares up inside me. "I don't need you or anybody else to tell me that, Coop."

"Maybe you do."

We let a couple of minutes silence pass between us, both wondering if we've overstepped the fragile line of friendship. Coop puffs furiously on his cigar. I stare at the piano as if it's mocking me. Coop finally breaks the impasse.

"Look," he says, "let me know if you see this Tony and Karl again. Get a description, a license plate, last names if you can, and we'll see if we can find out who they work for. Hired muscle isn't Vegas style these days, but from what you tell me, I bet both of them have a rap sheet. There's got to be something else going on for you to draw this kind of interest."

"Thanks, Coop, I really appreciate it."

"Hey, Wayne Newton will do it every time."

"Okay, you guys, what are you cooking up?" Natalie asks as she joins us with yet another shopping bag. I wonder if she's seen our exchange and waited for the right moment. She collapses in a chair. "That's enough shopping for me," she says. "Take me to the pool."

I get up for my last set. "What's on the agenda for tonight?"

"We're going to have a sumptuous dinner at one of the finer establishments," Coop says.

"Oooh, you didn't tell me." Natalie is all smiles, mocking Coop.

"Want to join us, sport?"

"No thanks, I have a previous engagement. You guys have fun." I head for the piano.

"Give me a call tomorrow," Coop says, turning serious again. "We don't leave until tomorrow night. I might even take a couple of days sick leave and let this beauty go home so you and I can have some bachelor time before I go back to serve and protect the people of Santa Monica."

"We'll see about that," Natalie says.

They wave at me as they go up the escalator, and I work my way into the last set on the beautiful piano at the Fashion Show Mall.

LATE-AFTERNOON DOWNTOWN is slow. It's too early for the serious gamblers, but the camper crowd with coupons and cups of nickels is out in full force, carrying drinks from casino to casino. I cruise the area for a few minutes and finally find a free space with a parking meter. I leave the Jeep just off Fremont Street and go looking for Sonny Wells.

Pappy had said he sometimes played in a storefront, so I start at the Union Plaza and work my way down the south side toward the Four Queens and beyond, checking doorways, listening for the sound of a saxophone. No luck anywhere.

I cross the street a couple of blocks beyond the Queens and start back up on the other side. Halfway up, I spot a thin black man unrolling a small piece of carpet in the doorway of a furniture store. He has a scraggly salt-and-pepper beard, a Dodgers cap perched on his head, and is wearing jeans, a white T-shirt, and scuffed tennis shoes that are definitely not Air Jordans.

I watch for a few moments as he unpacks a battered tenor case and takes out a horn that belongs in a pawn shop window. He arranges the open case on the carpet, blows a couple of notes, adjusts the reed, and takes a deep breath. Sonny Wells is going to work.

Some of the tone is still there, but his fingers stumble over the keys. He's trying for "Darn That Dream," having a hard time with the melody. How did Sonny Wells end up here? I wonder. Drug abuse, prison, bad breaks? This is the same tenor player who stood toe to toe with Dexter Gordon and Art Pepper in the clubs on Central Avenue in Los Angeles.

A couple of college-age kids walking by pause for a moment, listening. "Blow, dad, that's cool," one of them says. They drop a silver dollar in the sax case and move on. Sonny raises one finger in acknowledgment, but his eyes never open.

How is it so many jazz players end up like this? If he'd lived, would Wardell Gray be here? Would Charlie Parker? It's not likely a violinist from the symphony would be playing for change on a street corner. Jazz is always different.

I walk over and squat down in front of Sonny. He almost finishes "Dream," then stops playing and takes out a crumpled pack of cigarettes and pats his pocket for a match. Only then does he glance at me. I offer him my lighter and light a cigarette of my own.

"You know 'The Chase'?" I ask.

Sonny takes a deep drag of his cigarette, exhales a cloud of smoke, and laughs, shaking his head. "I know it," he says. "Don't mean I can play it."

"I know the feeling." He takes in my tux pants and white shirt, the bow tie loose around my neck.

"You giggin' down here?" he asks.

"No, just hanging out. Pappy Dean said I should look you up. Evan Horne. How you doin'?"

He looks at me closely now, his eyes wary. He takes my hand gingerly. His fingers are long and thin, and his nails are clipped short. "You the dude wants to know about Wardell?" His eyes, clouded with fatigue, wander somewhere over my shoulder. "I think I was supposed to play with Pappy last night. You there?"

"Yeah, I waited for you. What happened?"

"Oh you know, man, I just—" He holds up his hands help-lessly. "I'm just tryin' to get my shit together, you dig?"

I sit down on the rug with him. "Mind if we talk?" I take out a twenty-dollar bill. Sonny's eyes never leave the bill as I drop it in the sax case. He looks at me as if I might change my mind and take it away. When I don't, he palms it deftly, and it disappears into his jeans pocket.

"Talk all you want, baby. I got nothing but time, and my audience hasn't arrived as yet." He laughs again, a mocking rattle of hopelessness.

"Pappy says you knew Wardell, you were around when he died."

"The Moulin Rouge, Benny Carter's gig," Sonny says. "I almost got on that band."

"What happened?" Cars roll up and down Fremont Street, and the casino lights cast neon shadows over both of us.

"What always happens. Somebody else gets the gig, or I don't make it. You know how us junkies are."

"Wardell too?"

"Wardell too, only he could stay straight enough to blow. Wardell was a smart dude, man. He was always reading books, but when he got here, he wanted to score some smack, thought I could connect for him. I knew Wardell in L.A."

"I know."

"What else you know?"

"I know Wardell died in the desert, Sonny. What I don't know is how or why."

"Yeah, I know that story, but I know the real story too." He smiles slightly, as if he knows a big secret. "Yeah, there was smack, but there was a woman too. Wardell always had him a woman."

"What woman?"

Sonny thinks it over. He seems to waver and looks out at the street. I look too, for Tony and Karl, but all I see are tourists in shorts and T-shirts. "Look here," Sonny says, "I got my gig. You got a phone?"

"Sure." I write my number on a card. Sonny looks at it and puts it in his pocket. I wonder if he'll remember to call, but at least I know where to find him.

"You live around here, Sonny?"

"Later," he says. He flips the butt of his cigarette in the street and picks up his horn. The interview is over.

I stand up, drop my cigarettes in his sax case, and head for the Jeep, dodging cars. Over my shoulder I hear the mournful strains of Sonny's saxophone, struggling to find its old self, the cry of acceptance. I turn and wave at Sonny as I recognize the tune.

It's an old standard Paul Desmond recorded with Dave Brubeck—"Don't Worry About Me."

9

I PICK UP the freeway downtown and head north on I-95 for Louise Cody's house. Following her directions, I take the Lake Mead exit and continue west to the Desert Shores development, one of the many planned communities that has sprung up and out in Las Vegas to accommodate the nearly million people that now live here.

Desert Shores, I think, is something of an oxymoron, but when I see the manmade lake, beach club, and sail boats moored in front of the waterfront homes, I don't know. Lakes in the desert? And I thought there was a water shortage in Las Vegas.

I wind through a maze of streets with incongruous names like Shark Tank Way, Sail Crest, and Rusty Dock Avenue to Louise Cody's home, a two-story stucco at the end of a cul-de-sac, painted some kind of southwestern pink. Louise's Mercedes is parked in the driveway. The lawns are neatly trimmed, and some of the homes on her block sport desert landscaping, which seems strange with a huge manmade lake just a few blocks away.

Louise greets me warmly at the door. There's music playing and wonderful smells coming from the kitchen. There's no other word for her. Gorgeous. She's probably put on a few pounds since her dancing days, but in a flowing pantsuit, large gold hoop earrings, and understated makeup, Louise looks gorgeous. She gives me a show-business kiss on the cheek. I catch a whiff of expensive perfume, and I feel like I'm going to have dinner with Lena Horne.

"How about a glass of wine?" Louise asks. She pours us both a glass of Merlot. "To the Moulin Rouge," she says, clinking expensive crystal with me. "Make yourself at home. I'm just going to check on dinner. I hope you like lamb."

"Sounds great." Louise disappears into the kitchen while I wander around the living room. As I expected, her home is expensively decorated. A large white sofa is the room's centerpiece, opposite two comfortable lounge chairs with a glass-and-chrome coffee table in the middle. The sound of pianist Gene Harris's trio oozes from the speakers of a state-of-the-art stereo system next to a big-screen television.

Through the sliding glass patio doors I can see a small pool and Jacuzzi, lights shimmering in the water. Over the back wall is a view of the lights of Las Vegas miles away. The real estate business must be good.

"I got a good deal on this place," Louise says, returning from the kitchen. "It was originally one of the models."

I can easily imagine her showing homes, charming prospective buyers into signing on the dotted line in such a graceful way they probably think they're doing Louise a favor. "Very nice, very nice."

"Well, I hope you're hungry." She leads me to an oak dining table, elegantly set, that overlooks the pool. She serves salad on chilled plates and lamb curry with rice pilaf from steaming casserole dishes. There's Indian nan bread on the side and more wine. By the end of dinner, I feel a warm glow, entertain thoughts about calling Cindy, and wonder why Rachel Cody would want to leave all this.

We keep to small talk over dinner, getting acquainted, both

of us studiously avoiding talk of the Moulin Rouge or Rachel. Louise tells me about her real estate career. I briefly recount my struggles in the music business and give the Lonnie Cole case a quick once-over.

Musically, Louise and I are on the same wavelength. She gets up several times to play tracks from CDs ranging from Gene Harris to Carmen McRae to Miles Davis and Ahmad Jamal.

"Coffee?" Louise asks. She wears the satisfied expression of a hostess who knows she's impressed her guest.

"Fine," I say. I haven't seen a single ashtray, but I'm dying for a cigarette. Again, Louise reads my mind.

"Let's go outside. It's cool enough now, and you can smoke." She brings two large mugs outside to the patio table. Louise obviously doesn't trust her good china to a pool deck or a musician.

"What is this?" I ask, taking a sip.

"French Vanilla. I get it from the place we met at the other day."

I get a cigarette going, let the warm balmy breeze wash over me, and decide this is a life I could get used to. We both watch the lights of Las Vegas for a few minutes, basking in the satisfaction of a good meal.

"I like living out here," Louise says. "I'm only twenty minutes from the Strip, but it feels like much more. I like the detachment."

"And Rachel didn't?"

"She did at first. When she moved back here from California after her divorce, I guess life with mom sounded pretty good. It was fine for a while. We got to know each other again, and I got to see what it feels like to go places with a thirty-six-year-old daughter. But a few weeks ago she became withdrawn. We'd always been very close, but suddenly we didn't talk. She began staying out late, and finally one day I came home from work and she was gone. Just packed a bag and left. No note, nothing."

"Any idea what set her off?" Even in this light I can see Louise is avoiding my eyes.

"None. She had decided to try singing again but wasn't having much luck."

"Did you encourage her?"

"You mean was I supportive? Yes, I suppose you could say that, although I guess not enough. This isn't a great town anymore for budding performers. I don't have to tell you that." Louise gets up. "I'm going to get some more coffee. Can I get you some?"

"You bet. I never pass up good coffee."

Louise goes back in the house, and I have a few minutes to decide whether to tell her about what I learned about Rachel from Pappy Dean. I decide not to mention the drugs. No need to worry her yet until I find out for myself. That is, if I find Rachel at all.

Louise returns with the coffee. "So," she says, sitting down again, "any Rachel sightings?"

"Afraid not. A couple of musicians recognized her from the photo you gave me. A bass player named Elgin Dean, and Sonny Wells, a saxophonist. Ever heard of them?"

"No." Her answer is almost too quick. "Have they actually seen her?"

"Dean has. They were both around in the Moulin Rouge days. Anyway, it's a start, and now at least we know she's still in Las Vegas."

Louise allows herself a smile, but it's forced. "Well, I guess that's good news then. Did this Dean or Wells say anything specific?" There's an edge to her voice I can't quite read.

"Not really." I don't tell her Sonny hasn't even seen the photo. I'm more interested in gauging her reaction to the names.

"Was Pappy Dean in the Moulin Rouge band?"

"No, I don't think so. At least he didn't mention it. Why?"

"Oh, I don't know, I just thought, well, it's not important."

She reaches for my cigarettes. "Do you mind? I quit, but every once in a while I feel like one."

"Sure." I push the pack and my lighter across the table. Her hands are trembling slightly as she flicks the lighter several times and finally gets her cigarette going. She takes only a couple of drags before she stubs it out."

"Bad idea," she says. "Will you excuse me for a moment?" She gets up and goes back into the house.

I wonder what's spooking her. Whatever it is, by the time she returns her composure is solidly back in place. She's carrying a scuffed cloth book about the size of a magazine. "This is for you," she says. "The diary of a very brief show business career."

I take it from her and open it to the first page. The handwriting is beautiful flowing script. I flip through it quickly. It's about three-quarters full, and all the pages appear to be numbered. Scattered throughout the diary, there are faded photos glued to the pages.

"Can you pick me out?" she asks as I study a photo. More than a dozen beautiful girls in elaborate costumes smile at the camera. "That was right after the first show. God, what a night that was. Press from everywhere, celebrities by the score, and a packed casino."

I flick on my lighter and look from the photo to Louise and back again. She hasn't changed much. "Right here, front row," I say, pointing to one of the girls.

"Yes, that's right," Louise says. "There was a *Life* magazine cover story as well. I've got it around here somewhere."

"I'd like to see it sometime."

"Anyway, take that with you," Louise says. "I want it back, of course, but maybe it'll be some help to your friend's research. I'd forgotten I'd listed the names of the musicians and celebrities who came to the club."

"Great, thanks," I say. "I'll be very careful with it. My friend will flip over this." I look at my watch. "Listen, I better get going. It's been a long day."

We leave the pool and go back through the house. "Thanks for a great dinner and this," I say holding up the diary.

"My pleasure," Louise says. "We'll have to do it again."

"Okay, but next time it's on me."

As we near the front door, Louise stops in front of some photos hanging on the wall. There's a couple of Louise and Rachel, some other obvious family photos, and one in the center that has already caught my eye.

"You might be interested in this one," Louise says.

It's a group shot, a line of dancers in costume on a stage. Over their shoulders, I can see some of the musicians.

"That was opening night at the Moulin Rouge, and that's me," Louise says pointing to one of the girls near the end of the line.

I bend in for a closer look. Louise was a beautiful young girl with a great smile. "It must have been an exciting night."

"Oh, it was. It definitely was," Louise says.

I wish I had time for a more detailed look to see if I can recognize some of the musicians, but Louise already has the door open. We say our good-nights, and I go out to my car. She stands framed in the doorway, waving as I drive away.

When I get to the lake, I pull over and stop, turn off the engine, and light a cigarette. I roll down the window and listen to the water lap against the shore and the sound of my own heartbeat. Louise Cody's journal rests on the seat beside me. I can't wait to see what's in there, but I already know what spooked her back at the house, and that's what bothers me even more.

When I'd told her about Elgin Dean and Sonny Wells, I never mentioned Elgin's nickname. She told me she'd never heard of either of them.

If that were true, then why did she call Elgin Dean "Pappy"?

WHEN I GET home, the phone is ringing as I unlock the door. "Evan? It's Natalie. I didn't catch you at a bad time, did I?"

"No, what's up? Coop doesn't want to see Wayne Newton again, does he?"

"No," she laughs, "nothing like that. He had to go back to L.A."

"What happened?"

"I don't know. Some case he's been working on. They've made an arrest and need him for the interrogation. We have the rooms through Monday, so he insisted I stay on."

I don't answer for a moment, thinking this over, trying to read Natalie's voice. I can't deny some attraction for Natalie, but she's Coop's, and Coop and I are friends. At the same time I don't think, or at least I hope, she's not calling me the minute Coop is gone to . . .

"Evan, you still there?"

"Yeah, sorry. Well, this is a drag for you. Are you going to stay?"

"I thought I would. I don't have to be back to work until Wednesday, but I don't want to just hang out by myself. I thought maybe we could have breakfast or something. Would you be okay with that?"

I sigh mentally. She knows exactly what I'm thinking. "Breakfast would be fine. About ten?"

"Great. I'm going to soak in the tub and turn in early. I'll see you in the morning."

"Natalie?"

"Yes."

"I'm really glad you're going to stay around."

"So am I, Evan. Good-night."

I hang up the phone, wondering where this is going. Probably nowhere, but the urge to call Cindy has passed. I strip off my tux, grab a beer, and open Louise Cody's diary.

I have some reading to do.

10

THE RIO HOTEL is on Flamingo just off I-15. If you're energetic and like the heat, it's within walking distance of Caesars Palace. The Rio's attraction is that all the rooms are suites, and the rates are a bit better than the Strip hotels. With a pseudo-Brazilian theme, the Rio features a Latin revue in the showroom and one of the better buffets in Las Vegas.

I park, go in, and call Natalie from one of the house phones. "I'll be right down," she says.

"Okay, meet me at the buffet entrance."

I get in line, and five minutes later Natalie arrives and catches me watching one of the Rio's cocktail waitresses glide across the casino in the revealing costumes they're famous for.

"Down, boy," Natalie says. She's looking fresh and scrubbed in tailored shorts, sandals, and a loose-fitting top. Her long blond hair is tied back in a ponytail this morning.

The buffet line is not too bad, considering it's Sunday morning. We pay and are seated quickly—Natalie insists on the smoking section for me—order coffee, and head for the food lines. She beats me back to the table and is already digging into ham and eggs.

"Oh, I love to eat like this," Natalie says. We make some small talk, do a little people-watching, which is always good entertainment in Las Vegas, and finish breakfast in record time. Over a second cup of coffee, the talk turns mildly serious.

"Look," Natalie says, "I know this is a bit awkward for both of us. I've dated Coop a few times, but there isn't anything serious between us. We're good friends, but that's all."

"Does Coop know this?"

"He does after this weekend. He wasn't that disappointed having to leave early."

I let that one alone, at least for now. "Fair enough."

I light a cigarette and marvel at my luck. "More coffee?" Natalie nods, and I signal the waitress for a refill. Natalie watches me, slightly amused.

"You don't know quite how to handle this, do you?"

"I guess not, considering the circumstances."

"Well, let me take you off the hook. I'm decidedly over twenty-one and not involved with anyone, including Coop, okay?"

"Better than okay."

"By the way, what did Coop tell you about me?"

"He said you were a meter maid," I say.

Natalie shakes her head. "God, I'll kill that big lug. I am in traffic division, but I don't ride around on one of those little motor scooters writing tickets."

"That was a hard image to conceive. So why police work?"

Natalie shrugs. "It's not a unique story. My brother was a cop, but he didn't make it back from Vietnam, so I decided to see what it was like on the way to law school."

"Sorry about your brother. Law school. That I could see."

"It was a long time ago. I'm glad you can see me as a lawyer. Speaking of that, how's your research coming? Coop told me a little about it."

"Well, last night I had dinner with Lena Horne."

Natalie's eyes widen. "Are you kidding?"

I bring her up to date and tell her about Louise Cody's diary and her resemblance to the great singer.

"You think she's lying?"

"I know she is. There's either another diary, or she's left a lot out of the one she gave me." I know I also want a closer look at the photo I saw at her house.

"This is really getting intriguing, isn't it?"

I don't tell her about Tony and Karl. "I'm way past the point where I can just walk away." I fill her in on Ace, Janey, and my comeback.

"This must be awfully frustrating for you," she says. She reaches across the table and touches my right hand. I don't know why, but I think she knows exactly what I'm feeling.

"Look, I've got a couple of things to do, but if you want, I'm told there's a very good quartet over at Spago in the Forum at Caesars Palace. You want to give it a try?"

"Sounds great. I think I'll get in a little pool time."

"All right, I'll pick you up about three." Before we say goodbye, Natalie takes my hand and gives me a light kiss on the cheek.

"I like you, Evan Horne," she says. Then she's gone, disappearing into the crowd.

TWO THINGS BOTHER me. As I told Natalie, Louise Cody's diary, while fascinating, was missing too much. It was the delightful journal of a young girl caught up in the glitz and excitement of show business on her first job. She'd kept an account of the rehearsals, the hustle and bustle of a new hotel-casino, and the inherent preparations for a new show. There was a list of celebrities who attended opening night—she even got to meet a couple—and, as she'd said, the names of the musicians in Benny Carter's band. Wardell Gray was there, but neither Sonny Wells nor Pappy Dean were among them.

But it was all surface impressions, as if it had been done last week, not thirty-five years ago. Journals can be enlightening when you look back on them years later, but only if you've made true entries at the time. Louise Cody hadn't. I don't know why I'm so sure. It's just a feeling, but one I'm going to work on.

The second thing that bothers me is the photo at her house, of the chorus line with the band in the background. Was it my imagination, or did she distract me from getting a better look at it? Was there somebody she didn't want me to recognize? I don't know how, but I have to have a better look.

Back at the apartment I leaf through the pages of the diary again, looking for some sign that will tell me what I'm looking for. The last entry is dated November 1955, when she'd come back to work for the last month of the casino's short duration. Wardell Gray had, of course, been dead for six months. There was no mention of his replacement, or anything else about the band.

I stare at the pages, trying to make sense out of it, but nothing jells. The ringing phone is a welcome distraction.

"Evan Horne. It's Pappy Dean." His deep voice booms over the phone.

"Yeah, Pappy, what's up?"

"Sonny Wells. He wants to see you."

"When?"

"Right now," Pappy says. "You gotta take Sonny when he's straight, or at least as straight as he can be, and Sunday morning that means church."

"Church?"

"Yeah, St. James. We got a band, an Irish priest who can't clap in time, but he's cool."

"Where is this church?"

"Oh, you can find it easy, right near the Moulin Rouge. H Street near Washington."

I MAKE IT in ten minutes. The church is emptying out from the morning service. A crowd of well-dressed people, mostly black, are getting in their cars, saying good-byes, and Pappy is standing on the top step in a suit and sunglasses.

"Go on in," he says. "Sonny's waiting."

The church is quiet and cool inside. There's a set of drums and what I think is Pappy's bass nearby in one corner next to the organ. Pappy does have one regular gig. Sonny Wells sits in the back, gazing at the altar as if he's waiting to take his turn in the confessional.

He's cleaned up considerably today, in a threadbare suit, faded white shirt with the collar tips curling up, and a thin black tie. He hasn't shaved, but his hair is slicked back and his expression is one of peace.

He recognizes me as I walk down the aisle toward him. "Hey, piano dude," he calls, waving his hand.

"How you doing, Sonny?" I sit down next to him in a pew. The quiet of the church reminds me of a concert hall right after a performance.

"I'm cool," Sonny says. "I'm always cool on Sunday." He looks at me searchingly. "Pappy says I should talk to you."

"Only if you want to."

Sonny nods his head and looks at the floor. "Wardell, man. You stirred up some memories with that name. I knew Wardell in L.A."

"I know, you told me the other day."

"I did?" He looks at me, puzzled, trying to remember and reconcile the recent with the distant past. "I tell you I was in that band? I took Wardell's place after."

"After what?"

"After they wasted him. Pay attention, man."

I try to keep my breathing steady. I want to shake him out

of this stupor, but I keep in mind I'm sitting in a church talking to a junkie who might want to fix any time now.

"What happened to Wardell, Sonny?"

"It was that woman. I told Wardell not to be messin' with her. She was somebody's woman."

"You remember her name?"

"Naw." He waves his hand in the air as if that's not important, then chuckles. "She was fine, though. I remember that. She was a dancer in the show. Long, pretty legs. Yes indeed, she was fine, and she dug Wardell too."

I wait silently, letting Sonny remember at his own pace, but there are so many questions I want to ask. Wardell Gray was in Las Vegas only two days before his death. I have another idea.

"You know this woman in L.A. too?"

"Sure," Sonny says. "I seen her with Wardell lots of times."

"And they came to Las Vegas together?"

"I don't know," Sonny says. "I just know they found his ass in the desert. I told him not to mess with that woman. They wasted him."

"Who is they, Sonny?"

Sonny looks at me and grins. "The Man."

"The police?"

Sonny grins again and shakes his head. "No, the other Man."

I don't get a chance to learn any more. Sonny pulls up the sleeve of his coat as if to look at his watch, but there's nothing strapped to his wrist.

"I gotta split, man, I got my gig." He gets up and shakes hands with me almost formally. "You be cool, man." He walks to the door. He never looks back once.

The other man? What else can he mean but godfather dudes?

———

SPAGO IS IN the Forum shops at Caesars Palace. When I invited Natalie, I had some reservations about jazz at a trendy restaurant like Spago. But my source was good. In fact, when we arrive, he's strapping on a tenor saxophone.

"You didn't tell me this was your gig."

Billy Mills blows a couple of notes before he answers. "It's not. I'm a sub today and glad to get the work." Billy takes in Natalie and shakes his head. "I thought tenor players were supposed to get the best-looking girls. See you after the set."

Natalie and I get a table close to the band. This patio part of the restaurant extends out into the Forum Shops area. There's a continual parade of passersby who stop occasionally to listen as the quartet begins the set with a Jackie McLean blues line.

The piano is much better than the one at the Hob Nob, but again there's no real bandstand, just a corner cleared away near a cash register at the entrance. We order a glass of wine and listen to three tunes before there's any real conversation.

I watch Natalie nod to the music, a slight smile playing on her lips. "I don't recognize any of these pieces," she says.

I lean across the table. "Billy tells me they're mostly the piano player's originals." He's a tall, thin man with glasses who kind of bounces on the piano bench as he plays. His eyes dart from the music spread out in front of him to the other musicians when someone plays something he likes.

The bassist, white-haired, bearded, and wearing an eye patch that makes him look like a model for the old Hathaway shirts, plays head down, intent on the music. Nearly hidden by the piano, the drummer pushes and prods the group with splashes of color on the cymbal.

I get caught up in the music. I'm as unaware of the crowd as the band is, mentally following the pianist's fingers through impressive single note runs and block chord musings. He's really good, and I'm envious. The set ends to polite applause. Except for a few faces I recognize from the Four Queens, this is obviously a tourist crowd who've wandered over from Caesars or come out for a day of shopping and smart lunches.

"They don't know who or what they're listening to, do they?" Natalie observes.

"Probably not. Billy tells me they've been here over a year. The manager is an amateur pianist himself. He talked Wolfgang Puck into a jazz group, and I guess it's working."

"Is that him?" Natalie asks, pointing toward the piano.

The waiters and waitresses wear pink shirts and bow ties, but this man is in a dark suit and slicked-back blond hair. He's talking to Billy, who's pointing toward our table. He shakes hands with Billy and then comes over, his hand already outstretched to me.

"Allow me to introduce myself," he says, bowing slightly. "I am Baron Jordan von Esebeck, and very happy to have you as our guest. Perhaps you will play later, yes?" The German accent is softened, probably by many years in the States.

"No thanks, Baron. I'm just listening today, but thanks for the invitation."

He takes Natalie's hand and kisses it, Continental-style. "Please then allow me to buy you a drink." He snaps his fingers at a passing waiter and points to our table. "Later I will subject you to my own playing if the band will allow it." He laughs at his own joke.

"I look forward to it," I say. The baron bows again and moves away.

"Charming," Natalie says. "I wonder how he plays."

"Billy tells me he's a Thelonious Monk fanatic, not bad, and of course the guys call him the Red Baron."

Natalie sips her wine and studies me across the table. "This is hard for you, isn't it? Coop told me about your accident. The music is still in your head. It must be frustrating to not be able to get it out."

"You're very perceptive, Miss Beamer." I try to be flip, but she's hit it on the head. Any other time I'd be glad to sit in and probably acquit myself very well. Maybe I would just be better being out of music altogether. "Most nights I alternate between feeling sorry for myself and being determined to prove the doctors wrong."

When the quartet starts again, I try to content myself with the surroundings—good music, good wine, the company of a pretty woman, and perhaps the start of something good. I'm doing fine until the baron stops at our table again with two glasses of chardonnay.

"The gentlemen across the way beat me to it," he says. "Enjoy."

That's when I see Tony and Karl. Wedged between them is a small, nearly bald man, who holds up his glass to us.

Natalie follows my gaze. "Who are they?" she asks.

"No idea." Do we leave now, or stay here in this very public place until they leave? My mind is racing, but there isn't time to act. Tony and Karl stay where they are, looking bored out of their minds, with Billy's sax practically in their faces. The other man gets up and comes over to our table.

He's dressed in an expensive suit and dripping with gold—watch, rings, and collar pin. He looks right at home at Spago. "Mr. Horne, allow me to introduce myself. I'm Anthony Gallio." I watch Natalie's eyes widen. "May I join you for a minute?" He pulls out a chair and sits down, engulfing us in a cloud of cologne. "And this lovely young lady is?"

"Natalie Beamer." She offers her hand to Gallio.

"A pleasure," Gallio says. He smiles pleasantly but immediately turns his attention back to me. "I think you've already met my associates." He nods his head toward Tony and Karl. Their eyes are riveted on our table. "I'm afraid I owe you an apology, Mr. Horne."

"Oh, how's that?"

"The unfortunate incident at the—Hob Nob, I believe that's the name of the establishment. Tony and Karl are, what's the right word, exuberant, perhaps even overzealous in carrying out their instructions. As a matter of fact, Tony is my nephew. He likes to please me."

"But they were your instructions?" Natalie is trying to signal me with her eyes.

"I meant merely for them to inquire about your interest in the Moulin Rouge."

"My interest is simply that that's where a musician I'm researching was playing when he died. It's ancient history, Mr. Gallio."

Gallio takes a sip of his wine. "Exactly. Perhaps we should all keep that in mind," he says. "I have some interest in the Moulin Rouge myself. I'm a businessman, Mr. Horne. I have a proposition on my desk at the moment that concerns the Moulin Rouge." He pauses a moment, glances once at Natalie. "Business deals being what they are, sometimes fraught with delicate negotiations, I wouldn't like to see circumstances complicated by outside interests like yours."

"I'm not sure I follow you, Mr. Gallio. How does the death of a saxophonist thirty-seven years ago affect a business deal for you?" The quartet has slipped into a minor blues. Out of the corner of my eye I can see Billy, his hands crossed over his horn, listening to the pianist. I've never wished more to be that pianist.

"Probably not at all. My concern is that musician's unfortunate death is your only interest." Despite his congenial air, the polite smile, Gallio's eyes bore into me. My expression must assure him he's made his point.

"Well then, we have no problem, do we?" Gallio smiles, sets his glass down on the table, and stands up. "Nice to meet you, Miss Beamer. Enjoy your stay in Las Vegas. Horne."

Gallio walks back to his table. Tony and Karl are already on their feet. Gallio peels some bills off a large roll and leaves them on the table. With Tony and Karl as escort, Gallio walks out past the quartet. As they pass the piano, Gallio pauses, whispers something to the pianist, and lays a bill on the piano.

Natalie takes a deep breath and a drink of her wine. "I think I need another drink. Do you know who that is?"

"Anthony Gallio, right?" I watch as the trio passes by the rail. Gallio and Karl look straight ahead, but Tony catches my eye and points a finger at me like a gun.

"Evan, Anthony Gallio is some kind of organized-crime figure, at least he was. I've seen him on the news, walking into court with his lawyers. And you just sit here calmly and answer questions. Jesus, what are you into? And what happened at the Hob Nob?"

"It was nothing. I'll tell you about it later." Good question, though. What business proposition is Gallio talking about with the Moulin Rouge, and what possible interest could someone in organized crime have in Wardell Gray's death?

11

MONDAY MORNING, WITH Ace off at UNLV, I lie around the apartment and the pool, reading over Louise Cody's diary and sorting through my thoughts on Gallio, Natalie, and everything else that's come my way in the past few days.

I make arrangements to meet Natalie later at the Four Queens, but discourage her from coming to the Fashion Show Mall. That's something I need to work out on my own and I feel strangely embarrassed to have Natalie around for that. It's as if I don't want her to see me struggling. Unreasonable? Strange? Yes, since I hardly know her, but that's how it's coming out.

Still, I know her well enough and myself even better to know it's time to call Cindy or take the easy way out and write her a letter. At the Fashion Show, Brent Tyler doesn't come around at all, so I guess he thinks I'm doing okay. I fill a couple of requests for some timid shoppers, but when Mary Lou relieves me I'm grateful. My hand is aching after my two sets.

My other distraction for the day is looking for Tony and Karl or Anthony Gallio. I doubt if he gets out much, and I wonder about his visit to Spago. It took a lot of persuasive talking to keep Natalie from calling Coop to tell him about our lunchtime guest. In the end she promised and went back to the hotel after a quick dinner. A lot of thinking for me—alone.

Leaving Mary Lou to entertain the shoppers, I swing by the apartment and change into some casual clothes, a sport shirt, jeans, and some boat mocs, before running downtown to the coroner's office to look up the records on Wardell Gray.

A bored clerk digs out the records and shows me the file. Everyone at least is telling me the truth about this. There's an incident report, just as Trask said, and cause of death is listed as drug overdose. I have a copy made just for the record. Maybe Ace can use it for his paper.

Since it's Monday, I decide to try the Four Queens. Besides Pappy, I've put out the word to anyone who might come across Rachel Cody. Maybe I'll get lucky. I head down early for something to eat and the first set without even checking who's scheduled to play.

I park in the Four Queens garage, but before I go in, I decide to drop by Sonny's storefront and see if his "gig" is going. The sun is starting its slow descent, glinting off store windows and casinos, but the temperature, according to a sign on a bank, is still 103.

There seem to be more people than usual out on Fremont Street, wandering from hotel to hotel carrying the obligatory cups of coins, some with drinks in their hands. The whole street is like a big party, and the eternal display of neon gives the street a surreal effect. It's like a movie set, shooting with lights in the sun.

I'm taking this all in, feeling almost like a tourist, until I near Sonny's spot. Three police cars, red lights flashing, are parked at odd angles, blocking two lanes. One of the uniforms is waving traffic around, and a crowd of curious onlookers has gathered around Sonny's store as if they've heard about a sale.

There are several uniformed cops keeping the crowd at bay, and a yellow police tape across the doorway. I almost don't want to see what the crowd is blocking off. I manage to shoulder my way through and bump into Detective John Trask.

He turns around and starts to say something, recognizes me, and waves me through the uniforms. I duck under the tape, not knowing what to expect. Sonny's carpet is there, and the open saxophone case with some change and a couple of forlorn dollar bills. His horn lies nearby, dented and bent as if it was ripped out of his mouth and thrown to the ground. The mouthpiece has fallen off and lies a few feet away. No sign of Sonny.

"What are you doing here?" Trask asks. He's got a pad and pen out.

"What happened?"

"Somebody reported a disturbance, some yelling, and called it in. Apparently a guy plays his horn here every evening."

"Sonny Wells."

"What?"

"Sonny Wells. That's the guy's name."

"You know him?" Trask takes me aside. He's not as friendly as he was the other night at the Sands with Coop.

"Yeah, he's a musician down on his luck."

"I know he's a musician, Horne," Trask says. "He left the goddamned saxophone."

"Lieutenant." We both turn to the voice of one of the uniforms. He's holding the mike from the black-and-white radio. "You better take this."

"Wait here, Horne." Trask goes to the car. He talks on the radio for a minute, listens, then comes back. "You better come with me." He takes my arm, and we head for his car, an unmarked Chevy. "Don't touch anything till you hear from me," he tells the uniform. We get in his car. He attaches a red light to the roof, and we're off.

He cuts over to Carson and back up to Las Vegas Boulevard, then turns north. At Bonanza he makes a left. For a minute I think he's heading for the Moulin Rouge.

"Another anonymous tip," Trask says, both hands on the wheel. "Jogger found someone in the desert."

"Is he dead?"

Trask shakes his head. "Don't know." He glances at me. "Why'd you say he?"

"It's Sonny Wells, I know it." I sit back.

A few blocks down Bonanza we see a police helicopter circling overhead. "They called it in," Trask says. He skids to a stop alongside a black-and-white and a blue-and-yellow paramedic truck. The crew is in a vacant lot near a convenience store I've already seen. There's a stretcher and two uniformed cops bent over something in the patch of desert. I turn and look back west, toward the Moulin Rouge, thinking of Wardell Gray.

Trask and I get out of the car and walk over. "Whatta you got?" Trask asks one of the attendants.

"He'll make it," the attendant says. "He's in bad shape, though. Somebody went after his head with a baseball bat or something like it. They also broke the fingers of his right hand."

I move in for a closer look. Sonny's face is covered in blood; his hands are folded across his chest, the right one in a splint and swathed in bandages. Both eyes are swollen shut. I step back and watch the crew superficially dress his wounds, get an IV going and get him ready for the stretcher.

"You know him?" Trask asks me.

"Yeah, it's Sonny Wells."

"All right, you wait over by my car. They'll take him to UMC—the University Medical Center. I don't imagine this guy has Blue Cross."

I walk back to Trask's car, light a cigarette, and lean on the fender. It's dusk now. The lights of downtown and the Strip beyond fill the sky as Sonny is loaded in the paramedic van and it roars off. Trask and one of the uniforms comb the area with flashlights, and in minutes it's over.

"Nothing," Trask says he walks over and joins me at the

car. "I'd like a statement from you about this Wells character."

"Now?"

"In the morning will do. How do you happen to know a homeless saxophone player, or shouldn't I ask?"

"I'll tell you in the morning. It's a long story."

We drive back downtown, and Trask drops me off at the Four Queens. "What about Sonny's stuff?" I ask before I get out of the car.

"What stuff?"

"His horn, the case."

Trask shrugs. "It's being handled. We don't know whether we have a simple mugging or attempted murder yet."

"We don't? Doesn't it look to you like Sonny was taken from his storefront out to the desert and beaten there?"

"Horne, what it is you do for a living? You're a musician, right?"

"Yeah."

"Fine. Do I come around and tell you what songs to play, what chords to use?"

I put up my hands in surrender. "Okay, okay. What time tomorrow?"

"Between nine and ten," Trask says. I open the door and am starting to get out when he asks one final question. "Why do you think the fingers on his right hand were broken?"

"Right or left, it wouldn't matter," I say. "It's hard to play a sax with one hand."

I slam the door and watch Trask drive off. Of course it does matter, and I know exactly why Sonny's right hand was broken. The message was clear, and directed to me.

INSIDE THE FOUR Queens I look for three people—Alan Grant, Natalie, and Pappy Dean. It's Pappy I see first, standing at the bar looking much like he did the first time I met him. He sees me, notices my expression, and breaks away from the people he's talking to.

"What's up?"

"Sonny. Somebody dragged him from his storefront out to the desert and worked him over pretty good."

"You were there?" Pappy asks.

"Right after."

"Damn! Where is he?"

"They said UMC."

Pappy nods. "Yeah, homeless motherfuckers go there."

"Sonny got any relatives here?"

Pappy shakes his head. "He got a sister somewhere in L.A., but nobody here. Guess I'll go by. You comin' over?"

"Yeah, I'll meet you." Pappy nods and takes off as we're engulfed in applause. Striding on stage to throw quips at the audience and introduce guitarist Kenny Burrell, Alan Grant is busy. That only leaves Natalie.

I stand at the entrance, and she comes out with the rest of the crowd as the lounge empties out.

"Where have you been?" she says. "I had a table inside."

"Something came up." I fill her in on Sonny. "I have to go over there," I say.

"Can I come with you?"

"Sure." Before we can leave, Alan Grant stops me.

"I didn't see you inside," he says. "Burrell can play, huh? Wait a minute." He fumbles through his pockets and comes up with a scrap of paper. "Think I got a line on that woman's daughter, the one who claims she's a singer."

"Rachel Cody?"

"I don't know if that's her name," Grant says, "but she was at Pogo's Friday night, least it sounded like her." He hands me the scrap of paper with an address on it.

"Thanks, Alan."

"Hey, you're not going to stay for the second set?"

"Not tonight."

Natalie and I drive over to UMC on West Charleston. When I inquire at the desk, we're told Sonny is still being treated and we'll have to wait. We find Pappy outside, pacing around smoking a cigar.

"Bad shit, man," he says as he sees us. "This your lady?" He gives Natalie a cool appraisal.

"Not exactly." I make the introductions, and we sit down on a bench. "Do you know how to contact Sonny's sister?" I ask Pappy.

He shakes his head. "Sonny never talked about her much. I think she lives in Compton."

A few minutes later a doctor comes out, carrying a clipboard. "I'm Dr. Straub. Are any of you relatives of"—he glances at the clipboard—"Mr. Wells?" It seems somehow strange to hear Sonny referred to as Mister.

"I'm his friend," Pappy says, getting to his feet.

"And you are?" The doctor glances from Pappy to me.

"Evan Horne. I made the identification for the police."

The doctor looks tired and as though he doesn't want to hear the explanation or spend very much time on this, the last in what is probably a long line of beatings, stabbings, and shootings. "All right," he says, making a snap decision. "I need to talk to you for a moment."

I follow him down the hall to a small office. He motions me to a straight-backed chair and leans over the desk, reading off the clipboard. "Severe lacerations, considerable loss of blood, compound fractures of the right hand, which is also attached to an arm full of needle tracks." Dr. Straub glances up at me.

"This man is a drug addict, heroin is my guess as to what we're going to find. This beating, combined with his extremely poor physical conditions—oh, did I mention the head wounds? Skull fracture, probably with a baseball bat. They seem to be popular these days. Jesus Christ!" He slams the clipboard down on the desk, kicks the door shut, opens a drawer in the desk, and takes out some cigarettes. "It's like this every night."

He lights us both cigarettes, takes a deep drag, and says, "He's not going to make it." He taps his ash in an empty soft-drink can. "What was it, robbery? Mugging? I don't understand the broken hand. That was deliberate."

"Like Chet Baker?"

"What?"

"Nothing. What happens now?"

The doctor shrugs and drops his cigarette in the can. It sizzles as it hits the liquid. "We'll try to stabilize him, but his system is so weak, I don't know. If there's a next of kin they better get here fast."

I leave him my number and promise to check back later. "Okay," the doctor says. "I'm here all night."

I go back out to Natalie and Pappy and give them the news. Pappy says he'll try and find someone who knows Sonny's sister. "That boy never hurt nobody," Pappy says. "He just wanted to play his horn ever since—" Pappy stops, catches me watching him closely. He ambles out of the hospital just as another emergency vehicle arrives with another casualty.

I take Natalie back to her hotel, and we go to the coffee shop, an open-air affair that faces the pool. We order coffee and watch the waterfall in the swimming pool for a few minutes before Natalie breaks the silence.

"Evan," she begins, "I don't want to push this, but Tony Gallio has lunch and joins us for a drink yesterday at Spago, and today Sonny Wells is found in the desert. Isn't that—"

"Just how Wardell Gray was found." I nod. "Might even be the same place, unless it's a shopping center or a parking lot by now. And yes, it's more than coincidence. On top of everything else, Sonny's right hand was broken."

12

"LET ME TELL you about Anthony Gallio," Coop says. "His nickname is Tony the Tiger. You know how he got that?"

"No." I look from Coop to John Trask. The Metro detective is content to let Coop talk. We're sitting in Trask's office.

"Somebody didn't pay off on time, gambling, drugs, tried to stiff Gallio, take your pick. So Tony and couple of friends took this guy out on some deserted road. Tony siphoned gas out of his car, poured it on the guy, and set him on fire. That's the guy you were having lunch with at Spago."

I shift in my chair and look through the window around the squad room. "I didn't have lunch with him. He just came over and sat down at our table."

Ringing phones and clacking typewriters cause Coop to talk louder. "Hey, he knows who you are. That's enough."

Trask has been listening silently through Coop's lecture. He opens a file on his desk, skims over it, and adds his own part. "Gallio was cut loose by the Chicago mob some years ago when he was involved in a skimming operation, so he's tried to go respectable now—several business holdings in Las Vegas, real estate, that kind of thing, but he's still connected, and there was some talk he was trying to get in with the UNLV basketball team, get an inside line on the games. Provided he doesn't embarrass anybody back East, he's on his own. Sometimes he's a loose cannon."

Trask flips through the pages of the file. "As for the two visitors you had at the Hob Nob, the ponytail is Gallio's nephew Tony. The other one is Karl Kramer, played a little pro football once, knew Tony in college. He's straight muscle and dumb as dirt."

Coop's eyes are still on me. "You get the picture now, sport?"

Not quite. I'd only been in Trask's office twenty minutes when Coop walked in and, I think, was pleased by the surprised look on my face. I wonder if he's come back for Natalie. We still have that to sort out. I'd only just begun to give my statement about Sonny Wells, such as it was, and now I was getting a lecture on organized crime figures.

"Let's go over this again," Trask says. "You've only seen Wells three times, is that right?"

"If you count last night in the desert."

"And how do you know him?"

I sigh and reach for cigarettes.

"No smoking in here," Trask says.

"Right. I told you, I'm helping a friend at UNLV do some research on the Moulin Rouge and the musician I told you about the other night, the one who was found in the desert."

"Wardell Gray, right? When was this again?" Trask has his pencil poised over a yellow legal pad.

"1955. Don't you already know this?" I look to Coop for confirmation. This is old ground.

"Humor me," Trask says. He throws down the pencil and leans back in his chair, rubs his face with both hands. "Maybe it's too early," he says. He looks at Coop as if to say, this guy is your friend? "1955? Who put you on to Wells?"

"I'd rather not say."

"I'd rather you did." Trask's gaze and tone are firm.

I look to Coop but he just shrugs. "I don't have any jurisdiction here, sport."

"Look," I say, "he's a musician, an old friend of Sonny's, but he didn't have anything to do with this. He was just helping me. If you guys start pressing him, he'll know it came from me." "You've been seeing too many cop shows, Horne. Nobody is pressing anybody. I just don't like the connections you seem to have with a guy found busted up in the desert and an organized crime figure like Anthony Gallio."

"Hey, I don't have any connection with Gallio."

"No? Then why is leaning on you—and that's what it was— to stop digging up the past? There's definitely some connection there."

"I have no idea what he has to do with the Moulin Rouge or Wardell Gray."

"Wardell Gray again. For a guy who's been dead for thirty-seven years, his name keeps popping up an awful lot."

"Yes, it does," Coop chimes in.

Before anyone can say anything else, the phone on Trask's desk rings. He nods a couple of times after answering and writes something on his pad. "Okay, thanks." He hangs up the phone and looks at me.

"Now we're really going to have to talk. That was UMC. Sonny Wells died twenty minutes ago."

I sigh and stare at the floor.

"What did I tell you?" Coop says. "Leave the past alone."

I ANSWER THE rest of Trask's questions. He doesn't ask about Louise Cody, and I don't volunteer her name or her daughter's. Trask promises not to contact Pappy Dean unless he lets me know first. That, I know, is simply a concession and courtesy to Coop if he keeps his promise. I also know I'll hear about it from Coop later.

Coop and I leave Metro and walk over to the Four Queens. "C'mon, sport," he says, "you can buy me breakfast."

We settle in the coffee shop. While Coop wolfs down hotcakes, I bring him up to date, with more details than I gave Trask, but avoid mentioning Natalie.

"I know what you're thinking," Coop says between bites of hotcakes.

"Really."

"Really," Coop says. "Two things. First, you think I don't care or I'm being too casual about Sonny Wells's death. Well, I'm not. Homicide is my job. That may sound like a line from a TV show, but it's true. I didn't know Wells, neither did you."

"Coop, he died after I—"

"Wait a minute. I'm not finished. Second, and more important, Wells's beef could have been over something else. He was an addict. Drug dealers get pissed when they don't get paid." He shrugs. "Sometimes they kill people."

"And sometimes they kill people to silence them."

"True," Coop says, "but you don't know that yet."

I know Coop is trying to make me feel better, but I'm just irritated. "What are you doing back here anyway?" I ask him.

Coop mops up the last of his hotcakes in a puddle of syrup and shoves his plate aside. "She called me."

"Who?"

He looks at me like I'm stupid. "Natalie, who else? That's one sharp lady, and by the way if you're worried that I'm mad about that situation, I am. Not about her or you, about me."

"I don't understand."

Coop signals the waitress for more coffee. "I knew the second or third date we weren't connecting. Besides, I can't go out with someone who likes jazz."

I know this is as close as Coop is going to get to letting me off the hook, so I don't press it.

"Just for the record, we had separate rooms."

"What?" It didn't register at the time, but I remember now Natalie telling me on the phone. *Rooms*, she'd said.

Coop looks away, then picks up a spoon and points it at me. "That's the only way she'd come. If you ever let that out I'll have you arrested." He pauses, looking at the Keno board. "My numbers. I should have played." Still looking at the board, he says, "She thinks a lot of you already, sport, and she thinks you're in over your head. Gallio scared the shit out of her." Coop turns his attention back to me. "This is Vegas, man. There are high stakes here, and all you've ever seen of this town is the view from the stage. These guys can play rough, as you've already seen with Sonny Wells."

"You think Gallio did that?"

"I'm not saying that," Coop says. "He might have had Tony and Karl rough him up, it got out of hand, who knows, but doesn't it strike you as some kind of warning for you to back off?"

That's exactly how it strikes me, but now it's personal. Sonny never hurt anyone, and now, maybe because he talked to me, he's dead.

"So, what are you saying?"

"My advice, which I know you won't take, is do just that. Back off. Let your professor friend do his research in the library, and you just play the piano for the shopping crowd. Better yet, let the gig go and take the next flight back to L.A. with me. Of course I know you're not going to do that."

Coop was right. I wasn't going to do that. "I can't, Coop, not yet." Our waitress brings the check.

"You can give that to him," Coop says. "He's kindly offered to treat me."

I lay a ten on the tray and wait for her to walk away. "How long are you going to be here?"

"I'm going back this afternoon," Coop says.

"And Natalie?"

"I gather she's staying around for a while." Coop allows

himself a grin. "Says she's met some piano player. She put in for some leave time. Don't jump her for calling me. She at least has some sense."

I nod. "Tell her not to worry."

"Tell her yourself, sport."

I PROMISE TO take Coop to the airport later. I drop him back at Metro to attend to whatever police business has brought him back to Las Vegas, and I head home to change clothes and look up the address of the Musicians Union.

The old building on Duke Ellington Way near the Tropicana is gone, as is the bar and rehearsal hall that was the site of many late-night kicks bands. Musicians who were weary of constricting gigs like Wayne Newton or Robert Goulet. At the union they could let it all hang out after-hours and forget for a few hours they were playing in hotel house bands to pay mortgages and keep up with payments on cars, boats, and credit cards.

The entertainment changes in Las Vegas have hit the union hard. Lot of members dropping out, the dissolving of hotel house bands replaced by tapes, and a couple of strikes have all taken their toll on this once-powerful organization.

They operate now out of an office on Sahara. I call first and get an appointment with a business agent, Larry Jenkins, a former trumpet player who's been in Las Vegas since the sixties. I tell him what I'm looking for, and he agrees to see me within the hour.

The lunchtime traffic crawls down Sahara, and the heat is relentless. Back in the VW, I miss the Jeep and wonder how people survived before air-conditioning. I finally make it to Credit Union Plaza and find Jenkins waiting for me inside.

He's a short, slim man with a shock of white hair, a gray suit, and an easy manner. We sit opposite each other in his small office. "I've already done a little checking for what you want,"

Jenkins says. "We have records going back to the sixties, but the other stuff is archived and in boxes in a storage warehouse."

What I want is a look at Benny Carter's Moulin Rouge contract, which would have to have been filed with the union. The contract would include the amount the band was contracted for, which I didn't care about, and would list the musicians Carter brought with him from Los Angeles, which I cared about a lot. I knew Wardell Gray would be on that list, but I wanted to see if there were any other familiar names.

"Is there any way those records can be checked?" I ask Jenkins. "It's for legitimate research. You can check with the university on that. I'm just doing legwork for a friend over there."

"I'm sure it is," Jenkins says. "That's not the problem. If we still have those contracts, the trick will be finding them, digging them out. We could draw a blank. Things were a lot different in the fifties."

"What do you mean?"

Jenkins shrugs. "There were a lot more under-the-table gigs then. Contracts weren't always filed, there were a lot of ringers from other locals coming through. This is a right-to-work state, so the musicians could have been nonunion guys."

Jenkins pauses and looks at a photo on the wall. It's a shot of a big band with Frank Sinatra standing in front of it, a mike in one hand, a drink and cigarette in the other. "I worked at the Sands all during the Rat Pack era. Man, that was a swinging time," Jenkins says.

"You weren't by chance around here during the Moulin Rouge period?"

Jenkins shakes his head. "No, I didn't settle here till the sixties, after a lot of road time with Woody Herman and Stan Kenton. There are some musicians still around who were here then. Somebody might remember who was on that band. That might be a better bet."

"There is one musician I wanted to check on. Ever heard of Sonny Wells, play tenor?"

"Doesn't ring a bell, but let me check." He picks up the phone and punches a button. "Pat? Check out member locator for a Sonny Wells, saxophonist. Yeah, I'll hold." Jenkins puts his hand over the receiver. "You know if Sonny was a nickname?"

I shake my head. Jenkins drums his fingers on the desk. "Pat? Yeah, okay, thanks." He hangs up the phone. "No record of Sonny Wells as current member, but that doesn't mean much. Since the last strike a lot of guys dropped their membership. The hotels got us by the balls on the last contract."

I stand up to go. "Well, thanks for your help. If anything turns up I'd appreciate a call." I leave Jenkins my number and Ace's.

"No problem," Jenkins says. "I'll ask around. Maybe we'll get lucky. But those files? They'll be awfully dusty by now."

I JUST MAKE it to the Fashion Show for my first set. The crowd is light today, and even the food court is slow. I sit at the piano for a minute trying to think of something to play.

"Two o'clock, Horne. Let's hear some music."

I turn and look over my shoulder to see Brent Tyler coming down the escalator, his cellular phone in his hand. I bet he sleeps with it. He walks over and stands by the piano. I hit a couple of the keys.

"This could stand a tuning, Brent."

"No kidding. I'll get right on it." He takes a pad and pen out of his pocket and makes a note, then he's off on yet another mall mission.

I try a couple of standards, and already I can feel the first twinges of pain in my wrist. It seems to start earlier every day, but I feel adventurous. I decide to try "Lush Life."

Billy Strayhorn wrote it for Duke's band when he was only sixteen. It's a difficult song to sing, with its strange intervals and complicated chord progression, and it's just as hard to play. I stretch for the high notes of the melody and miss while a shooting stroke of pain climbs up my arm. I get through it, but Strayhorn would not be happy with my version. I go for some easier tunes for the rest of the set. Despite the climate-controlled mall, I'm in a sweat by the end of the hour.

I sip a Coke and smoke two cigarettes on the break and wonder what I'm trying to prove, enduring pain and frustration. It's just not happening, and I wonder more and more if it ever will. I knew from an early age I wanted to do nothing but play the piano. When I heard my first Bud Powell record, jazz had me by the throat, and that's what I've worked toward ever since.

Now, sitting here in a shopping mall, a hundred feet away from a grand piano that needs tuning, I get a glimpse of my future. If things don't get any better, what's the most I can expect? Cocktail lounge gigs with drunks hanging over the piano requesting their favorite songs and singing along? Not for me. I want to be part of a rhythm section, backing some bitch tenor player, or lead my own trio. If I can't do that, then maybe I should give up the whole thing.

I finish my shift and turn things over to Mary Lou, envious of her dexterity on the keyboard, her painless playing. I stay around for a couple of tunes and think she's got a future in music.

Outside, the VW is cooking in the late-afternoon heat. I crack the windows and turn on the AC full blast and head for home to wait for Coop's call. A short dip in the pool and a couple of Henry Weinhards and I'm almost back to normal when the phone rings.

"Any time, sport," Coop says. "My flight is at five-thirty."

"I'm on the way."

I pick up Coop in front of the Rio and we head for McCarran Airport. Turning onto Paradise, we enter the airport complex and pass a sign that thrills Coop.

"Will you look at that," he says. "Wayne Newton Boulevard."

I glance over at him. "You're right, Coop. You and Natalie would never have made it."

"Yeah, well, I don't see some fucking jazz musician's name on a street sign."

"That's exactly the point."

I maneuver through the airport traffic and pull up in front of the Southwest Airlines doors. Coop grabs his bag, gets out of the car, then leans in the window.

"Watch yourself, sport. Trask tells me he'd really like to nail Gallio. He might try to use you. If it gets real sticky, give me a call." He turns away and walks into the terminal.

Trask won't have to try, I think. I'm going to be real cooperative.

13

ACE MUST HAVE been waiting for me and heard my car. He comes outside and walks me back along the side of the house to the apartment. "Message for you," he says, handing me a piece of paper. "Dr. Straub at UMC. What happened? Was there an accident or something?"

"It's nothing, Ace," I say, unlocking the door. I go inside the apartment, and Ace follows me. "I was a witness, they took the guy to the hospital, and I was able to identify him, that's all."

"Who? What guy? Witness to what? C'mon, Evan, what's going on?"

I look at Ace and shrug. "Okay, hang on a minute." I flick on the AC and grab a couple of beers out of the fridge. I hand Ace one and bring him up to date with a very edited version of the attack on Sonny Wells. I still leave out Gallio, his nephew Tony, and Karl. Ace listens intently. With every sentence his mouth drops open farther.

"You mean this musician, Sonny Wells, was killed in the same place Wardell Gray was found? Jesus Christ!" Ace gets up and begins pacing around the room. "I don't know, Evan, I just don't know."

"Look, Ace, let's not jump to conclusions. Wells was an addict. This could have been a drug deal gone wrong, a mugging. It happens every day." I knew what I'd said wasn't convincing. I'm sounding like Danny Cooper, and I realize as I hear my own voice that it's more for my benefit than Ace's.

He sits down again and points at me with his beer bottle. "I don't like any of this, Evan. Maybe we should just forget the whole thing. I'll find something else to write about." He suddenly notices his beer bottle as if he's just discovered it in his hand. He takes a long drink, then looks at me for several moments. "You're not going to quit on this, are you?"

We both know it's not a question. "No."

"Well, what do I say? Be careful?" Ace is genuinely troubled by all this, but there's nothing I can tell him.

"You don't have to." I look at my watch. "Look, I gotta get out of here. When did Dr. Straub call?"

"About an hour ago. Said he'd be on duty tonight."

I'd given Pappy and the doctor both numbers. "Okay, I'll talk to you later. If Pappy Dean calls, tell him I'll be at Pogo's later." I usher Ace out, jump in the shower, and change into some light khakis, loafers, a cotton shirt.

The VW is still an inferno as I drive down West Charleston to UMC. I go in the emergency entrance and find the usual collection of the injured waiting for treatment, arguing with nurses, and trying to get some help. I've never liked hospitals, and since my accident I like them even less.

Dr. Straub is bent over a counter at Admitting, filling out some forms. "Be with you in a minute," he says, nodding at me. He looks tired already, and he's probably only been on duty a couple of hours. He finishes the forms, hands them to a nurse, and thumbs toward his office. "C'mon, let's go back there."

He grabs another Coke, and we settle in his office. "I guess you heard about your friend. There wasn't much we could do."

"I know. Thanks, I appreciate your efforts."

Straub shrugs. It's all in a night's work for him. "We've got him downstairs in the morgue, but there's been no word from any next of kin. Didn't you say something about a sister in Los Angeles?"

"I'm not sure. The police are trying to run that down now. Is that what you wanted to talk to me about?"

"No, there's something else," Straub says. "I was with him when he died. He was trying to talk but all I heard was 'See Lavonne.' "

"Lavonne?"

"Yeah, that's what it sounded like to me. Mean anything to you?"

"Not a thing." I lean back in my chair. A woman's name, I suppose, but not one I've ever heard. "Maybe it's his sister."

"Well," Straub says, "it could have been anything. Death-bed utterances usually aren't coherent."

Maybe, but I think Sonny wanted me—or maybe Pappy Dean—to hear it. Who the hell is Lavonne?

"There's one other thing," Straub says. "Who's going to claim the body if you can't get hold of the sister? If there's no next of kin available, it's a county burial, the modern-day equivalent of Potter's Field."

"Have you heard from Trask at Metro? Did they order an autopsy?"

Straub nods. "Already done. Severe brain damage from head trauma, and his system was full of dope."

"Just like Wardell."

"What?"

"Oh, nothing. Just thinking out loud." I get up to go. "Well, thanks for passing on the message. I'll get back to you if there's any news on the sister."

"Do that," Straub says. He stands up, stretches, and rub his eyes with his hands. "Well, I got bodies to sew up."

I STOP AT a sports bar on Decatur. While I'm waiting for my order, I get some quarters and make a few calls. Natalie is out when I call the Rio. I leave a message for her and try to track down Pappy Dean, but there's no answer at his place. Detective Trask has already gone for the day, so it's strike three.

I sit at the bar and watch a couple of innings of a Dodger game on one of the six TVs suspended over the bar. I spend twenty minutes getting through a sandwich and french fries, pay the check, and try Natalie again. This time she's in.

"Evan, I was wondering if you were going to call."

"Why wouldn't I?"

"I don't know. Did you see Coop?"

"Yeah, just put him on a plane a little while ago. Look, I understand why you called him. It's all squared away, so don't worry about it."

"I didn't know what else to do. Gallio is a dangerous man, Evan."

"Yeah, Coop filled me in." I pause a moment, looking around the bar. "Natalie, Sonny Wells died this morning."

"Oh, Evan, I'm sorry. Do you think—?"

"I don't know what to think yet. I've got to find Pappy Dean and see if he's come up with Sonny's sister. I know one place to look, and there's someone else I want to find who might be at the same place. Want to tag along?"

"Of course, that's why I stayed around."

"Okay, I'll pick you up in about fifteen minutes in front of the Rio."

I drive back to the Rio and spot Natalie in a crowd of people waiting for their cars from valet parking. She's wearing a white blouse and white jeans that make her tan seem even darker. Her long blond hair is loose over her face, and the scent of subtle perfume enters the car with her.

I head up Flamingo and turn north on Decatur, conscious of Natalie beside me, watching me.

"Where are we going?"

"Place called Pogo's. It's been a jazz joint at least one night a week for more than twenty years, according to Pappy. He hangs out and plays there sometimes. The other person I'm looking for was spotted there a few nights ago."

When we stop at a light, I look over at Natalie and realize how glad I am to see her. With some women, you're captivated immediately because of how they look, what they say. That's how it had been with Cindy Fuller. With others, after a while they slowly work their way into your soul. I know the first part is true already for Natalie. Immediate captivation. I'd have to wait for the rest to see if it was going to happen, but I have a good feeling about her.

"Coop told me you put in for some leave. How long can you stay?"

"I don't know. I have at least a week coming. Coop arranged it for me."

Thank you, Coop.

I continue down Decatur and start looking for Pogo's after we cross Washington. We find it a few more blocks north in a small shopping mall. The sun disappears just as we pull up and park. There are red streaks in the sky to the west, and the temperature, according to a sign on a bank, still hovers around a hundred.

We go in and stop just inside the door. There's a rectangular bar right in front of us, a pool table in the back to its right. Two guys in jeans and T-shirts with beepers clipped to their belts are shooting eight ball. To the right is an area of booths and tables so dark we can hardly see anything. In the back a tiny alcove, which must be the bandstand, is barren—no piano, music stands, nothing. The floor is littered with napkins and ciga-rette butts and peanut shells.

"Another glamorous jazz club," I say to Natalie. "Let's get a beer."

Natalie follows me to the bar. There are half a dozen customers nursing drinks, watching ESPN on the TV over the bar. We order a couple of beers, and I decide to try the bartender with Rachel Cody's photo. He's a tall, heavyset man with a brush cut and glasses, in jeans and a white shirt with the sleeves rolled up. When he brings my change, I show him the photo. With all that's happened, looking for Rachel Cody has become secondary. Maybe it's time to start.

"Ever seen her in here?" I say, laying the photo on the bar.

He picks it up, glances at me, and studies the picture. "Why?"

"Why what?"

"Why do you want to know?"

I shrug and smile casually. "She's a singer, I'm a keyboard player. Friend of mine told me to look her up."

"Why don't you just call her?"

"I tried one number. I guess she's moved."

He lays the photo back down on the bar. "Keyboard, eh? Who wrote 'Un Poco Loco'?"

"Bud Powell."

" 'Relaxin' at Camarillo'?"

"Charlie Parker."

He smiles and holds out his hand. "I'm Cal. Welcome to Pogo's. Sorry about the quiz, but some people don't like to be found, if you know what I mean."

"Sure, no problem. I'm also trying to catch up with Pappy Dean. Has he been in tonight?"

Cal smiles again. "Well, I know you're okay if you know Pappy. Naw, he stops by sometimes during the week, but we only play here on Fridays."

"Hey, Cal, how 'bout a couple of brews?" one of the pool players calls.

" 'Scuse me," Cal says. He goes over to draw the beers for the pool players.

Natalie picks up the photo. "She's very pretty. Who is she?"

"Remember when I told you I had dinner with a woman that reminded me of Lena Horne? That's her daughter." I fill Natalie in on Louise Cody and her missing daughter. Natalie smiles and hands back the photo. "You really are becoming a detective, aren't you?"

Before I can answer, the door opens and Pappy Dean's huge frame fills the doorway. He comes over, nods at Natalie, and puts his hand on my shoulder. "No music here tonight, man."

"So I've been told. I was hoping to run into you. You know about Sonny?"

Pappy frowns and shakes his head. "Yeah, I checked with the hospital this morning. They told me." He waves at Cal, and the big bartender sets down a glass of cognac on the bar. "C'mon, let's go over there," he says, indicating the darkened booths.

Natalie and I take our beers and follow Pappy to a corner table. The booth is cracked vinyl with the stuffing showing through in some places, and a chipped Formica-topped table. We all slide in around the table. "Any luck finding Sonny's sister?"

Pappy shakes his head. "One guy I know who might have known her thinks she might be dead too."

"If we've got a name, we could check DMV in Los Angeles," Natalie says.

Pappy and I both look at her. "You a cop?" Pappy asks.

"As a matter of fact, I am."

Pappy looks at me and raises his eyebrows. "Martha Wells. I'm only tellin' you cause I want to see Sonny buried right, ya dig?"

I light a cigarette. It's so dark I can hardly see Pappy's eyes. "Look, if we can't find her, I'll handle the funeral. You just tell me what you want."

"Why you wanna do that?"

"I just do, okay? So let's not argue about it."

"Who's arguin'? I can help you out some, and I'll pay you back for the rest."

"Don't worry about it, Pappy. Sonny didn't deserve to die like that."

"We gonna find out who did it?" he asks.

Natalie looks at both of us. "You guys are amazing. If anybody finds out, it will be the police. They will handle this."

"You with Metro?" Pappy asks.

"No, Santa Monica. I'm in traffic," Natalie says.

"You think Sonny Wells, a black junkie musician, is going to get a lot of attention from Metro?"

Natalie doesn't have an answer for that.

"Okay," Pappy says, looking back at me. "You got some ideas?"

I light another cigarette. In the flare of my lighter, I ask Pappy, "Who's Lavonne?"

Pappy's expression closes down like a curtain. "Lavonne who?"

According to the doctor at UMC, those were Sonny's last words: 'See Lavonne.' "

I take a drink of my beer and continue to watch Pappy, but he's not going to volunteer anything.

"Pappy, you've got to trust me."

"Why I got to do that?"

He's right. I can't think of any reason he should. The three of us sit in silence for a minute, trying to think of a way to break the tension. I hear the door open and Natalie catch her breath. "Look," she says.

I twist around in the booth to get a look. A blond glances our way, but I know she can't see us clearly. She takes a seat at the bar and waves at Cal. He comes over with a drink, then leans in closer to speak to her, glancing toward our table a couple of times. She looks over and shakes her head. When I look at Pappy, he's staring at her with what seems to be fascination.

"I'll be back in a minute," I say. I get up and make my way to the bar. I'm finally going to get to talk with Rachel Cody.

I take a seat next to her at the bar. "You're Rachel Cody, right?"

She turns and gives me the most hostile look she can muster but says nothing. Out of the corner of my eye I can see Cal watching us while he dries some glasses.

"How 'bout if I tell you I'm a record company executive and I want to sign you to a contract?"

Rachel lights a cigarette and stares straight ahead. "How 'bout if you just fuck off." Her voice is deep and husky. The blond hair is the same as in the photo, but the expression is very different. Her eyes are hard, and she's tense and drawn.

"Okay, how 'bout if I tell you your mother is looking for you? She's worried, she can't understand why you've just disappeared."

She stubs out her cigarette, finishes off her drink, and swivels on the stool to face me. "Look," she says. "I don't know you, but if you know my mother, you just trot back and tell her I'm going to stay disappeared. I don't want to see her, I don't want to talk to her, and I don't want to talk to you, okay?"

She grabs her purse from the bar, brushes past me as she hops off the stool, and heads for the door. I think of something else and follow her outside. She's unlocking a late-model Camaro. I make a mental note of the license plate and call out to her.

"Rachel, Sonny Wells is dead."

It's almost unnoticeable, but she does pause, then glares at me, her eyes blazing. "Who the fuck is Sonny Wells?" She jerks open the door, gets in, and roars off in a spray of gravel.

I go back inside. Natalie and Pappy are laughing about something. "904BNE," I say to Natalie.

"What?"

"904BNE. Write it down. It's a license plate." Natalie fumbles in her purse for a pen and something to write on. She comes up with a business card and writes the number on the back.

Pappy seems more relaxed now, as if he's glad Rachel wouldn't talk to me. "She don't like you," he says.

"God," Natalie says, "what did you say to her?"

"I just passed on a message from her mother. What do you think?" I ask Pappy.

He's hunched down in the booth, the Panama hat on the back of his head. "You gave her the message, she don't want it, so let it go."

"He's right," Natalie says. "Maybe she just really doesn't want to be found."

"But why?"

"*Why* gets you in trouble, piano man," Pappy says.

We get up to leave. As we pass the bar, Cal waves. "Come back on Friday and play," he says.

Natalie and I walk Pappy to his car. He drives a huge Chrysler station wagon. His bass, Trouble, rests in a canvas case in the back. There's a sticker on the window, This Car Protected by Smith & Wesson.

Pappy heaves his bulk inside and starts the engine. "I'll call you tomorrow about the funeral. I gotta talk to the preacher."

"All right, Pappy. See you."

We watch him drive off and stand for a moment in the parking lot.

"What was that Lavonne stuff about?" Natalie asks.

I have the same feeling I had when I caught Louise Cody using Pappy's nickname. "I don't know, but Pappy does."

14

NATALIE AND I drive back in the direction of the Rio and my apartment. We finally get to the inevitable point where it's her place or mine. "It's still early," I say. "Are you hungry?" We're at a traffic light on Decatur and Charleston.

"Not really." She cracks the window on her side a bit as the VW's AC struggles to cool the car. "Smells like rain."

She's right, and it's the weather that finally decides the dilemma for us.

Overhead the sky is black, and in minutes large drops splatter against the windshield, followed by booming cracks of thunder. A spiderweb of lightning flashes across the sky. By the time we reach Sahara, it's as though someone is pouring buckets of water over the car. The streets flood quickly, making the intersections like ponds, with cars throwing up huge sprays as they try to plow through faster than they should.

I lean forward and peer out the windshield. The wipers are as useless as the VW's feeble headlights. Natalie grabs the overhead handle as I roll through another intersection. Several cars are pulled over, and a couple are stuck, their drivers with the doors open, standing up on the door frames, looking for help.

"We better get out of this, hadn't we?"

"Yeah. Flash floods. I remember hearing a few years ago there were Caddys and Mercedeses floating upside down in Caesar's parking lot." I turn up Desert Inn and stay behind a van, using its taillights to lead the way. "Guess it's my place."

When I look over at Natalie, I catch her smiling at me in the glow of the dashboard light. "Well, at least this is original. You didn't run out of gas."

A few blocks from my place the rain subsides slightly, enough for me to see the turnoff to Ace's street. His Jeep, with four-wheel drive and plenty of height, is in the driveway. We get out and make a dash for the apartment, but we're soaked in seconds under the deluge. We duck under the patio covering, with the wind whipping at our clothes.

In another flash of lightning, I see a reflection in the glass big enough to be Karl. I push Natalie aside. She cries out as I spin around, feeling a rush of adrenaline course through my body.

"Hey, Evan, I thought I heard you drive up."

"Jesus Christ, Ace, you scared the hell out of me." I lean against the sliding glass door for a moment to catch my breath.

"Sorry, who did you think I was?" Ace says.

Ace suddenly becomes aware of Natalie. She's staring at both of us, her hair in wet strings over her face. "Hi," he says, sticking his hand out. "I'm Ace Buffington."

Natalie shakes his hand and looks at me. "Say hello to Natalie Beamer, Ace." The three of us stand there for a moment listening to the wind and thunder.

"Well, let's get in out of this," Ace says, as a plastic patio chair rockets across the yard and flips into the pool.

"Yes, can we?" Natalie says.

I get the door unlocked and we all go inside, Natalie and I dripping on the carpet. I go in the bathroom and get a couple of towels and hand one to Natalie. She puts it over her head and starts drying off.

Ace stands there watching us and finally says, "Look, I've got a great idea. I've got a nice bottle of chilled chardonnay next door. You guys get dry and come on over. Anyway, Evan, I've got something I forgot to give you this afternoon. I want you to hear it."

Natalie stops drying her hair and looks at me from under her towel. I shrug at her. "Sure, Ace. Sounds good."

Ace claps his hands together. "Great. Hey, your friend needs something to change into. I'll be right back." Ace goes out and I look at Natalie.

"Sorry, this isn't exactly what I had in mind."

Natalie smiles. "I don't know. A bottle of wine sounds good if he's got some cheese and crackers to go with it."

Ace is back in a minute with a white terrycloth robe. "Here, this should work," he says, handing it to Natalie. "It's clean. I just washed it not too long ago. See you guys in a few minutes."

Natalie goes in the bathroom to change while I get into some jeans and a T-shirt. When she comes out, her hair is brushed back off her face and the robe is cinched around her waist. "I hung my clothes over the shower rail," she says.

The robe looks good on her. I catch a flash of tanned thigh and an expression in her eyes as she walks across the room that makes me wish we weren't going to Ace's.

"Like you said, it's early," Natalie says, reading my look. "C'mon. Let's not keep the man waiting."

Ace works fast. By the time we get to the main house, he has three wine goblets on the coffee table next to a tray of cheese and an assortment of crackers.

"Sit down, sit down," Ace says, motioning Natalie and me to the large sofa. He pours wine in all the glasses and raises his in a toast.

"To good friends," he says. We clink glasses and are treated to a pure musical note. "I love that sound."

"They're beautiful," Natalie says, holding her glass up to the light.

"I got them for Janey," Ace says. He looks at me and I can

see the trace of pain in his eyes. "Excuse me for a minute." He sets his glass down and goes off to the kitchen.

While Ace is gone, I tell Natalie about Janey. "They were very close. I don't think they spent a night away from each other the whole time they were married."

"He seems like such a nice man," Natalie says. "It must be very hard on him."

"That's why he's so wound up about writing this Wardell thing. It's keeping him busy, giving him some kind of focus."

Ace comes back with part of a sliced ham, some small plates, and another helping of composure. "Just in case you're really hungry."

"Yes," says Natalie as she begins cutting into the Brie and forking a couple of slices of ham on her plate.

"How about some music, Ace?"

"Right, I forgot," Ace says, snapping his fingers. He goes over to a wall unit that houses a complete stereo system and puts on a CD. The sound of a very familiar tenor saxophone suddenly fills the room. Ace adjusts the controls to his satisfaction, then comes back with the case and hands it to me.

"Wardell Gray. Just found this at Tower Records this afternoon. Must be a new reissue."

There's a photo of Wardell Gray on the front of the plastic case. *Wardell Gray Memorial, Volume I* is the title. I turn it over. On the back is a list of the tunes, several as alternate takes— "Twisted," "Easy Living"—and a few versions of a tune called "Southside." The personnel is also listed: Al Haig, piano; Tommy Potter, base; Roy Haynes, drums.

We listen a few minutes as Wardell shows us how to play tenor saxophone while we drink the chilled wine and munch on Brie, ham, and crackers.

After the fourth version of "Twisted," Natalie is looking more and more puzzled. "Why so many versions of the same song? What's it called?"

" 'Twisted.' "

"Yeah," Ace says. "Annie Ross put lyrics to Wardell's solo."

"Annie Ross the actress?"

"That's right," Ace says. "She used to sing with Lambert, Hendricks & Ross."

"I didn't realize it was the same person," Natalie says. "I'd like to hear her lyrics sometime."

"You will," I say. Ace has quite a collection. In addition to hundreds of CDs, Ace has a vinyl collection that goes back to 78-rpm records.

"Record companies do this a lot on reissues, especially for someone long gone like Wardell. They have the master tapes, so they include all the takes that were done on that particular recording session. The original album probably had only one take of each tune."

"Are they all different?" Natalie asks.

"If you listen very closely a number of times, you'll hear some slight difference in each take. The producer or leader chooses the best one for release, but in jazz sometimes the first take *is* the best."

Ace refills our glasses as we polish off most of his ham and cheese. Natalie, leaning back on the sofa, a smile on her lips, listens intently as several versions of "Southside" play. She recognizes "Sweet Lorraine" and smiles happily at her discovery. When the CD finally ends, she says, "What was the name of that last one?"

I don't recognize it either. I pick up the CD case and look for the title. I've suddenly had enough wine. I set my glass down and stare at the case.

"What's the matter?" Natalie says, noticing my expression.

"That last track, it's called 'Lavonne.' "

Ace looks from me to Natalie. "I don't get it."

I look again to make sure there's no mistake, and of course there isn't. "The doctor at UMC told me Sonny Wells's last words were, 'See Lavonne.' " I explain to Ace. I look at Natalie. "You saw Pappy's reaction when I asked him about the name La-vonne." Natalie nods her head. "So that's what that was about."

Ace is still confused. "So who's Lavonne?"

"That, Ace, is the final jeopardy question."

"Jesus," Ace says, jumping to his feet. "This could be the key to the whole thing. We've got to figure this out!"

"Ace," I say, "settle down. Let's not get carried away. We don't know if it means anything. Lavonne may just be Sonny's sister."

"Yeah, I suppose," Ace says, looking clearly disappointed.

I'm not sure if I'm just caught up by Ace's enthusiasm or whether I believe it myself, but I want to be sure. I have him play the track several times to see if there's some musical clue I'm missing.

There's a nice piano intro, two choruses by Sonny Clark, followed by Frank Morgan's alto and Teddy Charles's vibes. Wardell finally comes in for three choruses before they take it out. If there's anything there, I don't hear it.

"Where was that recorded?" Ace says. "Maybe it's some-thing to do with the location or the date."

I look at the notes again. "Different band, and this was in L.A. on February 20, 1953."

"No," Natalie says. "I think it's the name Lavonne."

"Maybe it's an anagram," Ace says, brightening again. "Hang on a minute."

He gets some paper and pencils. We all spend twenty min-utes trying for names with the same combination of letters, like some bizarre variation of Scrabble. The best we can come up with are Val Neon and Al Nevon. Finally, I throw my pencil down.

"We're trying too hard to stretch this. If it's anything, and we don't even know that for sure, it's just a name. A lot of jazz tunes, especially blues, are named for women."

"Yeah," Ace says, scratching his head. " 'Nica's Dream,' 'Along Came Betty,' 'Donna Lee.' "

"Why do you suppose that is?" Natalie asks, smiling at me over her glass.

- "I'm not even going to touch that one," I say.

"Well, it won't keep me awake," Ace says. He gets up and stretches his arms over his head. "I'm going to kick you guys out and go to bed. I've got classes in the morning."

"Thanks for the wine and the robe," Natalie says.

Ace sees us out. The storm has gone as fast as it came. The sky has cleared now, with only a few clouds hovering around the moon. Natalie and I go back to my place. This time there's no dilemma. There's a rustle of terrycloth on skin, and somehow we manage to squeeze together on the twin-size bed. They do have their advantages.

In the morning Natalie is awake and up before me, already brushing that long blond hair. She looks down at her white jeans. "They're a little wrinkled, but at least they're dry. The bathroom is all yours."

I stand under the shower, thinking I've been spending far too much time alone lately and maybe liking it more than I should. Maybe that's going to end now. Natalie and I have a lot in common, including a taste for a single twin bed, but there's still a lot to work out, and I have a letter to write.

To pay Ace back for the wine party, we decide to invite him to breakfast. "C'mon, Ace, you've got time before your first class." He's half dressed when I knock on the door.

"Yeah, I guess I do," Ace says, checking his watch. "Give me fifteen minutes."

We decide on a place at the Lakes, another of those master-planned development communities built around water. Last night's rain has eased the heat somewhat, so we sit out on the patio with a view of Las Vegas while the misters' fine spray keeps us cool.

None of us has come up with any names that make sense from Lavonne. it's been fun trying, but as Dr. Straub said, deathbed utterances usually aren't coherent anyway. We talk music, teaching English, and Natalie's impression of police work. Then halfway through this relaxing breakfast I see something that brings me back to the reality of the past few days.

I just happen to glance through the window inside the restaurant. A couple, who appear to be arguing over their morning coffee, are at a table where I can see them but they can't see me. Even in this glass-diffused view, Louise Cody still reminds me of Lena Horne.

Seated opposite her, dressed as immaculately as he was at Spago, is Anthony Gallio.

They must have come in through another entrance. I wonder if Karl and Tony are nearby. Louise looks upset. Gallio seems to be pressing her about something and occasionally wags his finger in her face. Finally, he picks up the check and angrily heads for the cashier, leaving Louise alone at the table.

She looks on the verge of tears. She glances around to see if anyone is watching her, then takes out a compact from her purse, checks the mirror, and brushes her hair with her fingers. A minute later and she's gone too.

In a few moments, I see Gallio pull out of the parking lot in a white Cadillac. He looks our way once, but I know he can't see our table. He's just checking traffic before he turns into the street. Louise Cody follows a couple of minutes later and drives off in the opposite direction.

"So what do you think, Evan?"

"About what?" All this time Ace and Natalie have been talking. "Sorry, I was thinking about something else."

We finish breakfast, Ace and I argue over the check, and Natalie is trying to figure out what's bugging me. I signal her with my eyes that we'll talk about it later.

By the time we get back to the apartment, the sun has

climbed and begun its relentless daily baking of the city. As I unlock the door, I glance over at the pool. "That's what I'm going to do," I say to Natalie. "Want to join me?"

"You're forgetting I don't have a swimsuit, and I don't think Ace's neighbors would appreciate midmorning skinny-dipping. You go ahead, but only after you tell me what you saw at the restaurant."

"Anthony Gallio and Louise Cody. They were inside, arguing about something, it looked like. They left separately."

"That's the second restaurant we've been at with him," Natalie says. "Well, at least he didn't join us this time."

"I'm just glad he didn't see us."

"What do you make of those two together?"

"I don't know, but I think it's time I had a talk with Louise." I change into swim trunks, grab a towel, and head for the pool. "If you want something to do, maybe you could call a couple of places and get an idea about funeral services."

"Sure," Natalie says. "I'll try the police and see if they've located Sonny's sister if you want."

"If you get John Trask, you might see if he'll run that license plate for Rachel's address."

Natalie frowns at that. "I don't know. Trask is Coop's friend, not mine. I don't know if I'd be comfortable with that."

"I'll leave it to you. I won't be long."

I pull one of the patio chairs out of the pool and, using a net on a handle, fish out some remaining debris from last night's storm. I dive in and feel the rush of cold water wash over me. I swim a few laps, dive around some more enjoying the moment alone.

I climb out and lie on my stomach for a few minutes. The sun's warmth feels good now. I think about Wardell, Sonny Wells, and Louise Cody and Tony Gallio. What are they doing together? And why is Rachel so hostile toward her mother? Does that have something to do with Gallio as well?

I raise myself up and look at the pool again. One last dip, then I'll give it up. I dive in again, swim down to the bottom, and shoot up out of the water like a porpoise. One more time. I touch bottom, then shoot for the surface. My eyes closed, I feel for the edge of the pool and put both palms out to pull myself up, when I feel a shooting pain in my right hand.

I open my eyes and see a huge shoe. When I try to pull my hand away, the pressure increases. When I look up, I see Karl smiling down at me. There's another form I catch briefly out of the corner of my eye, but before I can identify it, Karl has me by the hair. He pushes my head under water and holds me there till I think my lungs will burst.

He yanks me to the surface. I'm sputtering, choking; I almost get some breath when he dunks me again, this time longer. He jerks me to the surface by the hair once more and drags me half out of the pool, then resumes his stance with his size-thirteen shoe on my right hand.

I lie on the deck half out of the water, gasping for breath, without enough energy to pull my hand loose, even though the pain is sharper now. Finally I look up past Karl and see Tony, sitting in a deck chair, dressed immaculately in suit and tie.

"Well, Horne, we have your attention now, I see." I try to pull my hand loose from under Karl's foot, but he just adds pressure. "Now don't annoy Karl," Tony says.

He gets up and squats down in front of me, his face only a few inches from mine. "My uncle is not pleased with you, Horne. He thought you both had an understanding the other day at Spago, but apparently that's not the case. That's why I'm here today, as you might have guessed. Now what are we going to do about you, Horne?"

"The same as Sonny Wells?"

"Who the fuck is Sonny Wells?" Tony looks up at Karl. "Do you know Sonny Wells, Karl?" Karl shakes his head. "You see, Horne, we don't know Sonny Wells or what happened to him."

Tony grabs me by the hair; Karl increases the pressure on my hand. "This is the last time, Horne. If you don't back off, the next time we'll have to take you to see my uncle Anthony, and I guarantee this is fun compared to what that will be."

"Hold it," Natalie says. I hear her voice over my shoulder. She's standing, I guess, at the other end of the pool. As long as she keeps water between her and Karl she'll be all right. "I've already called the police," she says. Good girl.

Karl eases his foot slightly, enough for me to pull loose. I grab his other leg. It's like pulling on a tree trunk, but he's off balance. I pull as hard as I can. He topples over me and into the pool with a loud splash that sends water cascading over the edge of the pool. Tony stands up and backs away a few feet. He looks from me to Karl, sputtering and splashing around in the pool. When I realize what's happening, I almost laugh.

"He can't swim," Tony yells. He starts around the pool. I drag myself out of the water. What saves Karl is the size of the pool. His thrashing has taken him backward toward the shallow end. "Stand up, you idiot," Tony yells. "Stand up."

Karl's eyes are wide with terror until he suddenly feels the concrete under his feet. Natalie circles around the pool until she's near me. Tony moves closer to the shallow end, but he doesn't want to get his shoes or suit wet. Karl keeps backing up, then trips on the steps, plops down, and almost falls over backward. He scrambles to his feet.

Tony reaches him and drags him up to the edge. "Come on, you idiot."

"I'm sorry, Tony." He's blubbering now, struggling to his feet.

"I meant it," Natalie says. "The police are on the way."

Tony pushes Karl. "Move, move," he says. He glares at us and points his finger at me. "We'll see you again, Horne."

Then they're gone. We hear car doors slam and screaming tires on asphalt.

I drop into a deck chair and inspect my hand. It's already swelling, the skin is broken in a couple of places, but I don't think it's broken. I'm not going to play any piano today.

Natalie takes my hand gently in hers. "We'll need to get that x-rayed," she says. "Let's get some ice on it."

I try to close my fingers into a fist, but it's no use. We go inside. I stretch out on the couch while Natalie gets some ice and wraps it in a washcloth. "Did you really call the police?"

"I was on the phone with Trask when I looked out the window and saw them. I just wish I'd had my gun with me."

"I'm glad you didn't." The ice feels good against the pain shooting up my arm. I close my eyes and try to think of something else.

There's no sound of sirens, but it's only a few minutes until Trask and another detective arrive.

15

TRASK AND HIS much younger partner, a short, compact man with dark hair and eyes named Dave Ochoa, look around the pool, but of course, there's nothing to see now. The water is already drying on the pool deck as I explain to both of them what happened.

Trask listens in silence. He's not happy. "Inside, Horne," the detective says. "Dave, get a statement from her."

"My pleasure." Ochoa has hardly been able to take his eyes off Natalie. He must spend all his money on clothes. The blazer-slacks ensemble is definitely not off the rack.

"Relax, Dave, she's a cop too," Trask says.

"Really?" Ochoa says, smiling at Natalie. He dons his aviator-style sunglasses. I'll have to introduce him to Brent Tyler.

Trask and I go inside the apartment. I've changed into shorts. I have a towel around my neck, and my hand still wrapped with ice and a small hand towel. I've given up trying to flex my fingers. The whole hand is throbbing now.

Trask, looking weary, sits down opposite me. "Okay, Horne, let's get a couple of things straight. I'm not your friend like Danny Cooper, I didn't go to high school with you. The favor I did was for Cooper more than you, but that was a one-time thing. Now we're in a new game. First, do you want to file assault charges on those two goons? We can pick them up, but Gallio will have them out before we get the paperwork done."

"No, I think I'll just let it go."

"That's the second smartest thing I've heard you say yet. For your sake and your lady friend's, not to mention the guy who owns this place, the smartest thing would be for you to tell me you're on your way back to L.A. By the way, who does own this place?"

"Ace Buffington. He's a professor of English at UNLV."

"Ace?" Trask looks skeptical, but he writes it down in his notebook.

"Yeah, Ace. That's his name. He plays a lot of tennis."

"Well, I suppose I should be grateful you didn't tell me his name was Robin Masters. You're definitely not Magnum."

"Ace doesn't have anything to do with this."

"Oh, really? Isn't he the guy you're doing legwork for?"

"Yeah, but he doesn't know about Gallio or any of the rest of it."

The ice cubes are melting and dripping on the carpet. "Let's have a look at that hand," Trask says. We go over to the kitchen sink. Trask peels off the towel and lets the ice cubes drop into the sink. His touch isn't nearly as gentle as Natalie's, but he's done this before.

"You better get down to Emergency and have this taken care of. Then we'll talk some more." He takes a card out of his wallet and lays it on the counter. "Just in case you lost the first one. Call me."

I figure I've gotten off easy. Trask goes outside to get Ochoa. I pull on a T-shirt with one hand, slip into some rubber sandals, and watch through the patio door as Trask says something to Natalie, with Ochoa looking on. He hands her a piece of paper, then thumbs toward the apartment.

After they're gone, Natalie locks the door for me and we head for UMC, with her driving the Bug.

"How'd you do with Ochoa?"

"He asked me to dinner," Natalie says.

"What was that Trask gave you?"

Natalie keeps her gaze straight ahead. "Rachel Cody's address. He ran the plate for you, but he said if you're foolish enough to follow that up, which he thinks you will be, you should be careful."

"Why?"

"It's in an area called the Naked City—heavy gang activity, drug deals going down in broad daylight—very bad area."

"Did he tell you where it is?"

Natalie shakes her head. "No, he said you'd figure it out yourself."

At UMC we only have to wait for forty minutes with an array of people suffering from various cuts, sprains, and injuries from a couple of minor traffic accidents. I wait another hour for X-ray results. The good news is, there's no break. I tell the doctor on duty I caught my hand in a car door.

"No kidding," he says.

"Actually two Mafia guys tried to drown me. The big one crushed my hand."

"Whatever," the doctor says. He's already lost interest in me by the time an ambulance pulls in with a stabbing victim. The ER doctor wraps my hand loosely in an Ace bandage and writes me a prescription for pain killers.

"Where do I get this filled?"

"Try a pharmacy."

We stop at an Albertson's supermarket and wait another thirty minutes on a vinyl bench for the prescription, wondering why it takes so long to shove twenty tablets into a bottle and type a label. Back at the apartment I swallow two Percodan with a large glass of water and stretch out on the couch. In minutes I'm out for the count. When I open my eyes again, Natalie is sitting on the edge of the couch looking down at me, holding a glass of water.

"Hi, sleepy. How do you feel?"

"Better, I think." I sit up and reach for a cigarette. "How long have I been out?" I down the whole glass of water in one gulp.

"Couple of hours."

"What time is it?"

"Nearly three."

"Oh shit, the gig."

"Already taken care of. Brent Tyler wishes you a speedy recovery and got a sub for a couple of days. I told him you'd call. I also made arrangements for the funeral service. It's tomorrow at eleven, Bunker Brothers Mortuary." Natalie frowns at me and consults a scrap of paper. "Can you afford this?"

"Yeah, it's not a problem. I did okay financially with Charlie Crisp."

"The country singer?"

"I know, it doesn't fit, but he was pretty generous. I saved him a lot of money."

"Coop told me a little bit about it," Natalie says.

"I'll tell you all about it sometime."

"Well, you still look sleepy. If it's okay, I'm going to check out of the Rio and bring my stuff over here."

"It's more than okay."

"Good, I was hoping you'd say that. What about Ace?"

"Don't worry about Ace. I don't think his moral standards are in jeopardy. I'll square things with him."

"If you say so. You get some more rest, and I'll be back soon with something to eat."

With Natalie gone, I drift off, thinking about the ever-widening hole I'm getting into. Sonny Wells is dead, maybe because he talked with me. I've been warned off by two goons who work for an alleged Mafia connected figure, who wants me to stop looking into Wardell Gray's death, then roughed up considerably, enough so that I can't play my gig, and Rachel Cody is holed up somewhere in far less luxurious digs than her mother's planned community. The Naked City? Lots to look forward to, but I've come this far, so why not? As the Percodan kicks in again, it all starts to blur. I drift off into a delicious dreamlike state of euphoria.

I WAKE UP in the dark to Oscar Peterson's piano on the stereo and the smell of Chinese food on the coffee table. I hear Natalie rattling plates in the kitchen.

"What time is it?"

"Nearly nine," she says, coming into the living room. "I decided to let you sleep. Feeling better?" She sits down next to me on the couch. She's changed clothes, and her hair is in a ponytail again.

We both look at my hand. The swelling has gone down considerably, but the pain is still there, though now it's little more than a dull ache. I try and flex my fingers. There's movement, and that's something. I've been here before.

"This looks very good," I say, eyeing the egg rolls and little boxes of Mongolian beef, peppers, and steamed rice. We eat in silence, listening to Oscar romp through a set of standards. It's a live performance from the old London House in Chicago. When the tape ends, Natalie gets up to put something else on.

"That's okay, leave it," I say.

"How about some coffee with our fortune cookies?"

"Yeah, sounds great." I get a cigarette going while she brings the coffee. My head seems clear now, but the temptation to close my eyes again is compelling. Natalie leaves me alone for a few minutes but finally says, "Have you decided what you're going to do?"

"About what?"

Natalie shrugs. "Wardell Gray, Gallio, Rachel Cody?"

"If you're asking am I going to pack it in and go back to L.A., the answer is no, and don't tell me that's what I should do."

"I don't imagine many people tell you what you should do, and if they do, you probably do just the opposite."

I laugh. "I think you've got me figured out already."

"Yeah, that's what worries me." She reaches into one of the paper bags and pulls out two fortune cookies. "Let's see what the future holds for us."

"You first."

She cracks hers open and takes out the slip of paper. "Your ambition is a positive driving force," she reads.

"That sounds an awful lot like law school."

"Okay, smarty, your turn."

I break open the cookie and look at mine. "Working for a higher purpose is more fulfilling than just making a living."

"Oh, that's deep," Natalie says.

"Well, I'm not doing too well at making a living, so maybe my higher purpose is solving Wardell Gray's murder."

I meant it jokingly, but Natalie's face is troubled. "Is that what you're going to do?"

"I don't know. I just know I've got try."

I DON'T KNOW how or when I fell asleep or how I got tucked into the twin bed next to Natalie. I know I took two more Percodans sometime after we ate, and talked some more. I just know when Natalie shakes me awake it's morning, and she's standing by the bed dressed in a dark pantsuit with a cup of coffee.

I stand under the shower for ten minutes, switching at the end to cold water for as long as I can stand it. More coffee, and

I'm ready for whatever today brings. I rewrap the hand in the Ace bandage. I can move it some, and the dull ache tells me it's not as bad as I originally thought.

I still don't feel up to shifting the VW's gears, so Natalie drives while I swelter, even with my coat and tie folded across my knees. We negotiate the midmorning traffic to the funeral home, across from Cashman Field on Las Vegas Boulevard. There are only a couple of other cars in the parking lot, and one of them is Pappy Dean's. He's waiting at the door, Panama hat, suit, and dark sunglasses in place. I put on my coat and tie and walk over to join Pappy.

"Shoulda been at Sonny's church," he mumbles as we go inside. "Wasn't time, I guess."

It's only a little cooler in the chapel. A short, thin black man with thick glasses nods to Pappy and introduces himself to me as Reverend Waters. He motions us to a seat near the front. There's one small floral arrangement in front of the closed casket. I check for a card, but there's none. There are some papers for me to sign, a check to be written, which Natalie has to make out for me, and the Reverend's brief familiar eulogy.

Just before he begins, Trask comes in and takes a seat at the back. A minute or two later a woman with a scarf over her head and wraparound sunglasses sits halfway down the left side. I watch Pappy glance at her and give what I think is a brief look of recognition. I turn and look at her closely, but her head is bowed throughout the service.

"We are gathered here today," the Reverend begins, "to pay tribute to Charles Wells, known as Sonny to his friends. Charles was a musician and so I'm told, a good one. Sonny fell on hard times later in his life and was the unfortunate victim of these violent times we live in." The Reverend's voice rises as he winds up. "Struck down in a senseless and brutal way by unknown assailants. We can only be comforted by the faith that the Lord knows the circumstances of Sonny's demise. Vengeance is mine, saith the Lord."

"Or mine," Pappy whispers next to me.

Before the Reverend Waters can wrap it up, Pappy gets up and retrieves his bass. I hadn't even seen it. He walks Trouble over near the casket and plays three choruses of the saddest blues I've ever heard come out of a bass. We sit for a few moments as the last note resonates through the chapel.

The Reverend Waters swallows once, recites the Lord's Prayer, looks over the nearly empty chapel and ends by saying. "Thank you for coming."

It's over so quickly, none of us seems to know what to do. We stand up and turn toward the exit. The woman in the scarf and dark glasses is already on her feet, moving toward the door. She stops for a moment, turns, and looks toward all of us. With those glasses I can't tell who she's looking at, but somehow, something clicks. I think I know who she is.

I follow her outside into the glare, past Trask, who starts to speak to me. She walks quickly toward her car.

"Lavonne," I call to her. "Is that you?"

Her back still to me, she stops, pulls the scarf off her head, and takes off her glasses.

When she turns around, a slight smile plays at her lips. Then Louise Cody gets in her car and drives off.

Behind me, his bass back in its canvas bag, Pappy leans on it and says, "Now you know."

16

I STAND IN the parking lot for a minute, baking in the unmerciful sun, staring after Louise Cody's car as it turns onto Las Vegas Boulevard. I take off my coat and loosen my tie. Suddenly my hand doesn't hurt so much. When I turn around, Pappy Dean is watching me, his forehead glistening with a sheen of perspiration, his arm round his bass.

Behind him, I see Natalie talking with Trask. I want to jump in the VW and go after Louise right now. Find out why she has held back so much, about Wardell Gray, Pappy Dean. I want to be angry but I can't.

Something back there in 1955 is haunting her today. That smile she gave me when I called the name Lavonne was not a taunt but her acknowledgement that I had figured out at least part of it. She would tell me the rest, the smile said, but not now. Louise will be waiting for me, and I have Pappy to deal with first, then Trask and Natalie.

"You're good, man, real good," Pappy said, "but I wish you hadn't done that."

"And I wish you hadn't lied to me, Pappy."

He looks down at his feet for a moment, then locks eyes with me. "Yeah, I guess I did, but I had my reasons."

"I'd like to hear them. We need to talk, Pappy."

He nods, takes off his hat, and wipes his brow with a large handkerchief. "Yeah, we need to do that." He glances back at Natalie and Trask. "That dude's a cop, right?"

"You know he is."

"Can you keep him out of it, at least for now?"

"Right now, he doesn't even know who you are. I'll do what I can."

"Do that. Louise don't need no trouble with the law, and neither do I."

"Where, Pappy?"

He thinks a minute then says, "Where else? Moulin Rouge in an hour."

"I'll be there. You have some answers."

Pappy lumbers toward his car, pushing his bass ahead of him. Natalie and Trask are already walking toward me. "What was that all about?" Natalie asks.

"Some ancient history."

She shrugs out of her jacket and starts walking toward the VW when she sees I want to talk to Trask. "I'll be in the car."

"That was Rachel Cody's mother?" Trask asks me.

"None other."

"What's she got to do with all this?"

"I don't know yet. Probably nothing," I say, trying to look sincere.

"Sure," Trask says, shaking his head. "Well, maybe your buddy can talk some sense into you."

"Coop?"

"Yeah, he's coming back up on this extradition thing. We picked up the other guy Santa Monica wants. I'll be in touch." He gets in his car, and now there's only one left in the parking lot.

I throw my coat in the backseat of the VW and join Natalie.

I tell her Coop is coming back to town. She glances at me as she starts the engine and pulls out of the parking lot.

"Is this going to be awkward?"

"No," she says. "Not at all."

We drive in silence for a few minutes. At the expressway, I tell her to turn right.

"Where are we going?"

"Home. I want Ace's car so I can drive. I have to go to the Musicians Union and then meet Pappy at the Moulin Rouge."

"You want some company?"

"I don't think so. He may not talk with you along."

Natalie smiles. "We could play good cop, bad cop."

"I don't think that would work with Pappy."

Back at the house I get out of the suit and, without too much trouble, convince Ace I can handle the Jeep with one hand. He offers Natalie lunch, and I leave the two of them to while away the afternoon.

At the Musicians Union I catch Larry Jenkins on his way out. "I was going to call you," he says, looking at his watch. "Come on back. I've got a few minutes." We go into his office, where he grabs a file folder off his desk. "We got very lucky. One of the business agents is kind of an amateur historian, thought he knew where this stuff was buried. I think this is what you're looking for."

I take the file and look inside. The contract, filed with Musicians Union #369 of Las Vegas between the Moulin Rouge and leader Benny Carter, lists the starting date, the amount, and the roster of musicians. Wardell Gray's name is there, as are several others that ring a bell from that era. One other name pops off the page. I thought it would be there, but actually seeing it is still a shock.

"Is it possible there was an amended contract, after Wardell's death?"

Jenkins shrugs. "Could be. Someone obviously replaced

him. I know there was another contract when Lionel Hampton came in. Why? You looking for someone else?"

"No, just curious. Can you make me a copy of this?"

"Yeah, I don't see why not. Hang on a minute."

While I wait for Jenkins, I run everything through my mind.

A lot of people have been either lying to me or leaving things out of the mix, and now I have some concrete proof to confront them with. I still don't know the why, but I think I am about to find out.

When Jenkins comes back with a photocopy of the contract, I ask him about Elgin "Pappy" Dean. The name brings a smile to his lips.

"Pappy Dean. Yeah, he's kind of a legend around here. You know he did a little stint with Count Basie sometime in the sixties?"

"Yeah, I'd heard about that. Has he always been in Las Vegas?"

"I don't know," Jenkins says. "There was the time he was on the road with Basie, but I seem to remember hearing he was gone, just kind of disappeared for a while years before that. Come to think of it, it wasn't long after the Moulin Rouge opened. Then there he was again, showing up on gigs all over town. Every once in a while he gets a big band together for some benefit or a night at the Four Queens. Why? You think he had something to do with this Wardell Gray thing?"

"I doubt it, but research is research." Jenkins nods absently and glances at his watch again. I thank him for his trouble and say good-bye.

"If you think of anything else, give me a call." He walks me out to the parking lot, and we head for our respective cars.

The Jeep feels solid under me and, more important, cool inside. I think about a cruise to Alaska and punch in the jazz station in time to catch most of a recording of Stan Getz at a club in Copenhagen. It's one I have in my own collection, but I'm always amazed at the grace of his elegant, fluid tone. Another gig I would like to have played at.

When I turn into the Moulin Rouge parking lot, large dark clouds loom over the mountains to the west. The sun has disappeared, but not the heat.

I park the Jeep in the half-full lot and survey the Moulin Rouge. Up close, the fifties glamour is gone, replaced now by peeling and faded paint. In the front window a poster is taped to the glass, advertising a blues jam session on Sunday night. It's as good a place as any for Sonny Wells's wake.

Inside it's dark and cool, and the bar is about half full, a mix of construction guys in work clothes at the bar and several solitary afternoon drinkers who've probably wandered in from the neighborhood to play the video poker machines. No sign of Pappy Dean.

The bartender takes my order for a draft beer and a roll of quarters. I down the beer, order another, and hit a full house on one of the poker machines on the fourth quarter.

"Those things are addictive," Pappy says, sliding on the stool next to me. He points to my glass and holds up two fingers for the bartender. I cash out my quarters and shove them across the bar for the beers.

"So tell me about Lavonne, Pappy." I light a cigarette while Pappy downs half his beer. The tie is gone, but he still has the suit and hat.

"How'd you do that?" Pappy asks. "Ain't nobody called that name for thirty years."

"Thirty-seven."

Pappy nods and grins. "Yeah, you right. Thirty-seven."

"Just before he died, Sonny whispered it to the doctor. I didn't know what it meant at the time, but when I saw the song title on Wardell's CD, I knew that had to be it."

"I was supposed to be on that date," Pappy says, another one of those good things that almost happened. "I would have been if I hadn't gone out on the road with some sorry singer."

"But you made the gig here, right?" Looking around the Moulin Rouge bar, I find it hard to believe this was a jumping place for six months, or ever.

Pappy looks at me over his glass. "Shit, you *are* a detective. Who told you that?"

"Just a guess at first, but your name is on the contract. I just came from the Musicians Union. Sonny was in the band too, wasn't he?"

"Yeah," Pappy admits. There's a sadness in his gaze as he stares at the blinking light on the poker machine in front of him. "We was both here, different times." He sighs and stares at the rows of bottles behind the bar. "Benny Carter had the band first, but Lionel Hampton came in later. When Wardell didn't make the second show that night, they brought Sonny up from L.A. a few days later. He wasn't Wardell, but he was in pretty good shape then and playin' good. I subbed here later for about three weeks."

"So Sonny and Wardell knew each other in L.A., and they both knew Louise?"

Pappy nods and looks over his shoulder as if he's afraid someone is listening. "Louise was hired in L.A. for the show. She used to hang around the Central Avenue clubs. That's where she met Wardell and Sonny."

"What really happened with Wardell?"

Pappy shrugs. "I don't know no more than you do, probably less. He didn't show up, and they found him in the desert a couple of days later, dead as a motherfucker."

"You believe the story about the dancer Teddy Hale taking him to the desert?"

"I don't believe no junkies when they high."

"You think someone could have gotten to Teddy, got him to give that story to the police?"

"Hey man, anything's possible." Pappy takes a drink of his

beer and lights a long brown menthol cigarette.

It's frustrating to be sitting where it all happened with someone who was there and get this kind of answer. Why is everybody so afraid of the past? "Why didn't you tell me you knew Louise? And you recognized her daughter's photo as soon as I showed it to you at the Hob Nob. What's Louise got to do with all this?"

Pappy turns and gazes at me hard. "Louise ain't got nothing to do with whatever happened to Wardell. You wanna know more, you talk to her. If she wants to tell you, she will."

I study Pappy for a moment, wondering how much he knows, how much he trusts me. "Wouldn't you like to know what really happened to Wardell and Sonny?"

"I know what happened to Sonny, I just don't know who did it." Pappy is silent for a moment. He lays the cigarette in an ashtray and rubs his big, calloused, powerful hands together. "I thought I knew what happened to Wardell."

"What do you mean? C'mon, Pappy, take a chance. I have no reason to draw you into this, but I can't help you or Louise without some help. I'm in the dark here. I think there's a lot you're not telling me."

"Lord have mercy," Pappy mutters. He turns and looks at me. "I don't know why I'm tellin' you this, but maybe I got to trust you. There was a guy, slick Italian dude, hanging around the club a lot, talkin' to Louise, and I know he saw her with Wardell, least I thought he did."

"And? Who was he?"

"I don't know the fool's name." Pappy's voice rises slightly. Two guys in work clothes, egging one another on at a poker machine, eye us for a moment until Pappy stares them down.

"Me and him got into it, right here in this parking lot when he was gettin' in his car. I told him to quit messin' with Louise. You know what he told me? He said, 'Nigger, you don't know who you're talking to.'" Pappy has both hands on his glass, gripping it so tightly I think it's going to shatter.

"Well, that was it. I didn't mean to, but I thought he was goin' for a gun. I used to carry a knife in those days, and—" Pappy drains his glass and signals for another beer. When he looks at me again, I see nothing but pain and remorse on his face. "I think I killed him."

I stare at my own half-empty glass. I can't look at Pappy, but I know he's watching me, waiting for my response.

"Is that why you left Las Vegas?"

"Damn," Pappy says, "you know everything."

"No, just putting some of it together."

"I was scared, man. I hooked up with a show going to Kansas City and stayed around there layin' low, thinkin' any day they comin' after me."

"The police?"

"Or that dude's friends. The police, 'cause there ain't no— what you call it?"

"Statute of limitations?" There is none on murder, and I make a mental note to find some way to check the files on that as well without implicating Pappy. Maybe there were two unsolved murders—three now, counting Sonny Wells.

"Yeah, that's it," Pappy says. "Statute of limitations." He runs the words slowly over his tongue.

"But you came back to Vegas."

"I know, man, it was weird. I couldn't think about it no more. I came back, laid low for a while, but there was nothing. Nobody was looking for me, police or godfather dudes. I asked around but nobody had heard nothin'."

I couldn't imagine even a remotely connected Mafia type not being avenged. Wasn't that the code? And if it was murder, why wouldn't the police have investigated and Pappy been a suspect or, at the very least, wanted for questioning? Something was wrong with the whole scenario.

"And all these years, you never heard anything?"

"Nothin', man, nothin'."

I anticipate Pappy's questioning look. "Even if I wanted to, Pappy, what you've told me would be your word against mine, and after all this time, well, it wouldn't amount to much. You know what I think? I think you didn't kill anybody."

I watch Pappy's shoulders relax slightly. "I wish I knew that for sure. Lord, I do."

"What about Louise? I think some of this—Wardell, Sonny, everything—is connected to Louise." I watch Pappy give me a long, searching look.

"When you know for sure, you let me know."

"They might be godfather dudes."

"They might be," Pappy says. "They might be."

17

AFTER PAPPY LEAVES, I use the pay phone at the Moulin Rouge and call Louise Cody. "It's Evan, Louise."

"I know. I've been waiting for your call." She sounds a little shaky, but she is waiting for me. She'll be home all evening. We settle on a time and hang up. I wonder what she's going to tell me.

I leave the Moulin Rouge and head the Jeep back to the apartment. Ace and Danny Cooper are sitting around the patio table. Natalie waves from the pool. She climbs out, dripping water from her black bikini on the deck. Wrapping herself in a towel, she shakes out her hair. All three of us watch her every move. I try to imagine her in a police uniform, but it's impossible.

I drop into a chair as she walks toward me. We're not going to flaunt it in front of Coop, but she touches my shoulder as she passes. "I'm just going in to change," she says. "Oh, Brent Tyler called. He wants to know how you're doing, when you'll be back."

I look at Coop, staring after Natalie. He hasn't missed anything, but he's not going to talk about it, at least not now in front of Ace. "Well, I didn't expect to see you back so soon," I say to him.

"Your friend is really interesting," Ace says. "He's been giving me the inside dope on police work."

"And Ace here has been filling me in on the politics of academia," Coop chimes in. "I don't know which is worse. Sounds like a snake pit in the English department. I thought these humanities types were gentle souls only interested in scholarly pursuits."

"Something new going on, Ace?" I ask.

"Oh no, it's not new, I just voted the wrong way on a department promotion. The new chair's subtle way to get additional votes for himself is to try and run by the promotion of a very undeserving professor who hasn't published anything in years and has two sexual harassment charges pending against him. My negative vote will no doubt draw some retribution."

"What will they do?" Coop asks. "Ban you from the MLA?"

Ace and I both stare open-mouthed at Coop. "How do you know about the Modern Language Association?" Ace asks.

Coop is enjoying the moment. "Hey, I took a couple of English courses when I was in college. How 'bout you, sport? What have you got to report?"

I glance at Ace, who if nothing else knows how to take a cue. He's already getting to his feet. "Listen guys, I've got a couple of more steaks. How about a barbecue?"

"Sounds good to me," Coop says. I nod my agreement, and Ace takes off for the kitchen, muttering about the MLA.

Coop and I let a few moments of silence pass, neither of us knowing how to begin. We listen to the water lap against the side of the pool and, I suppose, collect our thoughts. I know I do. Coop goes first.

"I had an interesting talk with John Trask. You've had a busy few days."

"You mean this?" I hold up my bandaged hand. "It's already better."

Coop doesn't smile. "They could have done a lot more. You're lucky."

"I know, Coop, I know."

"You going to be able to finish the gig at the mall?"

I flex my hand a few times. "I think so. I'm going to try out Ace's piano later, before I call Tyler."

Coop nods and lights one of his little cigars. "Well then, I guess the music world can breathe a little easier." He blows a cloud of smoke into the air. "Let's cut the shit, okay? You're in way over your head, and once again a brilliant police mind is going to make some suggestions."

"I'm all ears."

"Yeah, and nothing between them. Gallio's clowns will be back, not here maybe, but you'll be hearing from them or maybe Gallio himself. Unless Trask can put something together, Sonny Wells goes down as an unsolved murder by unknown assailants."

"You know better than that, Coop."

"No, I don't, and neither do you. There's no way to link Gallio to Wells's death, at least not yet."

"What are you saying?" I expected much more opposition than this—pressure from Trask, caution from Coop.

"Metro would love to nail Gallio, but he's always been too slick," Coop says. He glances toward the window. We can see Ace busy in the kitchen. "I'd keep your professor buddy out of this, okay? Gallio's been into prostitution, pornography, loan-sharking, probably skimming and money laundering, some drugs, but he's always managed to keep a legitimate front. It's hard to get anything on him. He's vulnerable somewhere, and you've obviously struck a nerve on something he doesn't want brought up again."

I wonder if I should tell Coop I'm sitting on Pappy Dean's confession. I decide to wait until I've talked with Louise Cody.

"Trask thinks this Louise Cody is tied in with this some way, and since you're the only one anybody feels like talking to, he's willing to give you some leeway. Within certain limits," Coop adds.

"What kind of limits?"

"For starters, you don't go off on your own and do something stupid. You also keep me up to date on what's going on, and I will advise you how to play things out."

"That doesn't sound so bad."

"No, it doesn't," Coop says. "And besides, you'll have the advantage of a crack police detective to sift through and sort out information."

I can't resist. "Who, you or Trask?"

"Fuck you, Horne."

"Gentlemen, such language," Natalie says. She joins us at the table. She's fluff-dried her hair, and her skin glows in the late-afternoon sun. The bikini is gone, replaced by white shorts, T-shirt, and sandals.

"Sorry, ma'am," Coop says. "Sometimes us boys just get carried away."

Ace opens the patio door and comes out with a platter of steaks. "Let me get this grill fired up, and we'll be eating soon. Coop, you want to give me a hand?"

"Sure," Coop says. He joins Ace at the barbecue, and they immediately get into a debate about charcoal versus Ace's gas grill.

"A cop and a professor," I say to Natalie. "This should be good."

"Two cops. Don't forget me," Natalie says.

"Not possible. Why don't you help Ace with the salad? I'm going to try out the piano."

"It's not too soon, is it?"

"I'll find out real quick."

"How did it go with Pappy?"

"More complications," I say, keeping my voice low. "I'll tell you about it later. I'm seeing Louise tonight. Want to come?"

"I wouldn't miss it."

I go inside and sit down at Ace's grand piano. I take off the bandage, flex my fingers, and gingerly touch the keys. It's a little out of tune, but with my hand, it doesn't matter much. There's no shooting pain up my arm, but if I think about it, I can still feel Karl's size-thirteen shoe on my hand. My fingers are stiff, and stretching even less than an octave is difficult. I run through a few scales, some arpeggios, miss more than a few notes, then try a couple of tunes—ballads only. Everything is stiff, but I'm optimistic. Another day's rest, and I'll be able to wow Brent Tyler and the folks at the mall.

That's all, though. If Wynton Marsalis, Branford Marsalis, or the whole Marsalis family calls tonight, I'll have to pass.

TAKING NATALIE WITH me is, I think, a good idea. If Louise Cody is nervous, maybe Natalie's presence can calm her down, make her feel more comfortable. When I tell Coop we're going to hear some jazz at Pogo's, I don't think he really believes me, but I get no argument.

"Have a good time," he says. "I'm going to educate old Ace here on the intricacies of country-and-western music."

"I didn't know there were any," Ace says, winking at me.

"You've got a lot to learn, professor."

With steaks in our bellies, we leave Ace and Coop mellowing out over the last of the wine and head for the expressway in Ace's Jeep. I fill Natalie in with a censored version of my earlier talk with Pappy Dean at the Moulin Rouge. I leave out his confession. She listens attentively and doesn't say anything for several minutes. When she finally speaks, it's with caution.

"You're getting in awfully deep on this, Evan. How much are you going to tell Coop?"

I keep my hands on the wheel, my eyes on the road. "Coop doesn't have any jurisdiction up here. How much do I have to tell him?"

"Enough to let him help. He didn't have to come up himself for this extradition thing. He could have sent anyone. It's really just a messenger job."

"Did he tell you that?"

"He didn't have to. He's here because he's worried about your involvement."

We lapse into silence again. Natalie is right, of course. I just feel like I'm so close to figuring things out I'm afraid if I tell all, Trask will cut me out of the loop. Natalie doesn't press, about this or anything so far. Maybe that's why I like her so much.

"Okay, if I feel like I'm over my head, I'll let Coop know."

"Maybe you won't have to" is her only reply.

When we pull into Louise's driveway, the door opens almost immediately. She must have been watching for us. The look on her face tells me how surprised she is to see Natalie, and for a few minutes I think it's a bad idea. I introduce them and watch a rapport gradually build up as Louise offers us coffee on the patio. Natalie is picking up all the signals.

"Maybe it would be better if I go," she says.

"No, no," Louise says. She pats Natalie's hand and smiles at me. "You stay right here." Louise is casual tonight in jeans and a baggy top. After exhausting all the small talk, she glances at Natalie once, then turns to me.

"Well, where do I begin?"

"You could start with Lavonne, I guess."

Louise smiles and shakes her head. "Lord, I never thought I'd hear that name again. I guess you know it was one of Wardell's tunes—at least, he recorded it. I guess I just thought it was a better stage name than Louise. What can I say. I was only seventeen."

"Tell me about the Moulin Rouge."

"Well, I guess you've read the journal."

"Of course, but I know there was more than that."

She nods and gives Natalie a smile. "He doesn't miss much, does he?"

"I'm just beginning to realize that," Natalie says.

"Yeah, there was a lot more. I was so young and so caught

up in the show biz thing, I didn't even realize what I was seeing sometimes."

"What do you mean?" I light a cigarette and nod yes to Natalie's offer of more coffee. She takes our cups and disappears into the house. Louise seems to relax even more and leans back in her chair.

"When that choreographer came to L.A. and auditioned girls—it was Wardell who told me about it—I just knew I had to be in that show. I was working in a little revue, knew all the jazz guys, and was head over heels in love with Wardell. That baby could play."

"And you knew Sonny Wells too, right?"

"Yeah, poor Sonny. He never could straighten up. He worshiped Wardell, wanted to play like him."

"He must have been close. Pappy says he replaced Wardell for a while."

Louise looks at me sharply, then relaxes again. "Okay, you got me there too. I knew the minute you left the other night, I'd slipped and called him Pappy. How much did he tell you about—?"

"Just about everything."

Louise shakes her head. "I guess it had to come out eventually. He was trying to protect me, I guess, but I don't think he killed anybody, do you?"

"No, I don't think so either, but don't worry, Louise, I'm not interested in that."

"I don't know why I believe you," she says, "but I do. Anyway, I got the job and they brought us to Las Vegas about two months before the Moulin Rouge opened. They had us staying in these nice little homes over on the west side, the Cadillac Arms, three or four girls to a house. There were twenty-seven of us. The band came in a week before opening night, and Wardell, that rascal, didn't even tell me he was in the band. Wanted it to be a surprise. That's why it was such a shock." She stops and looks around at Natalie, who arrives with more coffee.

"We only had two shows a night," Louise says. "A dinner show at seven-thirty and a late one at three in the morning so we could get all the Strip business. And we got them, every night."

"What did you do between shows?"

Louise shrugs. "Went back to the house, cooked, just a lot of girl things." She and Natalie share a conspiratorial smile. "We never went on the Strip. We weren't allowed to. It was right on our contract, but we didn't care. We were having too much fun. Sometimes we hung out in the casino just to see all the celebrities. When we opened they had two nights of press coverage from all over the country. There was even a photo of us on the cover of *Life* magazine, all the dancers. I couldn't believe how lucky I was to be part of that show." She pauses and looks at me sadly.

"Then it all changed, the second night. Wardell was in bad shape then, but he made the rehearsals okay. After the dinner show, we went home as usual, cooked, relaxed, then got ready for the late show. When we got back to the club, I knew something was wrong. The talk backstage was that Wardell was missing."

"What about Teddy Hale, the dancer?"

"Oh, he was there, knowing what he knew. They delayed the start of the show, but the audience was getting itchy, so finally we had to go on." Louise looks away toward the light of the city. "I never saw anything so sad as that empty chair in the sax section where Wardell should have been when we came out for the first number. But no one expected what happened. None of the musicians knew where he was, and Teddy Hale wasn't talking, but nobody seemed that worried."

I stub out my cigarette and stare out at the lights of Las Vegas. Miles missed some gigs too during his bad period, just didn't show up.

"Nobody would tell me anything," Louise goes on. "I was just this little girl dancer, and nobody knew I had known Wardell before in L.A. He wanted to keep it that way."

"Why?"

"I don't know. I think he was trying to protect me or something. When we finally got the word that his . . . body had been found in the desert, and Teddy gave his story to the police, we were all in shock."

"Do you believe Teddy's story, that Wardell died in his room and he panicked and took him out to the desert?"

"I don't know. I wanted to because the alternative meant somebody had killed him, and I didn't want to think about that." Louise stops and wipes a tear from her eye. "I don't know, I guess it's possible it happened the way Teddy said. He was scared, I guess. I know some of the musicians got on him for not telling the truth. Wardell was taken back to Los Angeles—he's buried there, you know—and poor Sonny came up to replace him. Have they found out what happened to him?"

"Not yet, but the police are working on it. Me too," I add.

"I'll bet," Louise says. "Well, after that, the show just went on as they say, but I started paying more attention to things, listening to the talk around the club."

"Like what?"

"Every single night, the casino bosses cleaned out the cashier's cage, took all the money out in bags. I saw them a couple of times myself. We started hearing that the club had never been planned to be so successful, but baby it was. Packed every night."

"You think there really was pressure from the Strip hotels?"

"I just know we weren't doing their business any good."

"What happened the night it closed?"

"We did the dinner show and went home, and somebody called us, told us not to come back, the door was padlocked."

"Just like that."

"Just like that. We didn't know what to do. The girls had come from all over the country, and we were just suddenly stranded here. We hung around for a couple of weeks, but it was clear the Moulin Rouge was over."

"Did everybody get paid?"

"Oh yeah. We got paid, I know the band got paid, but we heard some of the waiters and other staff didn't, and later I heard none of the bills were ever paid, food and beverage places. The three partners filed for bankruptcy, and that was it."

"Who were the three partners?"

Louise stops and glances from me to Natalie and back again before going on. "Anthony Gallio's brother was one, I'm sure of that."

Just the mention of Gallio's name causes Natalie to shift in her chair, and even more so when I ask the next obvious question. "What's your connection to Gallio?"

Louise expels a deep breath. "I let myself be talked into serving on a committee for the renovation of the Moulin Rouge. I put them off for so long, but they thought it was funny I didn't want to be in on it since I'd worked there. I don't know what exactly, but Gallio has some real estate development deal going, and I think it includes the land where the Moulin Rouge is."

I still don't see where this is going, or why Gallio could pressure Louise, or even what Wardell Gray's death had to do with all of it. I tell Louise about seeing her with Gallio when Natalie, Ace and I had breakfast, but not about Gallio's visit with Natalie and me at Spago. "It was from a distance, but you seemed really upset."

Louise is surprised. "I didn't know you were there."

"Neither did Gallio."

"God, this is such a mess," Louise says. "When I came back to Las Vegas and got into real estate, I met Gallio, not knowing about his brother. He was very nice, very charming, and tried to rekindle some old fires."

Louise pauses again and won't look at either one of us. I glance at Natalie, and she cautions me with her eyes. Finally Louise looks up.

"I told you I was very young, but there are some things I'm not very proud of. Anyway, he set me up with a development company after I got my broker's license."

"And now he wants inside information about the Moulin Rouge property."

Louise nods. "I think he wants to buy it up, build something new. There aren't many people interested in investing in the west side, not after the riots a few months ago, after the Rodney King verdict. It was only much later that I found out about Gallio's brother and realized he was the same guy hanging around the Rouge, really coming on to me. He'd seen me with Wardell a couple of times, told me I could do better than a nigger sax player. Well, I brushed him off, but I got scared when I realized he was one of the partners."

"And that's when Pappy got in the act?"

"Yeah, he was like a big brother to me, said he'd take care of Gallio and all his brothers, you know, talking big. I don't know what happened. All I know is I didn't see him or Pappy around anymore."

Wardell Gray, Sonny Wells, Pappy Dean, Louise Cody, and Anthony Gallio, all tied up thirty-seven years ago in the same secret. And now it's slowly but surely unraveling. There was still one other thing on my mind.

"Why didn't you write any of this stuff down in your diary?"

"I did," Louise says. "There's another diary I kept, the real one."

Natalie and I both stare at her. "You kept two diaries?"

"Crazy, huh? I had some wild notion I would write a book someday about the Moulin Rouge or at least something for Rachel, to show her what it was like then. I didn't want all that bad stuff in it so"—Louise holds up her hands and shrugs—"I kept two diaries."

It's suddenly so quiet I think I can hear the sound of cars on the expressway a couple of miles away. Two diaries. If the real one, as Louise calls it, is detailed enough, it could answer a lot of questions. If Anthony Gallio knows about it, he must be getting very nervous. "Louise, I need to see that other diary."

Louise slumps back in her chair. "Somebody else already has."

"Gallio?"

"No, Rachel. That's why she left."

Of course. Now it was starting to make sense. That would explain Rachel's flight, anger toward her mother, and hostility to me.

"And she thinks Wardell Gray was her father? Was that it?"

Louise looks from me to Natalie and almost laughs. "Wardell? God no, she thinks Anthony Gallio is her father."

None of us speak again until Louise stands up. "Would you excuse me for a moment?" she says. She goes in the house, and Natalie and I are left to ponder her revelation in silence.

When Louise comes back, she's composed but quiet. I still have a couple of more questions though, which she seems to expect.

"What did you tell Rachel about her father?"

"I told you I'm not proud of some things I did. I was always going to tell her, but the right time never seemed to come. When she was old enough to ask, I told her he'd been killed in Korea. I know I should have told her the truth, but the longer it went on the less I knew how to approach it. And now she's found out it was all a lie."

"I've got a lead on her now," I say. "Let me see what I can do. Maybe I can bring her around."

Louise nods, but she doesn't seem very optimistic. "She's a very determined girl."

"Just like her mother, I bet," Natalie says.

That brings a smile to Louise. "Well, we better be going," I say, getting to my feet. Louise walks us to the door. When we pass the wall with the photo of the Moulin Rouge band, this time she gives me time to study it.

"That's Sonny," she says, pointing to one of the saxophone players. "And that big hulk on bass is Pappy Dean."

I look at the photo. I wouldn't have known either of them. As we leave, Louise says her good-byes to Natalie but pulls me back for a moment as Natalie walks toward the car.

"You hang onto her, you hear," Louise says. "That's a good woman."

I give Louise a hug and join Natalie, and we head back for the expressway, both lost in our own thoughts for a few minutes.

"Well, what do you think?"

"I think Louise had an affair with Tony Gallio's brother," Natalie says, "and maybe Pappy Dean."

"Yeah, but where is he?"

"What do you mean? Gallio's brother?' Natalie glances at me sharply.

"That's the part I didn't tell you about Pappy. He thinks he killed some guy at the Moulin Rouge, right after Wardell's death. I think it was Gallio's brother."

I can feel Natalie tense and turn toward me. "Oh my God," she says. "He told you that?"

I nod and ease onto the expressway. I feel Natalie watching me. I glance at her, see her frown in the glow of the dashboard lights.

"Isn't it time to tell Coop all this now?"

"Maybe," I say, "but first I have to get that other diary from Rachel."

"I thought you'd say that," Natalie says. "I can help you with that."

Louise was right. Natalie is a good woman.

And I wonder if the man Pappy thinks he killed is Tony Gallio's brother.

18

I TAKE THE expressway down to the I-15 interchange and head for the Strip. At Sahara and Las Vegas Boulevard, the Strip, ablaze with lights and crammed with tourists and bumper-to-bumper traffic, beckons to our right. I turn left, back toward downtown, past Bob Stupak's Vegas World Hotel-Casino, into a maze of streets that covers several square blocks. The Naked City. Images of the old television series flash through my mind as I start looking for street signs.

"Maybe we ought to come back in the daytime," Natalie says.

Maybe she's right. The Naked City is an area of low-income housing, drug deals, heavy gang activity, and a few small, run-down shops and stores.

When I turn the first corner, the headlights pick up a group of teenagers standing around in a small park, laughing, talking, slapping hands. Young black dudes in baggy pants and baseball caps on backwards. Some wear scarfs tied on their heads.

I skirt the park looking for Boston Street, wishing we'd looked at a map first. Natalie holds the scrap of paper with the address John Trask gave me. "Twenty-six-ninety," she says, squinting at the paper. "If we ever find the street."

I turn left again and get a flash of the street sign. "Here we go." Twenty-six-ninety is a two-story apartment building halfway down the block, set back from the street and badly in need of repair. I park near the front behind two cars up on blocks and cut the engine.

A couple of dogs foraging in trash cans give us a look, then continue on their way. At the entrance a dim light illuminates the wall of mailboxes. A couple are standing open, their doors bent almost off.

"Let me try first," Natalie says. "You didn't make much of an impression on Rachel at Pogo's. Maybe she'll talk to me."

I hesitate. I don't want to pull any macho scene on Natalie, and she is after all a cop. "You sure you want to do this?"

"I can handle it," Natalie says. "If Rachel is willing to talk, I'll come and get you."

I watch Natalie get out of the Jeep and check the mailboxes, wishing for once I was in the VW. In this neighborhood the red Jeep is as out of place as Thelonious Monk playing with Lawrence Welk. I hunker down in the seat and light a cigarette, watching Natalie climb the stairs.

She rings the doorbell, glances toward the car. The door cracks open, and a shaft of light spills over Natalie. A few moments later she's inside. So far so good.

I check my watch and decide to give her ten minutes before I go in after her. Two girls walk by, give me the once-over, then continue on down the block talking loudly in Spanish. I scan the street, the rearview mirror, but see no one else until a man from the next building comes out to walk his dog.

I flip my cigarette into the street and check my watch again. No sign of Natalie. I'm just about to go in when the door opens and Natalie appears, says something to whoever is inside, then comes down the stairs and back to the car.

"Well?"

"She's not here," Natalie says, getting in. "That was the boyfriend. God, what a piece of work he is, zoned out on something. Doesn't know when she'll be back. I told him I was an old friend of hers and I'd come back tomorrow."

"Well, that's all we can do tonight, I guess. If we come back early we'll have a better chance of catching her. I have an idea Rachel sleeps late."

"I hope she isn't sleeping with that guy," Natalie says.

BY SEVEN-THIRTY THE next morning we're in the VW, drinking coffee out of paper cups from a 7-Eleven, back in front of Rachel's building. Most of the neighborhood is awake. School buses are picking up kids, people are going back to work. The Naked City doesn't look nearly so ominous in the light. Neglected is a better word. A few blocks away the Vegas World Hotel-Casino and Bob Stupak's tower mar the skyline.

"I think I'll go with you this time." I lock the car, and going up the stairs we pass a man in work clothes, carrying a toolbox. He nods to us, and we wait a minute outside Rachel's door until he's out of sight.

Natalie rings the bell several times before a skinny guy with long hair hanging in his eyes opens the door. He's barefoot and wears cutoff jeans.

"Yeah, what are you guys, Jehovah's Witnesses?" He glances at me, then peers at Natalie closer, recognizes her.

"Hi, Rick," Natalie says.

"Look, I told you Rachel's not here." Rick starts to shut the door.

"That was last night," I say. I step in closer. "We'll wait."

Rick decides it's not worth arguing about and opens the door wider. "Give me a break, man, I told you she's not here."

"What is it, Rick?" The voice comes from another part of the apartment.

"Rachel," Natalie calls. "I was here last night. We want to talk to you."

Rick shrugs, brushes the hair out of his eyes, and steps aside. "Sorry, babe."

"Who's we?" Rachel says. She comes into view, wearing an old robe, her hair sleep-tousled. When she sees me, she stops and glares. "What do you want? Don't you get it? I told you the other night I didn't want to talk."

"Rachel," Natalie says softly, "it'll just take a few minutes. It's very important."

Rachel sighs but cracks a tiny bit. "All right," she says, "if it'll get rid of you. I'll handle this," she says to Rick.

"Wow, man, this is really a drag, can't even sleep," Rick says. He shuffles off to the bedroom and slams the door.

"Sorry," Natalie says.

"He'll get over it." Rachel shrugs and sits down on the couch. She lights a cigarette from a pack on the table and shoves some newspapers aside until she finds a large ashtray full of last night's butts. She rubs her forehead as Natalie sits down next to her. I lean on the wall near the door.

The apartment looks like it does from the outside. Besides the couch, a couple of chairs, and a dinette set near the kitchen—all hand-me-down furniture—there's a small bookcase holding a suitcase-sized boom box. The shelf below is stacked with CDs and cassette tapes. Mostly singers, from what I can see—Billie Holliday, Carmen McRae, Sarah, and Ella. Rachel still wants to be a singer.

I let Natalie take the lead. "We saw your mother last night, Rachel," she begins. "She's still very worried about you, and of course she wants to see you. She didn't send us, though." She glances at me. "Evan has found out some things that you can help us with."

"Well, as you can see, I'm doing fine," Rachel says. She stubs out her cigarette angrily.

"C'mon, Rachel," I say, "you're not doing fine. You're living in a dump with a doofus. Stop beating up your mother for something that happened a long time ago."

Natalie gives me a warning glance, but it's already too late. "Yeah, something happened all right—me. It was me who happened. How'd you like to find out your father isn't who you think he is. That he's a—a fucking gangster. She lied to me all those years. Christ, I—"

I let her go. She has me there. I rarely see my mother and father these days, but I grew up in a fairly supportive environment. My mother encouraged my piano-playing ideas all the way, mainly because she played herself. My dad went along with it, although I'm sure he would have preferred I had chosen an athletic career. I watch Rachel, head in hands, no way to identify with her feelings. She's got to get the anger out first.

When she looks at me again, her eyes glisten with tears. "Why did she lie, why didn't she just tell me sooner?"

"She probably had her reasons. I know she didn't want you to find out the way you did. She was trying to protect you."

"Protect me. That's a laugh. From what? Her screwing around when she was a dancer at some nightclub? I've seen it, written in her own hand. No, I don't buy it."

I glance at Natalie. She encourages me with her eyes. *You're doing fine*, they say. "Whether you buy it or not, it's done, and you may have some of it wrong."

"Oh, really?" Rachel gets up and goes into the bedroom. She comes back and slams a small notebook down on the table. "See for yourself. It's all there."

Rachel gets up again and heads for the kitchen. "I need some coffee."

I pick up the diary and thumb through the pages. Same neat script as the other one. I want to sit down and read it through start to finish. Pappy, Louise, Gallio, and maybe the answer to Wardell Gray's death are in here. I know I'm not leaving without it.

I go in the kitchen. Rachel is slamming things around, getting the coffee started. "Well?" she says.

"Rachel, your mother could be in trouble. I need to take this with me," I say, holding up the diary. That stops her. She looks at Natalie, who nods her head.

"What do you mean?"

"Your mother saw a lot of things while she danced at the Moulin Rouge. There's information in here other people want."

"Who?" Rachel says. "She looks from me to Natalie, then smiles slightly. "Gallio, right?" When we don't answer she nods and taps her fingers on the countertop, staring at the water dripping into a stained Mr. Coffee. Everyone is silent until the gurgling stops.

"Take it with you, then," Rachel says finally. "I don't want it."

"Why have you kept it, then?" Natalie asks.

"What else have I got?" Rachel leans against the counter and throws her head back. Natalie moves toward her. As Rachel starts to cry again, Natalie reaches out and hugs her. It's a few minutes before Rachel speaks again.

"Jesus, I don't know. I always knew something was wrong, but I could never figure it out. This really hit me hard."

"Rachel," Natalie says, "your mother loves you very much. She can't undo the past, but a lot has happened since then. It won't ever be like you want it, but a lot of it can be straightened out. Give her a chance to try."

Rachel wipes her yes and gets a mug out of the cupboard. "You want some?" she asks. Natalie and I both shake our heads. Looking around the kitchen, Rachel manages a smile. "I don't blame you," she says, surveying the sink full of dirty dishes. "My mother would never allow a mess like this." She takes a sip of coffee and looks at me.

"Is she really in trouble?"

"She could be. I know just seeing you would make her feel better."

Rachel nods again. "Well, take the diary if it will help. I've got to think about all this." She looks at me again, trying to come to some judgment. "Why are you doing this? Did you know my mother before?"

"It's a long story. I'm trying to figure out some of the past too, but for different reasons. Can I tell her you'll at least call her?"

Rachel takes a couple of deep breaths. "Yeah, you can tell her that. I'll call her, but I'm not promising anything."

AFTER WE LEAVE Rachel's, Natalie and I stop for some breakfast on the way back to the apartment. I stash the diary under the front seat of the VW. While we wait for the food, ham and eggs and coffee, I use the pay phone and call Louise. She's very relieved to learn she'll hear from Rachel and thanks me.

Neither of us talks much, but I know Natalie will push now for me to turn this all over to Coop and John Trask.

I feel her watching me as we eat, trying to decide what is exactly the right moment to bring it up. Over a second cup of coffee, I barter.

"Okay, I agree, Coop needs to be brought up to date, and I'm going to do that today."

"Good," Natalie says. "It's really the only thing to do."

"But you've got to do something for me."

Natalie's eyes widen. "What?"

I tell her about The Breeze, the lawyer-DJ, and what I want him to do. "It should be all public record, so there's no problem, is there? We're not breaking into anyone's office or anything like that."

Natalie is not so sure. She stares out the window. "No, I guess not, but why is this important?"

"I just want to have a handle on things before I give it all up to the police, and I still want to know what happened to Wardell Gray."

"Maybe it's in the diary."

I shake my head. "I wish it was going to be that easy, but I don't think so. There might be something, but from all the people I've talked to, I think I know more about it than anyone, and I wasn't even around then. There's one other guy I need to talk to." I put up my hands before Natalie can protest. "Hey, Trask gave me the number. He's a retired cop who was on Metro during the Moulin Rouge days."

"And what if he doesn't know anything?"

"Well, then I guess Wardell Gray's death will remain unsolved."

"Maybe that's the way it's supposed to be," Natalie says.

I don't answer that one because I don't want to believe it. I pay the check and we head back to the apartment. Coop is gone but has left word with Ace he wants to talk to me.

"He seemed pretty serious," Ace says. "Said he'd check back here later."

"If he calls, I'll be at the mall entertaining the shoppers."

I shower and change into my tux. "You look mighty handsome," Natalie says. "You sure I can't come and watch you play?"

"No, you get hold of Breeze and try this retired cop's number. See if he can see me later today, sometime after four, okay?"

"God, you need a secretary."

"Don't I already have one?"

"Get out of here," Natalie says, laughing and threatening me with the back of her hand.

The mall is fairly quiet when I sit down at the piano. I decide to stick to ballads the first hour, a choice Brent Tyler seems to approve of. I'm just halfway through my first attempt when he shows up.

"What's that called?" He asks as I go into the bridge.

" 'I Thought About You.' Like it?"

Brent looks at my hand. It's still bruised, but the swelling is gone and I can move it fairly well if I don't get too tricky. "Yeah, I guess. Still like to hear you try some of those Carpenters songs."

"I'll dig one out, Brent."

He takes off and waves. "Good to have you back."

I spend my first break poring over Louise's diary. There's some of the same stuff from the first diary, the excitement of the show, how she got hired, but in this one Wardell is very much in evidence from their L.A. days. When she gets to the part about rehearsals for the Moulin Rouge show and Wardell's reappearance, there appears to be genuine surprise on her part.

They meet several times for long conversations, but he warns her they can't be seen together, and Louise seems genuinely disappointed at this until she realizes Wardell is trying to protect her. From what, she doesn't know. By the time I get to the opening-night pages, it's time to go back to work.

I've been too optimistic. My hand is functioning, but that's all. I can struggle through some easy songs, but the ache is there, getting louder by the minute. Two songs into the set, I look up from the piano and see I have more than my hand to worry about. Directly across from me, seated at one of the tables, are Tony and Karl, sipping coffee and staring at me. Tony smiles and raises his cup.

Aching hand or not, I figure the safest place for me is right at the piano, until they both get up and walk toward me. They step under the velvet rope, one on each side, while I try to concentrate on the changes to "Everything Happens to Me."

"Nice, Horne, nice," Tony says. It's only a distraction. Out of the corner of my eye, I see Karl move closer to the piano and reach out for the keyboard cover. I know he's going to slam it right down on my hands. I start to pull away when another hand comes into view and grips Karl's wrist tightly.

"Let's take a walk, bozo," Coop says. Before Karl can react, Coop has his thumb bent back almost to his wrist. Sweat breaks out on Karl's forehead.

"Tony," he gasps, his eyes wide with pain.

"Who the fuck are you?" Tony asks. I lean back, blocking his access to Karl, and keep playing. Nobody notices a thing.

"In the words of Virgil Tibbs, I'm a police officer," Coop says, smiling at Tony. "Now shall we walk away from here, and not interrupt this gentleman's performance?"

Tony backs off, and Coop, still gripping Karl's thumb, pulls him behind the escalator. I glance over my shoulder. Coop has let go of Karl, who's glaring and rubbing his hand. Coop flashes his badge too quickly for them to see it's not Las Vegas; his shoulder holster registers much more clearly, enough to really back Tony off.

"The exit is that way," Coop says, pointing toward the double doors leading to the parking lot. He stands there until they're out of sight, then walks back to the piano and stands just outside the rope.

"Interesting fans you have," he says. "Doesn't this mall have any security?"

I finish the tune I'm on and stop playing. "Thanks, Coop." I glance at my watch. "Ten minutes to go, okay?" Coop nods and goes for coffee.

Mary Lou shows up early with her briefcase full of music. "Quiet around here today, huh?"

"Yeah, really slow." I say good-bye and join Coop at a table.

"Natalie says we have things to talk about," Coop says. "I'd like to hear them, please."

I tell him about Louise, Rachel, the diary, and my speculation about what it all means. He listens in silence until I finish. "So what do you think I should do?"

"What you should have done all along. Call the fucking police."

"I did, remember. You were the one who introduced me to Trask."

Coop rolls his eyes at me. "That was before all this other

shit. Tony Gallio is not some disgruntled jazz fan who wants to keep Wardell Gray's reputation part of history. Those two I just threw out of here are serious."

"Why didn't you arrest them?"

"On what charge? Annoying the piano player? No, you stop all this detective bullshit and Gallio will go away."

"I don't think so." I hold up the diary. "He wants this for a couple of reasons. He's got some deal cooking for the Rouge property, and he doesn't want what's in here to get out."

"You," Coop says, pointing his finger at me, "have to give that and everything you know to Trask. I don't have any jurisdiction here, or I'd take it away from you right now."

"I will, I will. Tomorrow."

Coop sighs and lights one of his cigars. "That's what I thought." He reaches in his pocket and pulls out a piece of paper. "This message is for you. Natalie gave it to me. Your retired cop friend. Wants you to call."

"See, I am going to call the cops."

19

"BUDDY HERMAN, LAS VEGAS Metropolitan Police, retired. *Retired* is the operative word," Herman emphasizes in his gravelly voice as we shake hands. He's a short, stocky man with a leathered, sunburned face. His retirement uniform is a Hawaiian shirt, Las Vegas Stars baseball cap, baggy jeans, and black canvas shoes.

"Thanks for seeing me," I say.

"No problem. John Trask is good people. I don't have much time, though," Herman says, tapping on the small motorboat hitched to a Chevy Blazer that's seen better days. The name *Pin Puller* is painted on the stern. "I'm headed out to the lake."

We're standing in the parking lot of a diner on West Charleston, the sun beating down as usual. According to the thermometer on the bank across the street, the temperature is 108 degrees. I can only imagine what it must be like at Lake Mead, baking in an open boat.

"Feels great, eh?" Herman says. "God, I love the heat." He grins, takes in my tux pants, white shirt, and sweating brow. "You a waiter?"

"Musician."

Herman nods. "Well, let's go inside."

The diner is busy, and the crowd seems to be regulars. Herman waves to some familiar faces and trades quips with others as we make our way to a table. We both order iced tea from a waitress who looks like she wishes it was closing time.

Herman takes a long gulp of his tea and studies me across the table. "John Trask told me you were on the force during the Moulin Rouge era. You remember much about it?"

"Era? Is that what it was?" Herman snorts and gulps more tea. "They were only open six months. I remember it as a time of easy police work in a small town. Couldn't have been more than 15,000 people here then. 'Course, by the time I retired it was getting bad."

He looks out the window at the traffic flying by on Charleston. "This place is like L.A. now. Murders, gangs, drugs, you name it, we got it. Today they walk right in the casino and take the money. The boys would never have allowed these casino robberies. I knew some of them," Herman says. "Personally. They'd have these punks buried face-first in the desert. But that's ancient history." He holds up his glass to a passing waitress for more tea.

"The boys?"

"You know," Herman says. "Bugsy Siegel, the guys who started this place."

"Actually, that's what I'm interested in. One of the musicians at the Moulin Rouge was found in the desert the night after the casino opened. Wardell Gray. May 1955. You remember anything about that?"

"Sure," Herman says, "Trask reminded me. Colored boy, wasn't he? Trumpet player or something."

"He was black. Saxophone." I wonder about Herman's quick answer and try to keep the irritation out of my voice, reminding myself he is from another era.

Herman shrugs. "Colored, black, African-American, people

of color, that's the latest," he says with almost a smirk. "I can't keep up."

"You would if you were still with the police."

"Whatever." Herman rubs a beefy hand over his eyes. "Let me think. I wasn't the primary on that, but I remember it. He was found in the desert somewhere over on the west side, out by the railroad tracks."

"Trask says there wasn't any investigation, and there's no file. Do you know why that was?"

"Didn't need to be one's my guess," Herman says. "You find a guy in the desert two days after he's killed, no suspects, no motive, no witnesses, he's a known drug user. What are you going to investigate? We had some other guy in from the show for questioning."

"Teddy Hale?"

"Yeah, Teddy something. Said he and Gray had a dope party in their room and Gray fell out of bed, broke his neck." Herman smiles like he knows something I don't. "Right, fell out of bed."

"You don't think that's how it happened."

Herman shakes his head. "Naw, I think this Hale character bopped Gray. You look at the coroner's report? Cause of death was drug overdose, but there were head wounds from the proverbial blunt instrument."

"So why wasn't there an investigation then?"

"Already told you," Herman says. "Maybe this Gray character stepped on the wrong toes. This town was run differently then, if you know what I mean. If Gray annoyed somebody well connected, and they knew he was a dope addict—don't musicians take dope to play better?"

"Some did, but not to play better."

"Whatever. Anyway, they could make it look like an overdose pretty easy, dump the body in the desert, who would know?"

"Or who would care?"

"I'm not saying that."

"What are you saying?"

"I'm saying if there was no investigation, there was no need for one. Look, son, no suspects, no weapon, could have just been a simple robbery assault. Coroner files an incident report, and that's that, nice and clean."

This is the end of the line, then. If there's no file, no investigation, and I'm talking to a cop who knew of the case, then there's nothing else. Wardell Gray's death will remain under what's it's always been—a cloud of mysterious circumstances.

"Who were some of 'the boys' at that time? You remember anybody particular?"

Herman shakes his head. "Naw, we didn't have much to do with the Strip. They took care of their own problems."

"How about Anthony Gallio?"

"Gallio? The name is familiar, but I don't remember from where. What did he do?"

"It doesn't matter. What about another case, a stabbing at the Moulin Rouge, sometime after Gray was found?"

"A murder, you mean?" Herman looks genuinely puzzled. "No, I'd definitely remember that."

I lapse into silence. Either Herman was carefully coached, or he really didn't remember. Pappy seems sure he'd killed someone.

Herman glances at his watch. "Well, sorry I couldn't be more help, son, but I got to go. The lake is calling, and there's some fish out there with my name on them."

"Sure, thanks anyway." Herman reaches for the check, but I beat him to it. "I got it. Thanks again."

He gets up and starts for the door, then turns and comes back to the table. "You know what I'd do if I were you? I'd let that Gray boy rest in peace."

I PAY THE check and call Natalie from the pay phone in the diner. No messages or calls from anyone, including Breeze. Coop evidently hasn't told her about Tony and Karl's visit to the mall. When I tell her about the conversation with Herman, she senses the disappointment in my voice.

"You've done all you can, Evan. You're just going to have to accept that."

"Yeah, I know. I was just hoping Herman would have some first-hand information. If he's typical of the police in those days, they didn't care about Wardell anyway."

"Are you coming back to the house now?"

"I guess so. I want to check with Breeze first."

"I thought you said he was a jazz DJ. He sounds like a lawyer on the phone."

"He is. I'll tell you about it later. That's probably a dead end, too."

"All right, see you soon. I've got a surprise for you."

I hang up the phone and stare out the window of the diner, trying to put my finger on something Herman said or didn't say, but it eludes me. Like everything else lately. Herman said he wasn't primary on Wardell Gray's case. If he wasn't, then who was? And doesn't that mean there was a case, an investigation? I think there was a file on Wardell Gray.

But if there was one, who has it? And why would anyone want the file on a thirty-seven-year-old case to disappear?

NATALIE'S SURPRISE IS brewing in Ace's kitchen. She's taken over and is busily dicing onions and peppers, grating cheese, and stirring some ground beef simmering on the stove alongside a pan of refried beans. A stack of tortillas rests on the counter. Natalie, wisps of hair falling over her eyes, wields the knife with considerable skill.

"Ace told me you like Mexican food," she says. "Coop is

coming over later. He's meeting with John Trask." Her light kiss, which I'd like to go on much longer, is interrupted by the whir of the blender where Ace is whipping up margaritas.

"Coming right up," Ace says. He stops the blender, dips three large glasses upside down in a plate of salt, sets them upright on the counter, and fills them with his mixture from the blender. "Try these on for size."

Natalie stops her dicing long enough for a quick taste and licks her lips. "A tad too much tequila, maybe?" Ace and I try ours and disagree. "Okay, you guys win, now get out of the kitchen," she says.

"C'mon," Ace says, "I want to show you something." We take our drinks and go into his office. He turns on his computer and calls up a file folder labeled "Death of a Tenor Man." There are files with notes, police reports, history, and excerpts from books and interviews. "It's really coming together," Ace says. "You, mister piano man, have given me enough to go with my research for a very fine paper at the conference coming up."

I sit down and watch Ace happily scroll through his files. "I'd still like to talk with Pappy Dean," he says. "Think you could arrange that?"

"Yeah, probably," I say absently.

"What's the matter?' Ace asks, sensing the mood I can't seem to shake, even with an excellent margarita. "Come on, you found Rachel and maybe got her back on track with her mother."

"But in the process maybe I've exposed Louise Cody to some real danger unless I can come up with something to get Gallio to back off. And I still can't finish that paper for you with a definitive answer on Wardell Gray."

"Look, you can't be responsible for what Louise did thirty-seven years ago. She's going to have to deal with that herself. You found her daughter, that's what she wanted. You've also given me more material than I dreamed of for this conference coming up. I can shove it up the department chair's ass. Sorry, Natalie," Ace says, noticing her at the doorway.

She smiles at Ace's uncharacteristic venom. "I thought the humanities was the last bastion of gentle, scholarly exploration." She winks at me.

"Not when it comes to department politics. The knives really come out then. I'm just sick of it. Hey, don't get me started on this."

"What I want you to get started on is dinner. Let's not wait for Coop."

Ace shuts off his computer. "Yes, ma'am."

"I'll be there in a minute." Gallio is still a problem for Louise and maybe the Moulin Rouge. Breeze is perhaps the answer to that one. I phone his office and leave two more messages for him on his service.

Coop still hasn't arrived by the time we've had our fill of tacos and margaritas. Ace retires to his office and leaves Natalie and me sitting on the patio with coffee. Natalie obviously has other plans anyway. Her hand is warm in mine, and her eyes are pools of darkness. Inside the apartment, I suddenly remember the diary.

"Oh yeah, I'd like to see that," Natalie says, "if it won't break the spell or take too long."

"Right, I left it in the VW. Be right back. Hold that thought."

"I will," she says. "You can read to me."

I walk down to the lower walkway when from my left, something slams into me, and I go crashing into the hedge with Karl's huge body on top of me. He quickly pins my arms behind my back and jerks me to my feet. I turn my head, trying to see him, but I know it's Karl, and the hard object against my cheek is a gun. The hand holding it belongs to Tony.

"Your fucking cop friend in there, Horne?" Tony asks.

"No, no one."

Tony relaxes immediately. "Good. My uncle wants to have a few words with you. You don't mind coming along with us, do you?"

I don't have to answer. Karl drags me out to the street and shoves me in the backseat of their car. Tony slides in beside me. Karl gets in the driver's seat, starts the engine, and roars off.

How long will Natalie wait before she comes looking for me? And if she calls anybody, what could she tell them?

"Thanks for being so cooperative, Horne. My uncle will appreciate the fact that you're coming along," Tony says. He smiles and holsters his gun. "I'm sure I don't need this, right?"

I ignore him and lean against the seat, trying to get my breath back. Karl heads up Rainbow, then turns south toward Tropicana. At the next light he turns west, and I really get worried. There's some new housing developments out this way, but just beyond is open desert.

Tony senses my apprehension and laughs. "No, it doesn't work that way anymore, Horne. We're not taking you out to the desert, are we, Karl?"

"No," Karl says. "I'd like to take his cop friend out there, though."

"No, you wouldn't, Karl," I say.

Karl half turns in the seat to glare at me, but Tony shuts him up.

"Just drive, Karl. We're almost there, Horne," he says to me.

There is Spanish Trail, a very expensive, upscale planned community, complete with a tennis complex and golf course, where people like Steve Wynn and Andre Agassi and, apparently, Anthony Gallio live.

I feel momentarily relieved as we turn into the entrance past a security booth, thinking I should yell out to the guard, but there's no chance. Karl and Tony both nod to the guard as he waves the car through.

We drive for another few minutes, turning several times

through the maze of streets, then pull into the driveway of a huge home the size of a library. Karl presses a remote button, and the security gate rumbles open. I see a large gold letter *G* slide past us. Tony pulls the Lincoln in beside a Mercedes and a white Cadillac. The gate shuts behind us.

Tony jumps out and holds the door open. "Let's go, Horne. Inside."

The house is brick, lots of windows and two turrets dominating the silhouette. With Karl leading the way, we go in the house down a long hallway and step down into a tennis court–size living room.

"Wait here," Tony says. Not much choice with Karl just looking for a chance to show me his NFL linebacking skills. Tony disappears down a hallway. I glance around the living room. It looks like a setup for an *Architectural Digest* photo layout. In the soft lighting everything looks expensive and placed just so, right down to the angles of the photos on the mantle. Music comes from somewhere, an opera at very low volume.

Tony reappears and motions me. "This way, Horne." I follow him down the hall around the corner. "In here," he says. I step down into a room brightly lit by fluorescent tubes.

"Good evening, Mr. Horne. So nice of you to join us. Please have a seat."

"How could I resist Karl's invitation?" Gallio is seated on a high stool, bent over a workbench. Under a high intensity lamp, he holds something in his left hand and peers through a magnifying glass eyepiece. When he looks up at me, the glass picks up the light and shines like a spotlight. His right hand holds a small brush. In front of him is an array of paint bottles.

"I'm glad to see you've retained your sense of humor," Gallio says. "Can I offer you a drink?" Behind Gallio on a massive table that dominates the room is the most elaborate dollhouse I've ever seen.

There's a landscaped yard and garden, and through the windows of the house, I can see tiny figures in the various rooms, which are lit in varying degrees of brightness.

"Have a look," Gallio says while continuing his work.

I look in the window of what is obviously the living room. Its furnishings are identical to the room I was standing in only minutes ago. The scene is a party in progress. Miniature dolls, some holding drinks, are seated around the room or stand in groups. In one corner is a grand piano complete with a pianist seated on the bench, his hands locked on the keys.

"My hobby and my passion," Gallio says. He lays the brush on a cloth and carefully places the doll on the table. He takes the eyepiece out and switches off the lamp. "It's very delicate work, sometimes frustrating to get everything exactly right, but it relaxes me. I enjoy the control, the way I can change the scene. Watch, I'll show you."

From a glass case on the wall he surveys what must be hundreds of miniature dolls. He selects one of a woman in an evening dress and takes it to the dollhouse. He lays it aside for a moment, then, using some kind of device that looks like a long thin tube with pincers on one end, reaches into the living room scene and extracts the pianist. He carefully pulls it out through the window, takes it off the tube, and attaches the woman in its place. Back through the window, he seats the woman at the piano, removes the tube, and only then relaxes.

He holds the tuxedo-clad pianist doll carefully in his hand for a moment, staring at it. His fingers tighten around it. There's a light snapping sound, and one of the arms breaks off.

Gallio looks up at me and smiles. "You see," he says, "I can change the scene to suit my mood, but no matter how careful you are, accidents do happen." He tosses the doll aside into a small box of other damaged miniatures. I get the point.

"Okay. I know who you are, and I'm sufficiently scared.

What I don't know is what you want with me. I'd just like to go home."

Gallio studies me for a moment. "You're either a very reckless or a very stupid, foolish young man, or perhaps both. I haven't decided which yet, but your responses to my request will no doubt determine my choice.

"You are being treated so graciously because I know of your association with Louise Cody. Otherwise, well, let's not go into unpleasant matters. I've known Louise for many years, as I'm sure you know, and I've helped her considerably in the past, which I'm also sure you know. Now you are going to help me."

I don't have a clue what he's talking about. We stare at each other for a few moments before Gallio's impatience gets the better of him. "Do I have to spell it out for you, Horne? When we met at Spago, I alluded to some business propositions I have pending with the Moulin Rouge property, did I not?"

"Yeah, I guess you did."

"Well then, those propositions are nearing completion, but there are a couple of details that need attending to. I don't want the past encroaching on the present." Gallio pauses for a moment, measuring his words. "There's a certain journal Louise kept when she was at the Moulin Rouge. There are things in that journal that would be embarrassing to me and certain colleagues in other cities should they become public. I want that journal, Horne, and you're going to help me get it."

Now it was starting to make sense. Gallio, now displaying a legitimate front, wants to buy the Moulin Rouge property. His background would not sit well with licensing agencies, and his "colleagues in other cities" definitely wouldn't like the media spotlight focused on one of their own.

"Why should I help you, and what makes you think I can?"

"Because," Gallio says, leaning in closer, "you know where the journal is, and I can help your friend."

"My friend?" Is he talking about Louise again?

"That's right, your friend Elgin Dean." Gallio smiles when he sees my surprised expression. "There's someone else I want you to meet. When you do, your confusion will be allayed considerably."

Gallio presses a button in his workbench. In a minute he looks over my shoulder and nods. Tony has come back into the room. "Let's go, Horne."

"When you come back, we'll talk some more," Gallio says.

We go down another hallway off the living room. At the end of the hall Tony stops at a door and knocks lightly. "Uncle Carlo, got a visitor for you." Tony opens the door and motions me inside, then shuts the door behind me. I feel like I've stepped into a dream.

My first impression is one of coldness. This room is much cooler than the rest of the house. The air conditioning hums; it must be set on fifty degrees. Except for the metallic glow of a big-screen television, the room is dark. Directly in front of the television is a large recliner chair. I walk toward it, vaguely aware of the shapes of other furniture, a wall of bookcases, tables, and unlit lamps.

"Come in, please." A strange voice comes from the recliner and startles me. It's an eerie, mechanical sound, a droning monotone that gives me further chills. I move closer and glance at the television. A black-and-white film fills the screen. A man sits in an easy chair, staring at a painting of a beautiful woman on the wall. I know the scene, but I can't place it.

"Over here," the mechanical voice says. An arm appears from the recliner and points at an easy chair nearby.

I walk over to the chair and sit down. In the bright glow of the television screen I can see the slight resemblance of this man to Anthony Gallio. The glasses are thicker, like prisms when they're struck by the television light, but the features are similar. He's dressed in slacks, sports coat, and shirt and wears a scarf around his neck.

"Forgive me for not getting up, Mr. Horne. I am Carlo Gallio, Anthony's brother."

Now I understand the mechanical voice. He holds something like a small microphone to his throat when he speaks—a mechanical voice box to replace his own. The music on the television swells to a crescendo. I turn my head when I recognize the song. The man in the film has dozed off while staring at the painting.

" 'Laura,' " Gallio says. "You play this tune?"

"Sometimes." Now I remember the film. I must have seen parts of it on late-night television.

"It's my favorite film. Dana Andrews is the detective. Gene Tierney is Laura. Watch now. Here she comes."

I turn to the screen. The door to the apartment opens, and Gene Tierney enters the apartment. She looks at the sleeping Andrews, the painting of herself, then back at Andrews. He opens his eyes, comes awake, sees her, then jumps to his feet, staring at her with an expression of utter disbelief and confusion.

"You see," Gallio's voice box says, "nothing is as it seems. Do you know this film?"

"I think I may have seen it."

"There's been a murder. Andrews, the detective, thinks it's Laura, the woman in the painting. By now, he's fallen in love with the painting, but it's not Laura who was killed. It was her roommate. A romantic twist to the plot, don't you think?" Gallio picks up the remote control and presses the mute button. I continue to watch Andrews and Tierney mime dialogue.

"My own life has been somewhat similar, Mr. Horne," Gallio's voice box says. "Many people thought I had been killed, but as you can see, I was not. It's true I nearly died. My voice did die. A shame, perhaps. I had a rather good singing voice when I was young. And now I have this."

He holds up the voice box microphone, looks at it, then

returns it to his throat. "There are, of course, other, more advanced procedures available now, but my health won't permit them, and I've grown used to this. It's a rather frightening sound, don't you agree? Most people are made uncomfortable by it."

"What happened?"

"I was young, full of bravado, as we are prone to be in our youth. In a rather stupid display of machismo, I mistakenly underestimated my opponent's skill with a knife. My vocal cords were severed."

I lean back in the chair and take a deep breath. The shiver I feel comes not from the room temperature but from what I understand now. No wonder nobody came looking for Pappy Dean. No wonder there was no murder reported. There wasn't any murder, and I'm sitting in a freezing room staring at the man Pappy thinks he killed—Anthony Gallio's brother Carlo.

"Enough about me," Gallio's voice says. "I'm not sure why my brother wanted me to see you. He's been very tense lately, worried over some business deal to do with the Moulin Rouge property. Strange how the past comes back to haunt us. There were many voices at the Moulin Rouge. Mine was lost there.

"Anthony told me you are investigating the death of one of the Moulin Rouge musicians. He wants your help in some way, Mr. Horne. I'm not aware of the details, but I can tell you this much. My brother is a determined man. I suggest you honor his request for help. As for your suspicions that I or my brother had something to do with that musician's death, they are unnecessary. His name again, please."

"Wardell Gray."

"Yes, that's it. Those were exciting times, Mr. Horne. I was opposed to the decision made about the Moulin Rouge, but I had no say really. I assure you, this Wardell Gray was not important enough to be a problem. It's my understanding that he died by his own hand, the result of drug abuse. If he was taken to the desert, he was already dead."

I listen to Gallio's mechanical voice recite the past in such calm terms and try to reconcile this man with the one who fought with Pappy Dean in the Moulin Rouge parking lot. Could he have changed that much in thirty-five-plus years? Both Gallios had to be in their late sixties now. For the first time I entertain the thought that maybe Wardell Gray died like Teddy Hale said—simply falling out of bed and breaking his neck.

Gallio takes my silence for acceptance. He presses the remote button again, and we hear Gene Tierney and Dana Andrews talking, the music, a variation of Laura's theme, playing softly in the background.

"This is an excellent film, Mr. Horne. You should make it a point to see it in its entirety. I'm sure you would enjoy it." Gallio sets his microphone aside. His eyes close. The interview is over.

I get up and walk out of the freezing room. I feel another shiver pass up my spine as I shut the door behind me.

Anthony Gallio waits for me in the living room with Tony and Karl.

I stand for a moment looking at Gallio. He's enjoying this. "Does your brother know Pappy Dean is the one who—?"

"Stabbed him, ruined his life? No, of course not, nobody even knew who Dean was, or your friend wouldn't be alive now. If he was, he'd have suffered some very serious accident."

"And Wardell Gray?"

"You've made more out of that than there is. Nobody had to kill him. He was already dead. You prove different. Teddy Hale was hysterical, so we took Gray out to the desert and coached Hale on his story, persuaded him that was the best way to handle things. The show had just opened, and we didn't need any bad publicity. We had the cops in our pocket."

I bet they did, and I wonder if Buddy Herman was their man. Maybe Wardell would have died anyway, but that kind of death changes the future. With Wardell, it was promise never fulfilled.

"Why is this diary of Louise's so important?"

"Horne, do you know who you're dealing with? All you need to know is that I want that diary. You've got twenty-four hours to get it."

"Or what?"

"You don't want to know, Horne. You don't want to know."

20

IT'S NOT LIKE old gangster movies. I don't exactly get pushed out of a rolling car, but Tony and Karl don't provide door-to-door service either. They pull up near an open lot at Torrey Pines and Desert Inn.

"Don't forget, Horne," Tony says. "Twenty-four hours." They drive off, and I stand for a moment watching their taillights merge with the traffic on Desert Inn, wondering how I got here. I walk the two blocks back to Ace's house feeling stiff and sore and tired of being stepped on, beat up, and dragged around Las Vegas.

In the driveway there's a car I don't recognize, with an Avis sticker on the window, alongside Ace's Jeep and the VW. I stand for a couple of minutes just in the shadows of the house to see if Tony and Karl are following, but there's no one.

I unlock the Bug and pull the diary from under the front seat, lock it again, and walk around to the back of the house. Coop spots me first when I come around the corner.

"Here he is," Coop says. Natalie and Ace are standing with him by the pool. Coop takes in my disheveled clothes, the scratches on my face from the shrubs and looks to see if I'm favoring my hand. No damage there this time. "Taking up night jogging?" Coop says.

"I've been at Anthony Gallio's," I say, before anybody can ask me the obvious question.

Coop nods. "Let's talk."

We go inside. Natalie takes my arm. "Are you okay? I didn't know what to do when you didn't come back. I'll make some coffee," she says, and begins busying herself in the kitchen. Ace just looks bewildered. His academic world has been turned upside down, and for some reason he can't meet my eyes. Coop must have filled him in somewhat. He nervously paces around, looks at his watch, then goes into the living room and switches on the TV.

Coop and I sit down at the kitchen table. I feel his eyes on me, checking me out, assessing my attitude, and I know he doesn't like what he sees. He doesn't even mention the diary I lay on the table in front of us.

Before we can start, Ace interrupts. "Hey, look at this," he says, turning up the volume on the television. "Come in here."

We gather around the television and watch a blow-dried blond anchor stare intently at the camera.

" . . . and on a story you're going to see only on 'Inside Las Vegas,' " she reminds us, "we go now to our own Tiffany Walker at Lake Mead. Tiffany, what can you tell us?"

A graphic at the bottom of the screen says "Live at Lake Mead." There's a shot of a body partially covered in a blanket. Two feet in black canvas shoes stick out from under it. The camera pans away from the reporter to the shore, where a tow truck is pulling a small boat out of the water. I get only a brief glimpse of the name lettered on the stern. "Buddy Herman," I say.

Everyone turns to me. Natalie puts her hand over her mouth. Ace stares. "Who?" Coop wants to know.

Another shot of the reporter, standing near the water. She

squints in the glare of the television lights. Several men in warmup jackets with *Police* on the back move about in the background while Buddy Herman is zipped up in a body bag and loaded into the coroner's van.

"We don't have many details yet," the reporter says. "The victim has been identified as"—she glances down at a notebook, then back to the camera—"retired Las Vegas Metro Policeman Charles Buddy Herman, apparently the victim of a drowning. Lieutenant John Trask of Metro Homicide isn't talking yet. We'll have more details later in this newscast. Back to you in the studio."

"You know him?" Coop asks.

"I was talking with him this afternoon. It's the guy Trask put me onto when we met at the Sands." It seems like weeks rather than days ago.

Coop nods. "Trask will want to talk to you, since you may be one of the last people to see him alive." Ace is still staring at the television. Natalie hands me and Coop a mug of coffee. "C'mon, let's go outside."

We settle at the patio table. So many things are running through my mind, beginning with Wardell Gray in 1955, Sonny Wells, and now Buddy Herman tonight. Coop lets me get a cigarette going and gather my thoughts.

"Any ideas? You pick up anything from Herman?"

I shake my head. "He didn't have much to say, but I had the feeling he was almost reading lines from a script. I think there *was* a file on Wardell Gray. Remember Trask telling me there was no file? He also said Metro's computer records only go back to the sixties. Anything before that is in manila folders in storage boxes."

"And?"

"I think Herman took the file, maybe years ago, maybe even at the time of Gray's death. Nobody's going to remember after all this time. Thirty-some years, and nobody ever asks anything.

Then when they do go looking, there's no file. Everybody just assumes there never was one."

"Except you," Coop says.

"Look, Coop," I lean forward on the table. "Nobody cared about Wardell Gray. He was black, not very well known outside the jazz community, and it was 1955 in Las Vegas. Every account of Wardell Gray's death—newspapers, jazz history books, stories passed on by musicians—all say the same thing: death under mysterious circumstances. There's never been a reasonable, plausible explanation."

"There often isn't with murder," Coop says.

"You think that's what it was?"

"I'm not saying that. The point is, someone did care about his death, enough so that two more people have been killed. Gallio or someone connected to him isn't taking any chances."

"Right, Gallio. He as much as admitted that he and somebody else took Gray to the desert and coached Teddy Hale, who was the only witness, but he claims Gray was already dead. He said they had the cops in their pocket."

Coop bristles slightly at that. "Is that why Gallio pulled you in tonight?"

"Partially. He wanted to scare me, and he did. But what he really wants is this." I tap my hand on Louise Cody's diary. I feel a sudden chill, remembering Gallio's brother Carlo. "I also met his brother, the guy Pappy Dean thinks he killed."

"The bass player you were talking about?" Coop takes a sip of his coffee. "Let's back up here, sport. Start at the beginning."

I recount the whole thing then, turning it over in my mind as I talk. At one point, I'm aware of Natalie silently joining us, listening, watching me, and occasionally glancing at Coop to see his reaction. When I finish, Coop looks into his empty coffee mug for several moments. I have one question for him.

"Why Buddy Herman?"

"Like you said, if Herman took the file and Gallio knew you

talked to him, except for you, he was the last link in the chain. Now it's your word against Gallio's in a thirty-seven-year-old crime that's not on the books. And that's only if there was one. They may have intended to take Gray out, but it may be just as they said. He could have simply overdosed and been dumped in the desert."

"We both know different, Coop."

"Maybe about Sonny Wells and Buddy Herman, but not about Wardell Gray. Gallio's not stupid. He's covered his tracks well. I'd be willing to bet you can't put Tony and Karl at either Wells's or Herman's killing."

"No, but I think I can tie Gallio up with the Moulin Rouge. That's why he wants the diary. He wants to buy the property, apply for licenses to do whatever he's planning. If this stuff came out, his entire application would be in question, enough to delay it at least because of the publicity."

"You got some proof of that?" Coop asks.

"I can get it, I think. I've got somebody looking into it now."

"I should have known. When will you know?"

"By tomorrow, I hope."

"Okay. I've got an idea. Let me run it by Trask. I'll tell him you'll be down to make a statement about your talk with Buddy Herman in the morning. In the meantime, stay off the streets. It's dangerous out there."

"Coop?"

"Yeah?" He's already on his feet.

"Gallio gave me twenty-four hours."

IT'S AFTER MIDNIGHT when I stand under the shower for ten minutes, letting the hot water penetrate my bumps and bruises. Toweling off, I inspect myself in the mirror. Not too bad for having been sacked by a former NFL lineman. A few scratches on my face from the shrubs, but my hand is okay. It's what doesn't show that hurts.

Natalie is already asleep when I come out of the bathroom, breathing easily, her hair spread out over the pillow. I watch her for a few moments, then pull the light blanket up over her and tiptoe out of the bedroom, fighting the urge to go back inside and slide in next to her.

I go back to the kitchen, make some coffee, and grab Louise Cody's diary. There has to be something in here that makes Gallio want it so badly, something I can hold up to him and use against him. I put some Keith Jarrett solo piano on the cassette player with the volume way down and settle on the couch with coffee, cigarettes, and the diary, feeling like a student cramming for an exam.

I skim through the early entries, which sound much like the ones from the other diary Louise showed me. The voice is that of a young girl, stars in her eyes, set on a show business career, getting her first big break in a new show, new hotel-casino.

> April 1955—It's finally happened, but I still can't believe it. After four auditions, I've been chosen for the Moulin Rouge show in Las Vegas!!!! Yes! Yes! Yes! We leave next week to start rehearsals. I can't wait. I know some of the other girls, but there are more coming from all over the country. I feel really special, and I just know the show is going to do well. I looked at myself in the mirror and said, "Girl, you are something!"

Later, after she arrived in Las Vegas to begin rehearsals, Louise wrote,

> There's one part I don't like though. We're living in some houses built just for us—the Cadillac Arms, they're called. They're really nice, and my room-mates Marva and Josie are sweet girls. We're having lots of fun cooking, talking about our costumes, and helping each other with the dance steps, but the con-

tract we had to sign, well, I just can't believe it. Right up there on top, in big letters, it says we are not allowed to go to any of the Strip hotels. Not that we have time, but sometimes I feel like we're in a prison. I guess I shouldn't complain. The rehearsals are going well, and the band is coming in next week. I can't believe it. It's Benny Carter!!! Maybe—no, I won't even think about that now, it's probably bad luck.

May 1955—Maybe I should have thought about it more. We had our first rehearsal with the band this afternoon, and there he was, that sweet baby Wardell, sitting there in the saxophone section, smiling and winking at me real cool like. It's been so long since I've seen him. He looks tired though, and I know he's still into that bad stuff like he was on Central Avenue in L.A. I'm so glad he's here, but there hasn't been any time to talk much, and those men that run the casino have been getting too friendly, especially that Anthony Gallio and his brother. I just smile and take his compliments, but he's going to be a problem. I have to be careful though. I know he doesn't like me talking with Wardell. "Keep your mind on the show, sugar," he told me yesterday. Sugar? What does he *think* I'm thinking about? We open in two weeks.

—The band is fantastic. Benny Carter wrote all the music, but every time I dance by, all I can see is Wardell. I stayed around today to listen to the band's special numbers and Wardell's solos. That sweet baby can sure play his horn. Sometimes I feel like he's playing just for me, but I know that will never happen. He's got a wife and baby. He must miss them. We talked yesterday, and he took me out for coffee, carrying that little book of poems he always has with him. Sometimes I feel like he's a teacher and I'm his student. He talks different with me than he does with the other boys in the band, tells me I should read books.

But he told me to be careful of Gallio and the other men who run the casino. "This place ain't exactly what it seems," he told me. When I asked him what he meant, he wouldn't talk about it anymore, so I didn't press him. I think I know what he means.

I finish my coffee, thinking about that entry. What *did* Wardell mean? He was almost twice Louise's age and had been around long enough—Benny Goodman, Basie, Earl Hines—to know how things went down, especially in mob-run clubs. Living in Detroit, Wardell must have played in enough of them. He was also smart enough to know that if you just stick to the music, you'll be all right.

I go back to the diary. The rest of the entries lead up to opening night and confirm many of the things Louise has already told me.

Tuesday—Opening night and I still can't believe I'm part of this. I've never seen so many stars and celebrities. Joe Louis is the host, the heavyweight champion of the world! They just kept coming in big limos—Harry Belafonte, Sammy Davis, and the man, Nat King Cole!!!!—dressed so fine, and there were photographers everywhere, even some people from Life Magazine. They took pictures of us backstage and told us our photo would be on the cover. Mama will be so proud when she sees that. I felt like I was in a trance during the first show. I was so excited I almost missed my cue, but all it took was a wink from Wardell to settle me down.

The casino was packed with people, and everybody loved the show. The band was just cookin', and Wardell never sounded better. I hate to see him hang-

ing around with Teddy Hale though. Teddy's one of
the dancers. I know what he and Wardell are doing
before the shows, but I can't say anything to Wardell.
It's not my business.

Wednesday—The first show was just like last
night. More celebrities, a full house, photographers
everywhere wanting us to pose with people. Josie and
Marva and I went back to the house like we always
do to get something to eat and rest up for the late show.
I've never been so happy. We talked a lot about all
the gorgeous guys at the club, and they treat us like
we're stars. Hey, we are!!!!

But by the time we went back to the hotel, I knew
something was wrong. We were supposed to start at
two o'clock, but somebody came to our dressing room
and said there would be a delay. I peeked out in the
hallway and saw some of the musicians talking in
little groups. One of them who'd seen me talking with
Wardell told me they were waiting for him.

We waited forty-five minutes but finally had to
start anyway. The casino was packed again, and people were getting restless. When we made our first
entrance, I never saw anything so sad as Wardell's
empty chair in the sax section. Teddy Hale wasn't
there either. I hoped everything was alright, but I had
a bad feeling. Wardell never came back the whole
night, and nobody was talking, but everybody said
Benny Carter was mad.

Thursday—I don't know how I can write this.
Somebody called the house and told us Wardell was
dead. They found him in the desert, and the police
have Teddy Hale. I wanted to go right over to the club,
but I was scared. All I could think about was
Wardell's wife and baby. When we got to the club, it

was real quiet backstage. I tried to talk with one of the musicians. He told me Wardell overdosed. "You mess with that shit, baby, it's going to happen sometime." I cried then. I don't know why. I wanted to yell at Teddy Hale, but they told me it wasn't his fault. Wardell had been into this for a long time. We do the shows, but I'm so sad tonight I just want to go home. I laid awake half the night thinking about that poor baby lying out in the desert. I wonder who found him?

Friday—We had a meeting today. Mr. Gallio and some other men talked to everybody in the show and told us that it was too bad about Wardell, but that we had a show to do and we'd better do it right, told us not to even talk about it. These men don't care about Wardell. They just want to make money. Well, that's this business I guess, but it's not right. They already have another saxophone player, Sonny Wells, Wardell's friend. He even looks a little bit like Wardell, which makes it even harder for me to watch the band, so I just try to remember my steps and concentrate on the show.

Sonny Wells. There wouldn't have been time to bring someone up from Los Angeles right away, and I imagine Sonny scuffled with the arrangements of a show like this. He was a jazz player first. Still, Benny Carter would have pulled it together.

I remember somebody interviewing a jazz musician once. "Do you read music?" the writer wanted to know.

"Not enough to hurt my playing," the musician said.

Wardell's death was obviously a turning point for Louise. In the remaining entries all the joy is gone, but she starts making some closer observations, paying attention to what she sees and trying to make sense out of it. By mid-June she's getting more and more observant.

June 15—I still can't believe Wardell is gone. I've

heard his wife came up to claim his body and take him back to Los Angeles for burial. Not even a funeral for us to pay our respects, but everyone in the show gave some money for flowers. Everything is settled down now. The press is gone, but the casino is still full every night. I've been trying to remember something Wardell said when I look round the casino.

I stayed after the show tonight talking with my new friend Elizabeth, and while we were talking, I saw Mr. Gallio and those other men go in the casino cashier's cage and come out with bags. "There goes the money," Elizabeth said. "They do that every night." She's right, and she should know, she's a blackjack dealer. I've been watching, careful like, but it's true. I don't understand it. We get paid every week, so they must be saving some, and I know the band is getting paid because no one is complaining, but something is wrong. I can feel it.

June 30—I don't feel like writing in this anymore, but I've seen too much. Mr. Gallio is bothering me again, and his brother Carlo. They both want me to go out with them. Just lunch or dinner. Tell me. Marva and Josie both got boyfriends now, but they think I'm crazy to fool with those Gallios. Why'd he have to pick me? I know he could get me fired if he wanted. He got real mad the other night when I was talking to Pappy Dean, the new bass player. He was a friend of Wardell's too. He keeps telling me to forget the whole thing, but how can I do that? I saw Mr. Gallio talking to Pappy too, real angry like, but Pappy just stared him down. I'm afraid for Pappy too. They still take the money out of here every night. Where does it go? It just don't seem right, but I know I just got to shut my mouth and dance and look pretty. That's all they want us to do.

The entries get more and more sporadic, but the theme continues. Reading between the lines, it's clear Louise had some brief fling with Gallio, and then she either broke it off or Gallio got bored and went on to new conquests.

Gallio and his brother, and whoever else was in on the operation, were obviously skimming money out of the Moulin Rouge on a daily basis. Keeping the band paid was a good move. Nobody would complain or draw any attention to what they were doing, but something went wrong somewhere, because the hotel-casino closed without warning.

> I can't believe I'm writing this, but it's all over. We did the first show tonight as usual, then went home. Marva cooked, and we were sitting around talking about some new costumes when the phone rang. Josie answered, but her face told us something was wrong. When she got off the phone, she just kind of stood there for a moment like she was in a trance or something. Then she told us the club was closed, and we weren't even going to do the late show. We thought she was joking at first, but when we called around to the other girls, we got the same story from everybody.
>
> We sat up all night talking about it, wondering how long it would be closed. The next day we drove to the Moulin Rouge to see for ourselves, and sure enough, there was a padlock on the door. What was going to happen to us now? Some of the band tried to get in to get their instruments, but there was nobody around. No Gallio brothers, nobody. We were finally told after a few days that the club would not reopen, and we had one week to get out of our apartments.

So that was it. Less than six months and the Moulin Rouge was history, and had made history. Louise wasn't even aware of what she had been a part of. A white-owned interracial hotel-casino flourishing long before the bus boycott in Alabama. How much money could be skimmed from an operation like that in six months? And where did it go? Gallio's pocket? Back to Chicago to be laundered, used for other businesses? Nobody would ever know.

I close the diary, rub my eyes, and listen to the final strains of Keith Jarrett moaning his way through "The Wrong Blues," sounding almost like he can't find his way.

I know just how he feels.

21

ACE IS ALREADY up when I walk around to the house, sitting at the kitchen table, drinking coffee, staring out at the pool. I open the sliding door. "Got some for me?"

"Sure," Ace says. "Come on in. Where's Natalie? Still sleeping?"

"Yeah." I grab a mug and fill it with coffee and sit down with Ace. He shoves a manila envelope across the table.

"This came for you yesterday. With all the—well, I just forgot." I turn it over. It's Cindy Fuller's handwriting. Inside are several envelopes—a few bills, bank statements, junk mail, nothing important—and a note from Cindy.

> Dear Evan,
>
> Thought you might want these. I've been holding them for you, but I guess things are going okay in Las Vegas, eh? I got your letter. Evan, you don't have to explain anything. Maybe the timing was wrong for us, or maybe it will be better some other time. Meanwhile, I'm in and out as usual, you know, the friendly skies, but if you feel like it, call me when you get back.
>
> Love, Cindy

I put everything back in the big envelope and glance at Ace. "Cindy," I say, "just forwarding my mail."

Ace nods. He seems distracted, preoccupied. "You okay, Ace?"

"Yeah, sure. Exams today." He takes another drink of his coffee and doesn't even protest when I light a cigarette. "Look, Evan, I want you to know, if I'd had any idea any of this was going to happen, I would never have asked for your help. God, all I wanted to do was write a paper for a stupid academic conference that might get me a book contract. But all this, I just don't know."

I don't say anything, just let Ace get it out in his own way.

"My life has been research, papers, teaching, meetings, that kind of stuff. When Janey died, a little bit of me died with her. I saw this Wardell Gray thing as a way to focus on something, keep my mind occupied." He looks at me. "I mean, how do you deal with all this?"

"I don't know if I am dealing with it, Ace. None of us knew what we were going to find when we started. That's how things go. It's not your fault. Digging up the past uncovers the unexpected."

Ace smiles as if remembering something. "D. H. Lawrence had it right. Why doesn't the past decently bury itself, instead of waiting to be admitted by the present? God, I wouldn't like to think I'm responsible for setting all this into motion."

"You're not Ace, not even a little. Don't even think you are. If anyone is responsible, it's whoever killed Wardell Gray."

Ace says, "Yes, I think you might be right."

I push Louise's diary toward him. "I want you to do me a favor, Ace. Can you make a copy of this, keep it in your office?"

"Of course. That's the other diary you were talking about last night? Anything interesting in there?"

"Oh yeah, very interesting. Some of it may tie into your research. How important is the Moulin Rouge as historical landmark?"

"Vital, I would say. If Las Vegas had been a southern town, the opening of the Moulin Rouge might be considered by some to be the beginning of the civil rights movement. Don't forget, it was the first interracial hotel-casino. Discrimination was widespread in Las Vegas. Black entertainers performing on the Strip were denied accommodation at the hotels."

"That sounds like the opening remarks for a lecture. Louise mentions in here that the dancers' contract prohibited them from even going on the Strip."

"I'm not surprised." Ace glances at the diary. "The Moulin Rouge provided them a place to stay, and it clearly demonstrated that people in a mixed-raced crowd could enjoy themselves in a public place without a riot ensuing. Eventually the other hotels loosened their policies regarding black entertainers. My God, is that in there? Would it be all right if I read some of that?"

"I'm sure Louise would have no objection. What about after the Moulin Rouge closed?"

Ace says, "Still important. I'll have to check my notes, but I'm sure it was in the spring of 1960, the NAACP threatened to march on the Strip to demand integration. They finally met with the Nevada Resort Association and the governor. It was Grant Sawyer then. An agreement was reached that eventually led to desegregation on the Strip. Hell, it was signed at the Moulin Rouge."

"So this Moulin Rouge Preservation Society is pretty important, then?"

"Oh, absolutely. There's a campaign underway now to have the Moulin Rouge placed on the National Register of Historic Landmarks."

An organization Louise Cody is a member of. If Gallio manages to buy the property, the Moulin Rouge will disappear forever. Another good reason to stop Gallio.

"Well, there's a lot in here you can use."

Ace grins and lightly punches me on the shoulder. "By God, I am going to have a helluva paper, aren't I?" The wall-mounted phone rings before I can answer. Ace picks it up. "Yes, yes, he is. Just a moment." Ace hands the phone to me. "It's for you. Someone named Breeze?"

I take the phone from Ace. "Breeze, how ya doing?"

"Very well, my man, very well. I think I got what you were looking for. Even made some copies for you."

"When can I get it?"

"Well, I have to be in court at ten. How about I meet you at eleven?"

"Where?"

"Coffee shop at the Four Queens? It's close to the court-house."

"Fine. See you then."

"Evan, you are going to love this."

I hang up the phone and turn to Ace. "Don't even tell me," he says, getting up from the table. "I've got to go over to school and see how well I've molded those young minds in my charge."

"All right. See you, Ace."

Natalie is up but still looking sleepy in the robe and tousled hair. "Want to meet The Breeze?" I say.

"I wouldn't miss it. Give me fifteen minutes."

While Natalie gets ready I call Louise and Rachel, but there's no answer at either number. I have the nagging feeling that Gallio is not going to rely on me entirely to produce the diary. He just might try something with one of them, Rachel especially, although I can't be sure if he knows she had the diary. I leave a message on Louise's beeper before we leave.

"Where are we going?" Natalie asks, as I back the VW out of the driveway. The sun is climbing, and the heat is turned up full blast.

"Four Queens, then I have to swing by Metro and see Lieutenant Trask. Coop's probably there already. I also want to check on Rachel."

"Why?" Natalie wants to know.

"I don't know, just a feeling. I'd like to get her out of the picture just in case Gallio tries to lean on her."

I valet-park the VW and get a scornful look from the young attendant when I hand him the keys. "I won't be long."

"I can't wait," he says, giving me the parking stub.

We're early, so we decide on the breakfast special while we wait for Breeze. Even at this hour the casino is busy, and the keno junkies play through their breakfast.

"Feeling lucky?" Natalie asks, as she scans a keno ticket.

"Not really."

"Well, we have to play at least a couple of games. Give me some numbers."

All I can think of is my birthdate. "Nine, twenty-seven, fifty-seven."

"Great. I'll add mine." She marks the ticket with a black crayon.

"What are your numbers?"

"Never mind," she says, handing the ticket to a keno runner cruising the coffee shop.

We're on our second cup of coffee and third game when Breeze comes in. Today he's gray suit, dark tie, carrying a leather briefcase. The only nod to his music persona is a Las Vegas Jazz Society pin on his lapel.

"I'll have some of that," he says to the waitress hovering nearby. She pours him coffee and refills mine and Natalie's. He extends his hand to Natalie. "Jonathan Counts. I bet we talked on the phone. You must be Natalie."

Natalie smiles and shakes hands. "Hello, Mr. Breeze."

Breeze returns her smile. "Only on the radio. Today I'm Super Lawyer. Sorry I'm late," he says to me. "Judge was a drag, wouldn't let me have a continuance."

He sets his briefcase on the table and snaps it open. Rummaging inside, he pulls out a file folder and hands it over to me. "This, bro, is for you. Not as easy as I expected," he says.

I start thumbing through the file while The Breeze fills me in. "What you'll find in there is license applications, financial statements, real estate holdings, deeds of trust. Our Mr. Gallio is a very busy man."

I sift through the stack of photocopies. "I don't have time to go through all this, Breeze. What does it all mean?" Breeze sets his coffee cup down and folds his fingers under his chin.

"Gallio's real estate holdings are extensive. Individually they're small, but when you put them together, impressive. He owns the house in Spanish Trail; then there are some apartment buildings, a dry cleaners, part ownership in a restaurant, and some land on the west side that he is developing into a shopping center." Breeze pauses for a moment to let this sink in.

"The licensing applications are for food, beverage, and gaming, although there are several layers separating Gallio from the application. That took a few calls to a friend in Gaming Control. The major property sale pending at the moment is, guess what? The Moulin Rouge."

"He's going to open it again?"

Breeze shakes his head. "He's going to tear it down and start all over, but he's run into some snags with county commissioners. There's a group, which includes the present owner, who want to see the Rouge restored and get it historical landmark status. The other hangup is the Gaming Commission. They've got a Black Book here that frowns on organized-crime types applying for gaming licensing, but they can't get anything concrete on Gallio even though they know he's connected."

I look through the pages of the file and wonder how the Gaming Commission would like a look at Louise Cody's diary and someone to testify against little Tony and Karl. They'd like it even more if Gallio could be implicated in Sonny Wells's and Buddy Herman's deaths.

"How much would it take to smear Gallio's chances for license?"

Breeze shrugs. "Not much. The Gaming Control Board is very careful these days. They even went after Jackie Gaughan a few years ago, and he owns a bunch of these downtown casinos. Spotless record, straight as an arrow, but he had to go before the board anyway."

"And without a license?"

"Gallio's out of business before he starts. You can't run a casino without a license. What have you got in mind?"

"I'd rather not say."

"Good, I'd rather you didn't. There's one other thing."

"What's that?"

"Gallio may look strictly legit, but bad publicity would hurt him with his back-East connections almost as much as with the Gaming Control Board. You know who Tony Spilatro was? Tony the Ant, last of the Chicago family that was in Las Vegas, but he got to be too much of a celebrity."

I remember Trask bringing up his name.

"They were the ones found face down in an Indiana corn field."

RACHEL'S CAR IS parked out front when we pull up to her Naked City apartment building. So far so good, but I have a feeling something is wrong, something I should have thought of before. Gallio isn't really going to trust me to come through with the diary. He would take out some insurance, just to cover all the bases.

I try to tell myself I'm wrong, but it doesn't work. It takes nearly five minutes for Rick to come to the door, too long for Rachel to be in there.

Rick, clad only in cutoffs, is spaced on something. There's also a trickle of blood at the corner of his mouth. "Oh man," he says, "you guys are bad news."

We push past him into the apartment. Rick flops on the couch. He folds his arms over his chest and gazes at us through glassy eyes. The coffee table is overturned, and so are the chairs. A few of the cassettes are lying on the floor in front of the bookcase.

"What happened, Rick?"

He slumps over on the couch. I pull him upright and shake him. "Come on, Rick, wake up. Where's Rachel?"

"Leave me alone, man." He tries to pull away.

"As soon as you tell us where Rachel is." Natalie sits down next to him to hold him upright.

He stares at her with a pleading look. "Don't let him hurt me, okay?"

"Nobody is going to hurt you, Rick. We just need to know where Rachel is."

"They did, those guys," he says, looking at me again, trying to focus.

"Who, Rick?"

"Two guys, man. Bad dudes, one really big one, shoved me around."

"Tony and Karl," I say to Natalie. "They took Rachel with them?"

"Yeah, man." He looks at both of us. "I couldn't stop them. I—" His head flops back on the couch, and his eyes close.

"C'mon," I say to Natalie. "He'll sleep it off."

"Now what?"

"We've got to see Trask and Coop and then wait."

"For what?" She glances again at Rick.

"Gallio's phone call."

The diary for Rachel, that's how this is going to go down.

WE DON'T HAVE to find Trask or Coop. They're waiting for us back at the house.

"Rachel Cody is gone," I say to Coop. "Little Tony and Karl."

"We're way ahead of you, sport. Her mother called in, but we had to expect this."

Ace is back, looking bewildered by the invasion of his home. Trask is on the phone, while another plainclothes detective is setting up a tape recorder on the kitchen table. Trask barks something into the phone and slams it down.

"Okay, Horne, you're next. Let's go outside."

I follow him and Coop out to the patio. Trask is all business, but he's not angry. "Okay, Horne, your little nocturnal excursion has put a different light on things."

"I didn't exactly volunteer for that trip," I remind Trask. Coop signals me with his eyes. Do they think I'm enjoying this?

"I know," Trask says. "Coop filled me in, and he's made a very interesting suggestion. You're in this pretty deep now, enough so you can help us nail Gallio."

"What do you mean?"

"If he has Rachel Cody, he'll be calling here, and he'll more than likely have you as the go-between for the exchange. We've got the diary from your professor pal, so we can make a trade and also get something definite on Gallio. You're the only one who's been close to him lately, so it might work."

I look from Trask to Coop. "I don't think I like the sound of this. What am I going to have to do?"

"We'll decide for sure after the call, see what he's got in mind. Basically you'll agree to a location for the exchange, and we'll grab Gallio once it's made."

I glance from Trask to Coop. Both of them have made up their minds. "You don't really think Gallio himself will be involved in this? He's way too smart for that."

"He will if you insist," Coop says.

"Right," says Trask. "He wants that diary. I can understand why. I've just been skimming through it."

I glance toward the house. I can see Ace talking with Natalie as they watch the tape recorder being attached to the phone. I hope he made the copy I asked for.

"So, how is this going to work? Gallio will want me to come to his house in Spanish Trail."

"No way," Coop says. "We've got to come up with a place we can stake out with reasonable security."

"What do you mean, reasonable security? Can we do a little better than that? I'd like to get out of this in one piece."

"You and Rachel," Trask says. "Gallio isn't foolish enough to try anything, and besides, all he wants is the diary. So—"

"I know just the place," I say. I've already been thinking about it from the moment I knew Gallio had Rachel.

"I already know I'm not going to like this," Coop says.

"Where?" says Trask.

I look at them both for a moment, take a deep breath. "The Fashion Show Mall, while I'm playing."

"Out of the question," Trask says. "No way."

Coop watches me, and I can tell from his expression he wants to hear more.

"Why not? It's a very public place. Gallio certainly won't try anything there with a mall full of shoppers. I can have the diary on top of the piano where you can see everything. You can have some undercover guys around. He gets the diary, we get Rachel, and I'm in very plain sight."

Trask mumbles and mulls it over as if he's waiting for a vote of confidence from Coop. "It's not bad," Coop says. "We could control it maybe better than anyplace else."

"You'd have to convince Gallio," Trask says to me. "And do it exactly how I say."

"I'll convince Gallio. You guys work it out."

"What time do you play?"

"Two o'clock. I'm on till four."

Trask checks his watch. "Christ, that doesn't give us much time." He paces around the patio for a couple of minutes. Coop winks at me. Finally, Trask comes to a halt. "Okay, let's see what Gallio says and if he calls in time."

"He will," I say, "and anyway that's the only way I'm going to do it."

We don't have to wait much longer. The sliding glass door opens, and we all hear the phone ringing. Ochoa motions us inside.

"Okay," Trask says to me. "Take it."

Ochoa hits the record button on the recorder, and I pick up the phone on the third ring.

"Horne? I assume you know who this is?" I nod to Trask and Coop.

"Yeah, I know."

"Then you also know what I want," Gallio says, "and what I'm willing to do in exchange for your cooperation."

"You know Rachel might be your daughter," I say. I look at Coop and Trask waving their hands at me, mouthing, no, no, no.

"My what?" There's silence for a few moments, and for a minute I think I've pushed the wrong button. He's going to hang up. Hasn't he thought of this? "I'm tired of your games, Horne. Here's what you're going to do. You will come alone, I stress that word, to the Spanish Trail main gate, where the security guard is, and—"

"No," I say. "You want the diary, you come to me."

"Come to you? You think I'm going to just drive over to your house?"

"No, I don't expect that, but I want my insurance too. You be at the Fashion Show Mall at three o'clock with Rachel. The diary will be on top of the piano. You pick it up. When you're satisfied, you release Rachel."

"Tony and Karl will pick it up," Gallio says.

"No, you be there or it's no deal. We both know how much you want this, Gallio, so you come get it yourself."

There's another long pause while Gallio thinks it over. I put my hand over the phone and say to Trask, "I think he's going for it."

When Gallio comes back on the line his voice is quieter, more controlled, like it was at Spago. "All right, Horne, I'll be there."

"I don't mean little Tony and his playmate."

"I don't either," Gallio says. "Three o'clock. Horne?"

"Yes?"

"She's not my daughter." He hangs up, and I put down the phone. Ochoa presses the stop button.

Coop and Trask look at me as if I'm about to say the winning lottery numbers. "Well?" they say in unison.

"He's coming. Fashion Show at three."

"Yes!" Trask says, clapping his hands together. He grabs the phone and starts making calls.

Coop looks at me. "You got a big gig coming up, sport."

Ace and Natalie have been watching and listening to the whole thing. "Ace, have you got a large envelope I can put this in?" I ask, indicating the diary lying on the table.

"Huh?" Ace must feel like he's wandered into the set of a television police show. "Oh, sure. In my office."

I follow Ace to his office, where he digs out a large manila envelope. I slip the diary inside. "You did make the copy, right?"

"Yes, of course. Just like you said. It's in a locked file cabinet in my office at UNLV."

"Good, thanks, Ace. This will all be over soon."

I leave him and go back to the kitchen. Trask is still on the phone, Ochoa is making some notes on a pad. Coop and Natalie are talking quietly. "She'll go with me," Coop says. "Trask is arranging for some undercover, but you won't know who they are."

Trask hangs up the phone, stands up, and checks his watch again. "Okay, everything will be in place. You don't do anything but sit quietly and play the piano, got it?"

"He means it," Coop says. "No matter what else goes down."

"Don't worry," I say. "This is your show. I'm going to change." I take the diary with me. I change into my tux, make one call, and come back with the diary sealed in the manila envelope. By then they're all gone.

"Want to take the Jeep?" Ace offers.

"No, a nondescript VW Bug sounds right for this outing. Wish me luck, Ace."

Carrying my jacket and the diary, I go out to the car, sweltering in the heat, feeling ridiculous in the tuxedo. I toss the diary on the seat beside me and wonder what Brent Tyler would think if he knew his mall was about to be invaded by undercover Metro police and several organized crime figures, gathered to make a kidnapping exchange.

Especially when it is all going to be orchestrated by a piano player.

22

I SPOT OCHOA standing near the ice cream stand, licking a cone, trying to look casual, but his eyes are everywhere. Coop and Natalie are seated near the cappuccino bar, facing me, two paper cups on the table in front of them. I don't see Trask, but I know he's there somewhere.

We met briefly in the parking lot to settle the final details, make sure I know my part. Where is he? Outside, in radio contact with everybody undercover? Any of the shoppers walking by the piano carrying department store bags could be Trask's undercover people. I'm glad I don't know who or where they are.

"We want to keep this as low-profile as possible," Trask had said. He was emphatic. "You stay at the piano no matter what." Or under it, I think. Tony and Karl will be armed for sure. Gallio won't chance that. He just wants the diary and a clean getaway.

I look at my watch for what must be the tenth time. Still fifteen minutes to go. "These Foolish Things" pops into my head. As good a tune as any for the occasion. I play, smile at the passing shoppers, and try to focus on the music, but my mind is on Anthony Gallio.

Where is *he* going to come from? Down the escalator behind

me? He could come through Robinson's-May to the escalator. From the glass doors that lead to the parking lot on the food court level, or clear at the other end of the mall, upper or lower level? There were a lot of choices.

They'll arrive separately, of course. Tony and Karl probably with Rachel. Gallio from the opposite direction to the piano. I look down at the keyboard. This is one piano I'll never look at the same way again, even if I play after today.

At ten to three I see Pappy Dean, the first familiar face, come in from the parking lot doors to my right, in a sport shirt, slacks, and his ever-present Panama hat. Dark glasses hide his eyes. His head turns as he glances around briefly, gives me a nod, then heads for a Greek pita place and orders something at the counter.

I glance at Coop. He takes no notice of Pappy, but Natalie, I know, has seen him. She gives me a questioning look. I shrug back. It's not that I don't trust Trask and his men, but somehow, having Pappy around is a comforting sight. Maybe I just want a jazz connection. Besides, there's another reason I want him here. When I told him on the phone what I thought, all I got was silence, then, "I'll be there."

I'm not crazy about Natalie being here, but she insisted, and Trask finally caved in, but only if she stayed with Coop.

With my back to the escalator, I continue to play, keeping my eyes on Coop to gauge his reaction. I wish the velvet rope around the piano was something more substantial as I ease into a slow blues and mentally count off the minutes until three o'clock.

Halfway through the first chorus, Coop sets his coffee cup down and stares over my shoulder at a spot above and behind me. Gallio? Coop looks at Natalie and asks her something, but she looks confused. I turn slightly on the piano bench for a look myself.

There he is, visible to me only from the waist up, standing

erect on the moving stairs, descending toward the lower level, looking around the mall below him as if he's never been there before.

At first I think I'm seeing things, but there's no mistake, except mine in thinking I could trust Gallio. He's sent his brother Carlo.

I look back to Coop and nod. He speaks into the tiny radio microphone in his lapel. My eyes briefly scan the mall. Is the guy with the Dillard's bag one of Trask's men? His eyes are riveted on me at the piano as he sets the bag down on the floor.

Directly across from me on the upper level, I see Tony and Karl come around the corner by the bookstore. Rachel is between them. She's too far away from me to see the expression on her face. They stop at the rail and lean over for a clear view of the food court and me below. Rachel hangs back slightly. Good girl. Karl seems nervous. He keeps looking over his shoulder. Tony is cool all the way, probably enjoying this. I hope the couple next to them, also taking in the view, are Trask's people.

Out of the corner of my eye I see Carlo Gallio reach the bottom of the escalator. He steps off uncertainly, glances toward the piano, then walks toward me. He reaches the velvet rope and stops, seemingly confused for a moment. He pauses, then steps around the stanchion, spots the envelope on top of the piano, and looks at me expectantly.

I end the blues abruptly and go into the first few bars of "Laura." Carlo smiles slightly and nods. He reaches for the envelope, weighs it in his hand. I glance quickly above, at Tony and Karl. They're following his every move. So far so good.

Carlo Gallio's fingers fumble for the clasp. He gets it open and reaches inside, pulls out the diary, and holds it up for Tony to see as I continue to play. Coop gets up and moves back, behind the tables. I try to signal him with eyes to look above him. His view of Tony and Karl is blocked by the overhang of the upper level.

"Hey, Horne, glad to see you back," Brent Tyler says, coming up from my left. He looks at Carlo, then me. "What's going on? Who is this guy? I'm sorry, sir," he says to Gallio. "You're not allowed behind the rope."

At precisely that moment Tyler's cellular phone rings. He reaches into his back pocket. Shaken by Brent's movements, Gallio drops the diary and envelope, looks at me.

"Get out of here, Brent," I say.

"What?"

Gallio picks up the diary and shoves past Brent Tyler. "Hey," Brent says, as he bangs into the piano. "What the hell is going on?"

Gallio pauses at the escalator, still clutching the diary, then bypasses it entirely and disappears into the Robinson's-May store. The man with the shopping bag I'd seen earlier goes in after him. Ochoa trails close behind.

Some of the people at the food court tables have seen all this and are on their feet, pointing. Above, I see the couple at the rail slide over and move off with Rachel in tow, using the gathering crowd to block Tony and Karl. Coop is already sprinting up the stairs.

I don't realize I'm still playing. I stop and feel like I'm watching a movie, and the piano bench is the best seat in the house. Brent Tyler is madly dialing his phone, looking at me.

"I don't know what's going on, Horne," he says. Then into the phone, "Security? Get down to the food court on the double. Jesus Christ!" His eyes go to the upper level, where someone has screamed. Karl has his gun out, holding it over his head.

Coop is nearly on Tony now. He grabs for him, but Karl is panicking. He spots two men in green blazers rushing toward the rail, both carrying walkie-talkies. He skirts the security guards and jumps over Coop and Tony. Coop has Tony on the floor and is cuffing him.

Down the stairs Karl comes, knocking over some shoppers.

More startled voices, and he pushes people aside. He heads straight for the piano. Brent Tyler sees him coming, drops his phone, and runs the other way, but Karl doesn't even pause at the piano. I stand up and start to put as much of the piano between me and Karl as possible.

He runs past me, heading for the parking lot doors, and almost makes it except for Pappy, who's moved over to intercept him. Karl dodges to his left, but Pappy trips him, and he goes down. Karl's gun flies out of his hand and slides across the floor. Before he can get halfway to his feet, Pappy shoves him toward the glass door. Karl flies headlong, hits the glass. It doesn't break, but the impact causes the glass to spiderweb. Karl bounces back and lies moaning on the floor.

Two other undercover cops appear suddenly, cuff him before he can get up. Pappy picks up the gun and points it toward Karl. I open my mouth to yell, but nothing comes out. Karl's eyes widen; the undercover cops, frozen, stare at the barrel of the gun pointing between them. Pappy smiles at Karl, holds him in his sights for a few seconds, then lets the gun down and hands it to one of the guys holding Karl. I let out the breath I've been holding.

Coop leads Tony down the stairs. He glares at me as he passes the piano, but Coop pushes him toward the exit, through the startled crowd of shoppers gathering in groups and talking loudly. By now, with everything seemingly under control, Brent Tyler reappears and starts making appeasing noises to the crowd. More security has arrived, and they've blocked off the parking lot entrance.

Pappy, cool and calm, saunters over to the piano. "Thanks for calling me, man. I wouldn't have missed this. That's the dudes got Sonny, right?"

"Maybe, Pappy, maybe. You had me going there for a minute."

He nods. "What you said on the phone. It might be true.

Even if it isn't, that's how I think about it." He straightens up as Ochoa comes out of the department store with Carlo Gallio, who looks frail and tired. He pauses at the piano, looks at me, then stares at Pappy Dean.

He holds up the microphone to his throat. "A moment, please," he says to Ochoa in that mechanical voice that gives me shivers even here in the mall. He and Pappy stare at each other for several moments. Pappy takes in the throat microphone, the mechanical voice. A flash of recognition passes between them, and thirty-seven years seem to fall away. Gallio turns and looks at me once before being led off.

Pappy stares after Gallio for several moments. He looks at me. "I owe you big-time," he says. He slaps the top of the piano. "Don't forget tonight. I called everybody I know to get the word out. They don't come, they got me to answer to." He walks off shaking his head.

Natalie joins me at the piano. "Wow, I think it's time I filed my application for law school. That was scary!" She looks at Pappy's retreating figure. "Why was he here?"

"I called him."

"Why?"

"Something you said the other night, and I found more of it in the diary. I think you're right. Rachel might be Pappy's daughter."

We're soon joined by Coop and Trask as the crowd disperses and things return to some sense of normality. Brent Tyler pushes his way through, probably looking for his phone. He starts to say something to me, but I beat him to it.

"I know, Brent. I'm fired."

AT METRO HEADQUARTERS, I feel like I'm in a debriefing. Rachel is safely home with Louise, nobody got shot, Tony, Karl, and Carlo Gallio are in custody, but still Trask is not happy as he grills me in one of the interrogation rooms.

"You switched the diaries," he says. "We got zip on Carlo Gallio, and his attorney is already on his way. He'll be home for dinner." Trask slams his fist on the table between us. "You better tell me you didn't know Anthony Gallio wasn't coming."

"Not a clue, but it makes sense now. Carlo has hardly been out of the house in years, and he knows you have no interest in him or anything pending on him."

Trask nods, conceding the point with a sigh. "All Carlo Gallio did was pick up an envelope, something we were going to give him anyway. We can't charge him with anything and make it stick. Little Tony and Karl we can make with assault, illegal possession of firearms, maybe even attempted murder, provided you testify with Natalie as a corroborating witness."

"Oh, I think you can count on that, John," Coop says. He looks at me and smiles. "Right, sport?"

"I think I know how to get Gallio as well, at least put him on the run. We got Rachel back, but Gallio will soon know he's got the wrong diary, and he's not going to be happy about that."

"How's he going to know that?" Trask says.

"When you send Carlo home, give him the damaging one. I've got it in my car."

"Go on," Trask says. Coop smiles as if he knows where I'm going.

"If you publicize Tony and Karl's arraignment, put as much media attention on it as possible, connect them all to their back-East family, the folks in Chicago or wherever are not going to be happy with Gallio. They were very unhappy with Tony Spilatro, right?"

That brings a searching look from Coop before he and Trask exchange glances.

"You know, if you really knew who and what Anthony Gallio was," Trask says, "you wouldn't be sitting here telling me about this scheme."

"I don't want to know any more than I do, but I want to see Gallio out of commission." I explain to Trask about the Moulin Rouge campaign for restoration and Gallio's attempted purchase and application for a gaming license. "This all started out with researching Wardell Gray's death. That's going to stay a mystery, I guess. If there was a file, it went down with Buddy Herman in Lake Mead, but the exposure of that diary is surely enough to screw up Gallio's chance for a license and turn off the sellers."

"How are we going to do all this if Gallio has the diary?"

"I have a copy, and it's in a safe place. You simply get word to Gallio that if he so much as tries to buy a condo in Las Vegas, it gets published in the newspapers."

Trask and Coop both stare at me for several moments. It is Trask who finally breaks the silence. He looks at Coop and says, "Where did this guy come from?"

"He's got a point," Coop says. "We could send a note with Carlo to that effect."

"Or I could call him," I offer.

"No!" they both say in unison.

I hold up my hands in surrender. "Okay, you guys work it out." I'm suddenly very tired. "Can I go now?"

Trask sighs. "Yeah, I guess. I'll need a full statement on Tony and Karl, and you'll have to come back here to testify at their arraignment, but yeah, you can go."

"I'll catch up with you later," Coop says. "Natalie is outside."

I get up and shake hands with Trask. "You did okay, Horne," he says. "I wish I could have been more help with Wardell Gray. I'm sure I could fix things with that mall guy. What's his name? Tyler?"

"That's okay, thanks. I've had enough of mall gigs, and as for Wardell Gray, maybe Coop is right. The past should probably stay buried."

A HOT SHOWER, something to eat, a reassuring talk with
Ace, and I'm feeling pretty good.

Ace has seen the mall incident on the six o'clock news, but
he wants to hear a complete play-by-play, which Natalie and I
give him.

"What about the copy of the diary?" he wants to know.

"You keep it, Ace. Use whatever you want for your conference. When is that, by the way?"

"In September," Ace says. "I'd love for you both to be there."

"I'll do my best, Ace."

"You're leaving, I take it?"

I look at Natalie. "Yeah, this gig is over, and I didn't even
get two weeks' notice."

"Well, I've got exams to grade. School is going to be pretty
boring after all this."

Natalie and I drift back over to the apartment, both of us in
a kind of introspective mood. There are questions to be an-
swered for each of us. She's going back to work, at least for now.
I don't know what's in store for me next. More therapy and
rehab? It's getting old, and I've got to make some decision about
what I'm going to do with my life.

I let these thoughts wash over me, then suddenly jump to
my feet.

"God, I almost forgot."

"What?" Natalie says.

"There's one more thing. C'mon, we've got to go."

"Oh, Evan, can't we just stay here? Where are we going?"

"You'll see."

I'd be willing to bet Pogo's parking lot has never been this
full. Cars are jammed in at odd angles where the regular parking
has run out, so I pull down farther to a space in front of a real
estate office. We can already hear the music before we get to

the door. A hand-lettered poster is taped to the window: SONNY WELLS BENEFIT CONCERT—BRING YOUR HORN! When I open the door, a wave of jazz flows outside, ridden at the moment by a short, muscular tenor player in jeans and a black T-shirt with Dexter Gordon's face on its front. Knees bent, eyes closed, sweat pouring off him, the tenor player rocks slightly as Pappy Dean and the rhythm section chase him through the changes of "Just Friends."

Natalie and I push our way in. It's four deep at the bar, people shouting for drinks over the din of conversation and music. All the tables and booths are crammed, and some who couldn't find a seat have staked out space on the floor. The air conditioners and overhead fans are working overtime, but it feels hotter in here than outside.

Natalie and I elbow our way to the end of the bar and jostle for a position alongside the end of the bandstand. I pick up an empty beer bottle from the bar and hold it up for one of the bartenders. He eventually spots me, and I show him two fingers. Somebody passes the beers over, and I throw him a five-dollar bill, wave a hand to signal no change.

We turn at the sound of applause. The tenor player finishes his choruses, nods at the crowd, and steps down. To the left of the bandstand a line of saxophone players, horns on neck straps, licking reeds, nervously fingering keys—I count seven—shuffle forward a few steps closer to the band.

Pappy points at one, a reed-thin black man in a baseball cap, bright red shirt, and dark pants. He mounts the bandstand and whispers something to Pappy, who nods his head, then yells something to the drummer and piano player. At the end of the next chorus the rhythm section drops out entirely, leaving the tenor player to tell his story alone.

"This is what it's all about, isn't it?" Natalie says. I nod and smile at her and focus on Pappy. He grabs a towel off his amp, wipes his face, and gulps a beer. The drummer and piano player do likewise, and both light cigarettes and listen to the tenor's scathing sound. Pappy scans the room, catches my eye, grins, and waves a hand toward the waiting horns. Everybody wants to play one for Sonny Wells. Above the bandstand, someone has strung a banner across that reads REMEMBER SONNY! A jumbo brandy snifter at the pianist's feet is stuffed with money.

"This is incredible," Natalie shouts in my ear. I turn my head. I can barely hear her, listening to the tenor player come to the end of his second solo chorus. Drinks and cigarettes are set down as the rhythm section gears up to make their entrance. The tenor player blows through two more choruses. At times his tone is almost a cry. This is what I can do, he says. Then he half-turns toward Pappy, raises his fist in the air, and they go home. Everybody is on their feet at the end, shouting and applauding as the drummer closes things out with a final cymbal crash.

Pappy lays Trouble down carefully and moves toward the microphone, wiping his face again with a towel. His suit jacket is gone, his tie loosened. "Alright, y'all, settle down," he commands. He waits for a moment until there's reasonable quiet before he continues. "We got to give this rhythm section some rest, but let's remember who this night is for. We'll be back shortly. As you can see we got lots of bad-assed horns here tonight, so don't go away."

There's more applause, then Pappy glances toward me and says, "I see someone who might give our piano player a break if I can get him up here to play a couple." Pappy grins again and points in my direction.

Natalie touches my arm. "Are you going to play?"

"Doesn't look like I have much choice." I take a drink of my beer and look around the club. A lot of people look my way as Pappy pushes through the crowd toward us.

"You believe this, man," Pappy says. "Pogo's ain't never seen no shit like this. I told you I get 'em here." A tall thin man

in dark glasses, T-shirt, shorts, and sandals sidles up to us.
"Hey man, let's take a walk outside before you play," he
says. He pats his pocket and smiles.

Pappy gives him a hard look. "Get outta here, Juni." The
man called Juni shrugs and disappears into the crowd at the bar.
"Don't you be goin' with him," Pappy says. "He's got the
shit killed Elvis." He takes me by the shoulders. "C'mon man,
play one for Sonny. I know you can do it. We'll come up and
help you out if you get in trouble."

"I don't know, Pappy, it's going pretty good."

"C'mon, man, don't talk that shit. Play, man, play." He takes
me by the arm and pulls me toward the bandstand.

Pappy leads me to the piano and I sit down at the old scarred
upright. I flex my fingers and stare at the keyboard I know so
well while Pappy grabs the mike. "Let's hear it," he says to the
audience. "Evan Horne, a real friend of Sonny Wells."

There's some light applause, then the room becomes
strangely silent. I look up at the ceiling, searching for something
to play. The blues is all I can think of for Sonny Wells. Gene
Harris's "Black and Blue" comes to mind. I begin with a slow
left-hand figure, then lock both hands into the chord changes
and start moving through the melody line that has its own built-
in sadness.

"I hear you," somebody in the audience says. Another voice
murmurs, "Uh huh. Talk to me." I'm not sure where it comes
from. Head down, I start my solo, mostly block chords, mashing
keys, smearing notes, and feeling the first twinge of pain shoot
up my arm. But I play through it, and by the third chorus the
pain is gone. If this is to be my last time, I might as well go for
broke.

Suddenly, in my ear, I hear Pappy's bass walking with me,
huge dark tones that ring through, one note to another. "I ain't
here to help you," Pappy says, bending close. "I just want to be
along for this ride."

On the next chorus, the drummer joins us, entering with an Art Blakey-like press roll that begins as a whisper, then rises to a crescendo as he slams us down into the next chorus. I feel his stick on the cymbal, pushing and prodding at my back. I lean back slightly on the bench, shake out my right hand, then plunge into the keys while keeping the chords going with my left. I punch at the keys and pull out some lines I don't recognize myself, but as good as it is, as good as it feels, my hand is going fast, cramping up. The pain has come back to haunt me once again.

I glance over at Pappy, pulling on the strings of his bass, with me all the way. I need help. As we end the chorus, I nod to him and let a wave of applause wash over me. Now it's Pappy's turn. Hunched over his bass, Pappy doesn't need any help. I feed him the changes with my left hand, flex the fingers of my right, and listen to the drummer's brushes caress the snare. Maybe I'll get out of this yet.

Pappy's solo comes to a close, and he begins the walk home. I'm ready to take it out when another tenor mounts the bandstand and joins us. "I had to have a piece of this," he says. It's block chords all the way for me until the end, when he and I trade cadenzas. I manage to squeeze out one final run, and Pappy signals the closing chord. It's only then I'm aware of the audience as they erupt in an avalanche of shouts and applause.

Pappy leans over to me and says, "Maybe white men can't jump, but they sure can play the blues." He laughs and slaps my hand, and I surrender the piano.

"You cookin', baby," the pianist says as we trade places. "Cookin'!"

It all feels good—the club, the playing, the camaraderie of the musicians. But when I jump off the bandstand to join Natalie, I stop and turn to look at the piano. I feel a wave of sadness come over me, for I know this may be the last time.

CODA

PROFESSOR CHARLES BUFFINGTON is surrounded by colleagues in front of the Barrick Museum at UNLV. He's basking in the attention, smiling, shaking hands, accepting congratulations—even, I notice, from his nemesis in the English department. The news of Ace's paper has obviously been circulated, a practice Ace tells me is standard procedure during these conferences, especially since he leaked a copy to the dean.

I feel a bit out of place, but I promised I'd come by, at least for the beginning of the conference. Ace finally spots me and untangles himself from the crowd.

"How about this, Evan. I'm a star at last."

"Congratulations, Ace. You deserve it." It's great to see him so genuinely happy.

"Hey, that's not all. I faxed a proposal to this editor I know. He called this morning, and I may have a book contract with a pretty respectable university press." A momentary frown crosses his face. "He says I may have to give it some bullshit academic title, but it's the real thing, a book on the Moulin Rouge and Wardell Gray. It's a crossover book for me, but the English department can't ignore it. Merit pay and a promotion to full professor is definitely on the horizon."

I point at Ace's rival. "Even your buddy seems to be getting into the act."

"Sure, but don't be fooled. He just wants to take credit for being my chair. He's probably already trying to figure a way to quash the book deal. Well, fuck him. Let him try. I called in some favors and got a sabbatical approved for the spring semester to give me time to work on the book."

"Easy, Ace. You academic types are more vicious than record promoters."

"Not all of us. How did your testimony go?"

"Well enough to get a grand jury indictment on Karl and Little Tony. Sonny Wells and Buddy Herman's deaths are still down as unsolved, but Trask is going to keep the file open."

"What about Gallio?"

"When he realized there was a copy of the diary, he pulled out of everything, and Trask says he's made a couple of trips to Chicago. They're not happy with him there. He's got a lot of explaining to do."

Ace nods. "Well, you did all you could, and you certainly helped me with this paper. C'mon, let's go inside."

I follow Ace into the auditorium and take a seat near the back. The others file in amidst a buzz of conversation. They quiet down when a short slim man, a conference director, takes the podium to introduce the speakers.

"Thank you all for coming this afternoon. I hope no one had to cancel any classes, but if you did, I can assure you it's for a good cause." He pauses for a moment to accept the polite chuckles before continuing. "We're very happy to kick off the conference with a paper from one of our own English department members. We hope you all enjoy the city and the campus during your stay in Las Vegas. Now, without further delay, I'd like to introduce Professor Charles Buffington, who we've managed to get off the tennis court for this reading."

There's a smattering of applause as Ace strides to the podium like an actor about to receive an Oscar. He looks a little rumpled in his dark suit, but that's academic style. He arranges his papers in front of him, adjusts his glasses, and begins reading.

"This paper is the result of some pretty intensive research, and if you've been reading the local newspapers, some pretty intensive police work as well. I for one am happy to see the academic and local communities cooperate in the manner they have. I think we've gone a long way toward making the ivory tower a little bit more accessible."

Ace pauses for a moment to let his remarks sink in and give the department chair a meaningful glance. I have to admit, Ace knows how to play the room, and I know he's enjoying every minute.

"Before I begin this paper," he continues, "I would be remiss if I did not acknowledge a good friend to whom I owe a great debt in helping with the research. I believe he's sitting in the back of the room. Mr. Evan Horne."

I don't actually stand up, but I wave at Ace. Curious faces turn toward me, I suppose trying to place where they might have seen me before. I wonder if they'll mistake me for one of the faculty?

"The title of this paper is 'Death of a Tenor Man,' " Ace continues. "I should first explain that I'll be using some terms that are perhaps unfamiliar to many of you throughout the paper. For example, tenor man is an idiomatic expression to denote tenor saxophonist, generally in the jazz field. Apologies to my female colleagues, but tenor person simply won't work when referring to Wardell Gray. I think I'll begin with . . ."

I get up and slip out the door. I've read most of the paper already, seen the photos Ace as collected. Wardell, I think, would have been pleased to know that he was the subject of an academic conference and that the keynote speaker had written about him.

I cut across the deserted campus toward the humanities

building to get the rental car. Almost time to pick up Natalie.
We'll be flying back to Los Angeles together. Going down the
steps, I pass a campus security guard.

"Hot enough for you?" he asks. I wonder how many people
ask that question every day during the summer in Las Vegas.

"I don't know," I say. "Seems a lot cooler today."

The guard laughs. "You must be getting used to this dry
heat."

I'm not used to it, but September does offer the slight hint
of fall. The worst of the summer heat is gone. As promised, I've
come back to testify at the arraignment of Tony and Karl. They'll
do time, and Anthony Gallio's plans for the Moulin Rouge are
in a shambles. Trask thinks he had a lot of explaining to do in
Chicago.

Louise and Rachel Cody were reunited, and when I talked
to her, Louise told me the Moulin Rouge's place on the National
Register of Historic Landmarks was all but reality. She and
Pappy are seeing a lot of each other.

Natalie has been accepted for law school, and we're still
exploring our relationship. It's going well. The weeks I've spent
back in my Venice apartment have been good for reflection. I've
started physical therapy again. I just can't give up the piano.
Even Cindy Fuller is in my corner.

I get in the car and head for the Strip to pick up Natalie, but
at the light at Flamingo and Paradise I change my mind. There's
something I want to see. I drive through downtown and pull up
near the Moulin Rouge. One more quick look. I think of opening
night in 1955 and wonder if it will ever see that kind of excitement again. Probably not.

Then I drive north a couple of miles from the casino, I think
to the right place.

I pull over and get out of the car and walk into a vacant lot
near a convenience store. The trash is still there—crushed drink
cups, sandwich wrappings, overflowing weeds; even the aban-

doned truck tire remains—scattered about the lot of sand and dirt.

A few feet off the road I stop and stand still and listen. This is the spot where Wardell Gray's body was discovered. One of the great talents of jazz dead, like Charlie Parker, at age thirty-four, a lifeless heap dumped in the desert to be found by a passerby.

I listen again. For what? Spirits? The faint sound of a saxophone? So many thoughts flood my mind, but there's no epitaph for a tenor man here. Nothing but the wind blowing trash through the desert, the sound of traffic rushing by.

I reach in my pocket, touch the new rubber ball, and give it a squeeze.

So long, Wardell. The chase is still on.